"Interesting shirt. Your husband's?"

Susanna smiled. "No, it's mine." She picked up one end of the banner and fitted it over the stake. "I don't have a husband."

Flynn picked up the other end and followed her example. He raised one eyebrow. "Managed to get the shirt off his back, did you?"

"I'm a widow."

He had assumed she was divorced. She looked too young to be a widow. Awkwardly Flynn withdrew his foot from his mouth. "Oh, hey, I'm sorry. I didn't mean—"

He looked so contrite, Susanna was surprised. She came to his rescue. She hated seeing anyone in distress. "I'm sure you didn't. The shirt is from my son." She pointed to a towheaded boy in the field.

Flynn looked at the lettering across her chest. " 'World's Greatest *Dad*'? A little nearsighted, isn't he?"

She laughed. "No, the shirt was for Father's Day. My son said I earned it."

Dear Reader,

Welcome to Silhouette **Special Edition** . . . welcome to romance. Each month, Silhouette **Special Edition** publishes six novels with you in mind—stories of love and life, tales that you can identify with—romance with that little "something special" added in.

We've got a celebration going here this month! We're introducing a brand-new cover design for Silhouette **Special Edition**. We hope you like our new look, as well as our six wonderful books this month. We're pleased to present you with Nora Roberts's exciting new series— THE DONOVAN LEGACY. *Captivated* is the first tale, and it's full of magical love galore! The next books, *Entranced* and *Charmed,* will be heading your way in October and November. Don't miss these enchanting tales!

And rounding out this month are books from other exciting authors: Judi Edwards, Marie Ferrarella, Billie Green, Phyllis Halldorson and Betsy Johnson.

In each Silhouette **Special Edition** novel, we're dedicated to bringing you the romances that you dream about— stories that will delight as well as bring a tear to the eye. And that's what Silhouette **Special Edition** is all about— special books by special authors for special readers!

I hope you enjoy this book and all of the stories to come.

Sincerely,

Tara Gavin
Senior Editor
Silhouette Books

MARIE FERRARELLA

WORLD'S GREATEST DAD

Published by Silhouette Books New York

America's Publisher of Contemporary Romance

To Daddy, who got a late start, too.
Love,
Marysia

SILHOUETTE BOOKS
300 East 42nd St., New York, N.Y. 10017

WORLD'S GREATEST DAD

ISBN: 0-373-09767-0

First Silhouette Books printing September 1992

Printed in the U.S.A.

MARIE FERRARELLA

was born in Europe, raised in New York City and now lives in Southern California. She describes herself as the tired mother of two overenergetic children and the contented wife of one wonderful man. She is thrilled to be following her dream of writing full-time.

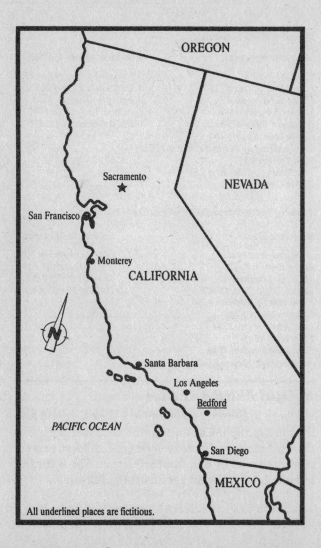

OREGON

NEVADA

Sacramento ★

San Francisco ●

Monterey ●

CALIFORNIA

Santa Barbara ●

Los Angeles ●

<u>Bedford</u>

PACIFIC OCEAN

San Diego ●

MEXICO

All underlined places are fictitious.

Chapter One

"What are we going to do without a housekeeper?" Michael stuck out his toes in front of him and wiggled them as he sat in the sports car, waiting for an answer.

Flynn O'Roarke looked down at the six-year-old on his right and smiled. "We'll manage."

Manage. He'd gotten good at that, managing, even when he was certain that he couldn't. He had managed because he had to. But God, it had been hard, hard to face life when Kelly wasn't in it anymore, smoothing the way, taking care of a hundred details he hadn't even known existed until now. His wife's sudden death after twenty-five years of marriage had made him as disoriented, as lost as a child. But Stephanie and Julia had still been living at home then, needing him. So, somehow, he had groped his way through the maze of pain and everyday living and he had managed.

And then the second blow had come, cutting him off at the knees, less than three months after Kelly's death. He had managed then, too, though he wasn't certain how he had faced the tragedy without Kelly beside him.

Six years earlier, Kelly had been there to hold his hand, to tranquilize his anger when his oldest daughter, Aimee, had come to him, tears in her eyes, and told him that she wanted to get married. The resounding no he'd uttered had softened to a yes when she told him she was pregnant. Pregnant. His brilliant, seventeen-year-old daughter, little more than a child herself, was with child. So, he'd said yes and he and Kelly had helped Aimee and Doug move up to San Francisco. Doug had been a likeable young man, full of ambition for their future. They'd all stuck together and made wonderful plans.

Flynn looked down at Michael as the boy pounded his brand-new mitt. Michael looked a lot like Aimee, so much so that at times it made Flynn's heart ache to see a familiar smile cross the boy's lips and know that he would never see it on Aimee's face again.

But he had managed. Somehow, when that call had come in the middle of the night from the highway patrolman at the hospital, he had managed to hold himself together, without Kelly to rely on. A prayer on his lips, he'd left his two younger daughters and gotten the earliest flight out to the hospital outside of Oakland. It had been just after the semester end. Doug, Aimee and Michael were driving down to Bedford to be with Flynn and the girls. A panel truck had changed their plans. Aimee and Doug were both gone by the time he had arrived at the hospital. He had allowed himself tears as he kept vigil at Michael's bedside.

Michael had managed to survive and Flynn had managed to go on, bringing the boy back to Bedford with him. Now he and Michael were struggling to find their proper roles in this new family structure they found themselves in.

But, at the moment, Flynn wasn't managing very well at all. Something had happened yesterday. Flynn had turned forty-five. Five years away from fifty. From half a century. Though the mirror before him reflected the image of a man who had never believed in overindulgence, who had exercised regularly, Flynn suddenly felt ancient.

Forty he had accepted, had laughed at when Kelly had given him a gag gift of a hot water bottle and a box of prunes. He had laughed because Kelly was with him and she made him feel young.

Without realizing it, he had depended on Kelly for too many things. After she died, he had sworn never to be that dependent again. But that decision didn't stop the feeling of floundering, of being emotionally adrift.

Fifteen months ago, he had been continuing a long-established pattern. He and Kelly were going to grow old together. He was going to watch his daughters mature and Michael grow up. As the boy's grandfather, not as his guardian. Then the pattern had blown up in front of him.

But somehow, he had managed. He supposed. One thing was certain. He promised himself never to be that emotionally dependent on another human being again. It was far too painful, being left behind.

Michael's voice brought him back to the present. "Are we going to get another housekeeper now that Mrs. Henderson had to move?"

Flynn picked his way through the tidy, serpentine streets of the residential development. "Do you want one?"

Discussing things with Michael made the boy feel more important. With Stephanie and Julia both away at college, that left just the two of them at home. The two of them to muddle through the maze of being thrown together and helping each other cope with the business of living each day. Flynn was still taking it one shaky step at a time, but Michael seemed none the worse for it.

Michael frowned as he tried to answer Flynn's question. "She was nice," he began with a sense of diplomacy beyond his years. "But she treated me like a baby."

"Can't have that." Flynn had sensed Michael's feelings and so had looked into alternatives. "I thought we'd get you into an after-school day-care center until we worked things out."

Michael looked up at him hopefully. "The one with the neat sportsman bus that picks Greg up?"

Flynn grinned. He wished everything was this simple. "That's the one."

"Great!" Michael almost bounced up and down. "Thanks."

He ruffled Michael's dark hair. "Hey, no problem. You're my favorite six-year-old grandson."

Up ahead, he saw the sign indicating Jeffrey Elementary School. He slowed down as a grassy lot behind the school came into view. There were several cars parked there already even though the game wasn't scheduled to begin for another twenty minutes. Flynn maneuvered his sports car into a space between two station wagons. The convertible looked out of place there, kind of the way he felt about himself and life right now.

With childish importance, Michael pounded the new mitt twice, then looked up as a thought struck him. "I'm your *only* six-year-old grandson."

Flynn pulled up the hand brake. "There's that, too." He stretched as he got out of the low-slung silver car. It had been a long day. They had all been long days lately. He thought of his own grandfather, the way he had looked when Flynn was six. Gnarled and hopeless, spending hours just looking off into space. He'd died when Flynn was ten.

With effort, Flynn shook himself free of the melancholy mood that had hung over him like a shroud since yesterday.

Flynn placed a hand on Michael's shoulder and guided him away from the curb, onto the field. There were several little boys dressed in blue shirts and white pants, running around, throwing and missing. God, he wished life could be that simple again.

He looked down and saw another frown on Michael's face. "What?"

Flynn didn't normally bring him to his practice sessions. For the past two weeks since practice had started, Mrs. Henderson had been the one who'd dropped him off. "I don't play all that great."

It was clear to Flynn that Michael was worried about disappointing him. The fact humbled him. Emotion stirred, but he banked it down. He'd had just about all the emotional stirrings he could handle right now. He probably would have sold his soul for some peace and tranquility.

Flynn touched the corners of the boy's sad little mouth, raising them up slightly with two fingers. "You'll get better. Before you know it, you'll be the star of the team."

Michael clearly hadn't explored that prospect. The smile that came to his lips was of his own making now. "Yeah?"

"Yeah," Flynn echoed solemnly.

Michael's expression turned eager. "Maybe you've got something there."

Flynn laughed. Being with Michael was always a joy. He hung on to that, even as he warned himself not to. He glanced around the field again, trying to locate someone who looked like a coach. Instead he saw a petite blonde, her hair hanging in her eyes, a look of deep concentration on her face. She was chewing her lower lip. She was also holding a hammer sideways and doing a rather inept job of pounding in a stake. A blue-and-white banner, proclaiming the team logo as well as all the players' names, was at her feet. The upper part of her body was encased in a light blue T-shirt that hung on her like a tent, but nonetheless did an interesting job of accentuating her body when the wind shifted. The words World's Greatest Dad were embossed across it in shiny, hot-pink letters.

Flynn shook his head as he watched her work doggedly at the stake. "Another woman going through her husband's closet and wearing his clothes."

Michael, having spotted one of his friends, began to dash off. He stopped for a moment longer. "Is that bad?"

Flynn hadn't realized he had said the words aloud. "Only if he doesn't want her to."

The six-year-old shrugged philosophically, his attention already directed somewhere else. "Maybe he does."

Flynn nodded, still watching. Hadn't anyone ever told her how to hold a hammer? "Yeah, maybe." He pointed toward a tall, genial-looking man with the word Coach on his sweatshirt. "Get some practice in, champ."

Michael eyed him hopefully. "And you'll stay for the whole game?"

"Absolutely. From start to finish," Flynn promised the retreating boy.

Flynn's attention was drawn back to the woman. There was no reason, he thought, for him to offer his help. After all, there were a couple of other men around, although they were involved with the boys. Besides, he didn't even know the woman. And if she wasn't smart enough to figure out how to hold a hammer, he really didn't want to. What would he have to say to a woman who hit a stake with the broad side of a hammer?

Still, he found himself drifting toward her, something male and protective and beyond his control getting the best of him. It was probably, he thought dourly, his Southern upbringing rearing its head.

The best part of Susanna Troy's days always revolved around Billie. When she was doing something with her seven-year-old son or for him, life seemed to have a certain warm glow around it, like a Christmas gift that went on forever. That was why, at the end of a long day filled with meetings and unresolved projections about the new rate-book calculations at Palisades Mutual, she had willingly come out to cheer him on to victory. More than that, she had come to do her bit as dug-out Mom.

Since the age of four, baseball had been Billie's prime passion. Totally ignorant about the fundamentals of the game, Susanna had quickly educated herself about positions and players' names. She had become familiar with things like ERAs and vital stats, all of which had meant nothing to her a short while ago. She had sewn the banner and toted it to and from the games, baked brownies, bought bandages and generally helped out where she could, even when she'd rather have been curled up on the sofa at home, watching a movie on the VCR or reading a good mystery.

Billie came first. He always did.

Having finally gotten the first stake into the hard ground, Susanna picked up the banner and measured off where the second stake had to go. She hoped it wouldn't be windy, like the last time. The banner had filled like a sail and then leaned completely over, taking the stakes with it.

With a sigh, she picked up the second stake, wishing the earth would soften up. Bedford had to have the hardest soil in Southern California, she mused.

"Here, give me that."

The impatient voice startled her. She hadn't heard anyone coming up. But then, the noise from the field was getting so loud, it probably would have drowned out a herd of stampeding elephants.

Susanna raised her head, unconsciously chewing her lower lip. The first thing she saw as a muscular upper torso straining against a washed-out blue T-shirt. She wondered if she would feel flesh or steel beneath her hand if she touched it. For a moment, she was almost tempted to find out. Lifting her eyes, she looked up into a rather somber, gaunt face with planes and angles that instantly made her think of a soulful poet, one who wrote testimonials to sorrow and pain. Because he lived it. She felt a funny little ache dance through her as well as something that was akin to anticipation.

And then she looked up into the greenest pair of eyes she had ever seen. Her thoughts evaporated completely, as did her breath. Susanna blinked, forcing herself back to the Jeffrey School playing field, Tuesday and a dozen eager little boys.

"Give you what?" she finally managed to ask.

She was prettier close up, more delicate-looking. Not that it mattered. Flynn nodded to the tool that hung suspended from her fingers. "The hammer." Though it was none of his business, he couldn't help asking, "Do you realize that you're holding it sideways?"

Susanna grinned. She felt rather than saw the fleeting look of appreciation that quickly flashed through his eyes and then disappeared as if it had never existed. She jiggled the hammer. It wasn't the first time someone had pointed that out to her. "It keeps me from smashing my thumb and it gives me a much broader surface to hit with."

In its own strange way, that made sense, but she still looked as if she was expending too much energy, seeing the results of her efforts. He made a movement to take the hammer from her and finish the job.

There were few things in life that Susanna hated, but one of them was being thought of as a "helpless little thing." She was used to doing things on her own, and had been doing just that for almost seven years, but at five foot two and a hundred pounds, frailty was a difficult image to shake.

She pulled the hammer back. "I'm perfectly capable of driving in the stakes myself."

His hand, surprisingly delicate and agile considering how muscular his body was, covered the handle just above her fingers. Warmth seared through her at the casual contact. Though it wasn't meant to be, there was something possessive about the gesture. She wondered if he blustered through life, used to getting his own way. It was easy to see how he could, with dark, good looks like his.

For some reason, he had a sudden flash of Kelly, of the way she had always forged through things. Of the way he had let her. Amusement highlighted his eyes for just a moment. "Most women are."

For a moment, Susanna considered using the hammer on his head, but with twelve little boys and two coaches nearby, there were too many witnesses. She surrendered the hammer to this overbearing chauvinist. If he wanted to flex his muscles, literally and figuratively, so be it.

Flynn took the hammer from her and swung hard. The stake sank into the ground at least four inches. Susanna suppressed a shiver. "Bad day?"

He hadn't realized quite how angry he really was at life until just this moment. He took a breath, struggling to get things under control. "The worst."

Probably his own doing, given his sunny disposition. "Your wife?"

He looked at her and noted that her eyes were a mixture of blue and gray and right now looked amused. He didn't care for being someone's source of entertainment. "Anyone ever tell you you ask a lot of questions?"

Susanna had had too much experience with hurt children to let a carelessly voiced sentiment bother her. "It's called conversation and you started it."

Yes, he supposed he had and he had no idea why he was even talking to this woman. He had come to be with Michael, to watch him play and offer encouragement. "I'm a widower,'' he told her, though he didn't know why he had offered this information.

She wondered if he'd been widowed recently. The wounds were still raw. She remembered what it had been like. It *was* incredibly hard. Obviously, his heart was not. Otherwise, it wouldn't have been hurt so much. Without thinking, she placed a hand on his forearm. ''I'm sorry.''

The concern he heard surprised him. Why should she care? They didn't even know each other's names. Her sympathy made him uncomfortable.

''Thanks.''

He thrust her hammer back to her. He watched as she bent over and dropped it into something cavernous that he assumed was a purse. If he was honest with himself, he'd have to admit that the length of her legs, which seemed to elongate before his eyes as she stretched, had captured all his attention. The contrast between her white shorts and tanned legs made her look exceedingly sexy. When she straightened up again, the long T-shirt came down and just covered her shorts, creating the impression that she had nothing on underneath. The thought and his warm response to it caught him unaware.

She looked inquisitively at the expression on his face. Flynn was stumped for something to say. He nodded at her apparel. ''Interesting shirt. Your husband's?''

She looked down, having forgotten for a moment what she had on. Then she smiled. ''No, it's mine.'' She picked up one end of the banner and fitted it over the stake. ''I don't have a husband.''

Flynn picked up the other end and followed her example. He raised one eyebrow. ''Managed to get the shirt off his back, did you?''

''I'm not divorced. I'm a widow.''

He had just naturally assumed that she was divorced. She looked too young to be a widow. The bitter taste in his mouth was like shoe leather. Awkwardly Flynn withdrew his foot from his mouth. "Oh, hey, I'm sorry. I didn't mean—"

He looked so genuinely contrite, she was surprised. And touched. Flashing a dismissive grin, Susanna came to his rescue. It was second nature to her. She absolutely hated seeing anyone or anything in distress. "I'm sure you didn't. The shirt's from Billie."

"Billie?"

She pointed to a tow-headed boy out in the field. As she did so, a ball went between Billie's legs. The boy scowled before he gave chase. "My son."

Flynn looked back at the bright pink lettering across her chest. "A little nearsighted, is he? World's Greatest *Dad?*"

She laughed. Flynn was struck by the depth of the delight he heard ringing in her voice. "No, the shirt was a gift for Father's Day last year." She saw his brows draw together in confusion. "Billie said he thought I had earned it."

She reminded him of someone who needed to be taken care of, not someone who had another life depending on her. He thought of his own experiences with Michael in the past year. There were times he hadn't thought he'd make it with his sanity intact. It must have even been harder for her. "Isn't it a little rough, being a single parent?"

"At times," she agreed. She took a clipboard from her bag. The batting schedule and playing positions were attached to it. She glanced at them before elaborating. "It's never easy balancing a child and a career."

Someone yelled, "Heads up," and Flynn's hand flew out automatically. He caught the misdirected ball and tossed it back onto the field. Warm-up, he noticed, was almost over.

When he looked at Billie's mother again, she was busy making notes. The wind was ruffling her blond hair, teasing the ends and brushing them against his bare forearm. Something tightened within him. Unconsciously, he took a step back. "So, you're not a housewife, or homemaker or whatever the popular term is these days for a mom who keeps the home fires burning. What is it that you do?"

She thought of her desk at work, overflowing with papers. "Mostly tread water."

Flynn tried to interpret the comment. "You give swimming lessons?"

Susanna shook her head, sliding the pencil into place on the side of the clipboard. "I'm an actuary."

Actuaries made him think of stuffy old men in three piece suits who had offices located on the top floor of insurance companies. Occasionally they recalculated mortality projections that told people when they were expected to die. Very cut-and-dried stuff. She looked more like someone who, if she got a haircut, could try out for the stage role of Peter Pan. "You're kidding, right?"

She saw the way his eyes measured her. "Do actuaries have a height requirement?"

He wondered if she was laughing at him and why that even mattered. "No, it's just that, when I think of an actuary, I think of someone old, someone—"

"Male?" she supplied, amused, when he hesitated. Her dad had been an actuary and she remembered his surprise when she had announced her intentions. It wasn't exactly a run-of-the-mill choice for a girl, even one who loved math.

Flynn shrugged as he shoved both hands into his pockets. "Yes."

Her eyes danced and he could have sworn a dimple was struggling to form in one cheek. "I'm neither."

His eyes swept over her again. Despite the baggy shirt, he could discern very firm, very high breasts beneath. An urge, warm and demanding, filtered through him, stunning him. It was a strange sensation for someone who had felt physically dead inside. "I noticed."

The man had the sexiest scowl she had ever seen and it was making her lose her train of thought. Again. She reminded herself that she had duties to see to. Looking over her shoulder one last time to make sure the banner was secure, she moved away from him. "Well, thanks for the help, but I've got dug-out duty."

He didn't move, although he knew that it would be wise to return to the sidelines. "You've got what?"

"I have to keep them in line." She gestured at the field. There were now about twenty boys running around, vainly attempting to execute successful throws and catches.

Flynn looked around the field slowly. Activity seemed to hum out there. It always amazed him to see how much energy a little boy could generate. He looked back at Susanna. "All of them?"

"No, that would take a superwoman. Just the ones in Cub uniforms."

He eyed her quietly. "Did you bring a whip and a chair?"

"They're not as bad as all that." Although at times, it was close, she added silently.

This he had to see. Maybe he could even pick up a few pointers. Fatherhood at this stage of his life mystified him. He hadn't had that much practice the first time around. Kelly had always been there, to see to everything. All he'd had to do was look proud and say the right words. "Mind if I hang around and watch?"

She shrugged, though something small and faraway was pleased that he wanted to. "Suit yourself."

"I generally do."

If this had been a hundred years ago, she would have said the tone was well suited to a legendary gunfighter riding through a small town. There was almost a warning note in the words. She wondered why.

She didn't have time to wonder for long. As she watched, the coaches from both teams, a total of five affable men who enjoyed reliving times when they ran faster and things like mortgages and insurance premiums had no meaning, got together to decide which team of eager, if slightly inept players went first. A red-headed boy with three times his share of freckles dusting his face and arms called the toss. The Pirates batted first.

Flynn stepped back as a flurry of boys in blue-and-white uniforms charged past him. Twelve little boys, all talking at once, crowded around the blonde and shouted questions.

Clipboard in hand, Susanna did her best to match each boy to his position. "Adam, first base. Billie, second. Nikky, left center," she read from the list that the head coach had handed her when she'd first arrived.

Having sent eleven boys onto the field, she was confronted with Drew. Drew was barely five and small for his age, but because his dad was one of the coaches, he had managed to get on the team comprised mainly of six- and seven-year-olds. He clutched a pair of red shin guards against his chest as he dropped an oversized helmet and mask to the ground. Despair was evident in his eyes.

"I'm the catcher."

Susanna bent down. "Yes, I know. And you'll be a very good one, too."

A smile began to form on the small face. Drew held up the guards. "You have to dress me."

Dropping down on one knee, Susanna grabbed the shin guards, either one of which looked to be about half as high as Drew, and took action. She had her doubts that he could move in the outfit, but refrained from saying so. "I thought you'd never ask."

Drew turned awkwardly as she struggled with the fasteners on the guard. "Huh?"

"Just a little humor, Drew. Best way to get through things that leave you confused." She tugged, but the last fastener refused to live up to its name.

She certainly did a lot of struggling. He wondered if she thought it was worth it. With a sigh, Flynn moved closer. "Need help with that?"

Susanna looked up. From this vantage point, the man looked twice as tall. Before she could answer, he was beside her, tackling the other shin guard. "Is riding to the rescue a sideline with you?"

He didn't have to look at her face to know she was grinning. A sudden image of Kelly flashed through his mind. The first time he had met her in high school, she had walked into him and dropped all her books on the ground. He had helped her pick them up. They were married a year later. "I minored in it at college," he answered flatly. "C'mere, sport, let's get you fitted properly." He realized how that had to sound and glanced in the woman's direction. If she took offense at his words, she didn't show it. That set her apart from a lot of other people he knew.

It was a little like watching twin copies of the Bad News Bears, Flynn thought. Two innings had stretched by and the game was tied ten to ten, not because of any phenomenal playing, but because the rules were mercifully different for six-year-olds involved in coach pitch. An inning ended with five runs or three tagged outs. In deference to coordination that hadn't yet developed, there was no such thing as a strikeout.

A red-headed little boy with the number three on his back swung hard and sent the ball sailing backward through the air. It landed at Susanna's feet. Flynn curbed the urge to retrieve it.

Scooping the ball up, Susanna threw it to the pitcher. Or at least she tried. It fell to the pitcher's left, about a yard short of its target.

Flynn laughed. So much for Supermom. "You throw like a girl."

She turned to look at him, unruffled. "There's a reason for that."

"Oh?" Flynn expected to hear some sort of involved explanation.

"I *am* a girl." She sighed. No, it had been a long time since she could have rightfully laid claim to that title. Brett had been part of her life then. She shrugged. "Or pretty close to one."

Flynn crossed his arms before him, curious about her response. Woman wanted to be considered equal, if not superior. His daughters had taught him that. "Haven't you heard that women are supposed to be able to do everything a man can—only better?"

She bit back the temptation to say that she could. He looked too eager for an argument. "I don't have to know how to throw a ball to feel secure, Mr.—" She cocked her head waiting for him to fill in.

"O'Roarke. Flynn."

"O'Roarke?" The name rang no bells. She glanced at her roster. "Which one's your boy?"

"Michael." He was about to tell her that Michael was his grandson but then the batter hit a double and Flynn's words were lost in the noise as she yelled encouragement to the right fielder who dropped the ball. She turned to look at Flynn.

"I'm glad you came to the game. Kids need to have their families show an interest."

The smile she gave him nudged away some of the darkness in his soul. He didn't know why the idea that she thought well of him appealed to him. It shouldn't. He didn't care what this woman thought of him. In all likelihood, he probably wouldn't see her again. Or if he did bump into her, he wouldn't recognize her.

She suddenly came to life, cheering an accidental catch on Michael's part. A small Pirate dropped his bat and shuffled off to the end of the lineup. "Way to go, Michael!"

Well, maybe he would recognize her again, Flynn amended as he clapped for his grandson. But that was as far as it was going to go, or as far as he would let anything go for a long, long time.

"That's three outs!" Susanna called to the fair-haired man in the center of the playing field. Nodding, he took off his glove and signaled the team in.

"You keep score, too?" Flynn asked. He moved as the team filed enthusiastically back into the area designated as the dug-out.

Susanna shrugged as Drew presented himself to her to be unharnessed. She was better at removing things, Flynn noted absently, than she was at putting them on. Interesting.

"Someone has to." Carefully Susanna pulled the protective pad from Drew's chest. The catcher's mask plopped down at her feet with a thud and she jumped back, colliding with Flynn who hadn't been quick enough to get out of her way. He was beginning to doubt that anyone was quick enough for that. She seemed to be all over, as energized as the boys she was involved with. Instinctively, Flynn reached out to keep her from losing her balance.

His hands felt steady, capable. Sure. He was a man you could trust, Susanna thought. But one who didn't give his own trust easily. She could see that in his eyes as he regarded her.

"This 'job' could be hazardous to your health," he commented dryly, releasing her. Her skin felt incredibly soft to the touch. He had an urge to discover if it was like that all over.

It was obviously not a good day for celibacy.

Susanna began waving the boys into batting order. "Only if I forgot the brownies."

"Excuse me?"

She looked over her shoulder. "I have to organize them, then I have to feed them after the game."

He glanced back at the various mothers and fathers who had straggled in to cheer on their sons. Why was she the only one doing things on the sidelines? "Who made up the rules?"

She laughed again. Flynn felt his body responding to the warmth of the sound even as something within him warned him not to. "No one. I'm an overachiever."

He could believe that.

Suddenly she swung around, looking down at a boy with a number seven on his shirt and mischief all over his face. He sat wedged in between two other players and was dusting them with dirt. Any minute, there was going to be a fight. "No, Chris, put the dirt down."

Eyes in the back of her head, Flynn thought, but then that went with the territory when you were a mother. His own had always known what he was up to, even when she wasn't anywhere in sight.

Number seven held up a fistful of dirt and seemed to be weighing his options. He put his hand down, but as Susanna turned away, he opened his fist and threw the dirt at her. Susanna swung around again, a reprimand on her lips.

Flynn beat her to it. Two strides and he was looming in front of the boy. "I wouldn't do that again." His voice was low, but stern. "Unless you'd like to be benched for the next three years."

The boy's eyes grew wide as he regarded Flynn, clearly buying into the warning. "Okay." He swallowed hard.

Susanna tried not to laugh as she listened to the exchange.

Michael beamed at Chris's retreat. "He lifts weights and works with space stuff. He knows astronauts," he added proudly.

Obedience came instantly with Flynn's references and the boys immediately settled down. "You guys better listen to—" His mind drew a blank as he turned to Susanna. "Say, what is your name, anyway?"

She plopped a batting helmet on number five's head. "Knock 'em dead, Jason." Turning, she extended her hand to Flynn. "Susanna Troy."

She smiled encouragingly at him when she saw that there was just the slightest hesitation in his eyes before he took her hand in his. It was almost as if he was afraid of making contact with her.

For the first time in a long while, Susanna found herself more than a little intrigued.

And very attracted.

Chapter Two

He had come strictly to watch Michael play baseball and to offer him a little one-on-one male bonding. Those had been his only intentions.

Instead, Flynn found himself watching both Michael and the exuberant woman to his left. Parents, he knew through firsthand experience, had a tendency to be prejudiced. Their own offspring was always the best. He'd been guilty of it himself. It was a normal reaction. Susanna, he concluded after watching her in action, was *not* normal. She cheered loudly for each and every boy on the team as soon as their bats connected with the ball, urging them to run. It was, Flynn thought, as if she regarded each boy as her own.

If she hadn't pointed him out, the only way Flynn would have known which boy was her son was by the way she tensed every time Billie came up to bat. But Flynn had a distinct feeling that she probably would have tensed even if Billie hadn't been her son. Flynn had noticed that she had a way of empathizing with each player and Billie had his own special problem. Billie swung in slow motion.

The first time he saw Billie swing at the ball, Flynn was certain he just hadn't been playing close enough attention. Little boys with bats in their hands swung energetically at everything. And so did Billie. At the empty air when he was taking practice swings. But whenever the coach who acted as pitcher threw a ball to him, Billie's swing inexplicably decreased until he swung the bat slowly past the space the baseball had just vacated.

Eight pitches and no contact. The coach's encouragement wasn't helping. Billie gripped the bat harder, his small shoulders rigid.

Susanna pressed her lips together, feeling Billie's growing agitation. She really wished he wouldn't put himself through this, but he desperately wanted to be on a baseball team. She couldn't forbid him to play. All she could do was just hope and pray his bat would make contact with the ball.

Some of the boys sitting on the ground, waiting their turn at bat, began chanting, "C'mon Billie, you can do it. Put a little power into it."

Billie missed again. The coach yelled another instruction to him.

"Let him concentrate, boys," Susanna murmured to the squadron of little boys at her feet. Her eyes remained fixed on the sweating Cub poised over home plate.

Twelve pitches whizzed by, each followed belatedly by Billie's bat. The coach pushed back his cap. "Someone want to help him bat?" he called out.

It was standard procedure after twelve misses. Otherwise, they would be there all night. Still, Susanna knew how much it had to hurt Billie's pride to have someone bat with him when the other little boys did it on their own. She turned to see which father was closest to the batting cage.

Flynn stepped in.

There was just so much agony he could tolerate watching. Flynn got into the batter's cage behind Billie. The catcher from the opposing team shuffled back to make room. Flynn hardly noticed him. He smiled down encouragingly at the slightly moist eyes as he positioned himself. Playing ball had been second nature to him when he was Billie's age.

"Let's show 'em how it's done, sport."

Billie sucked in air and nodded his head.

With his hands over Billie's, Flynn directed Billie's swing at the first pitched ball. And missed.

Billie craned his neck to look up at Flynn. "That's what I do."

Flynn heard the hitch of frustration bordering on tears in the boy's voice. With a slight movement, Flynn rotated his back muscles. "Just getting warmed up, sport. We'll do better next time."

Flynn crouched a little lower as the ball came toward them and guided Billie's aim. Contact. The ball went flying into deep left. Billie stared at the ball in open-mouthed wonder, the bat slipping from his fingers to the dirt.

"Run!" Susanna yelled.

Flynn turned and took a step toward first base, carried away by the enthusiasm in her voice before he realized she was shouting the directive at her son and not him. A small, self-depreciating smile touched the corners of his mouth as Flynn turned away. The look on Billie's face had made him feel good.

Hands shoved deep into his back pockets, he dropped to the sidelines. "You carry a lot of authority in that voice of yours," he commented as he watched a dark-haired boy dash in from third.

The runner reached home plate and Susanna scooped off his batting helmet, handing it to the next batter in line. Bases were loaded. Quickly, she noted the run on her pad.

"It's a gift," she answered Flynn belatedly.

She looked up at him and her expression softened. Flynn found he wasn't quite prepared for the look of gratitude that he saw in her eyes. It had a totally different effect on him than what he had seen in Billie's face. Why in heavens name should he feel aroused by the sight of gray-blue eyes and a face that could fit neatly between the palms of his hands? Grandfathers, he thought, weren't supposed to be aroused, only amused.

"Thank you."

She might have been thanking him for presenting her with an emerald necklace for all the feeling he heard in her voice. "For what?"

This was a man who didn't take gratitude easily or without suspicion, she thought and felt a twinge of sorrow. "For helping Billie."

Flynn shrugged noncommittally. "Someone had to."

"True, but it didn't have to be you." He didn't look as if he fit into this late-afternoon get-together of fathers and offspring. There was something that set him apart, a barrier he seemed to be keeping between himself and everyone else.

"I was closest." The look on his face warned her to drop the subject.

Susanna wondered why gratitude made him look so uncomfortable. "I'm glad you were." She was aware of his eyes on her as she turned her attention to the next batter. A hot flush stirred within her and she smiled. It was a nice feeling.

Susanna gave Billie the high sign. Her son beamed back, crouching, ready to run to second base on the next hit.

After what seemed like five incredibly long innings, the Cubs finally won. The score was twenty-five to twenty-four. That made them two for one for the season, Susanna told

Flynn as he helped her pull up the stakes for the banner. He told her he was surprised she knew the terminology.

"Self-defense," she quipped, handing Billie her hammer to hold.

Without thinking, Flynn began rolling up the banner. "Excuse me?"

Susanna bent to pick up a piece of discarded plastic that had been wrapped around a giant brownie not ten minutes ago. She threw it into a large garbage bag.

"Billie eats, sleeps and breathes baseball." She looked at her son fondly. The boy was engrossed in a conversation with Michael. "I had to learn the lingo in order to communicate with him." She went to take the banner from him, but Flynn had already picked it up and had it balanced against his shoulder. Lord, he looked powerful, she thought. "It's a little like mastering a foreign language." Picking up her knapsack and purse, she began to walk toward the parked cars.

The sun was going down. It would be cool soon. Cool and dark. Flynn watched the wind play with her hair and wondered what she would be like in the dark, against cool sheets—

Abruptly, he refocused his thoughts, wondering if his mind was going. "Is every game like this?"

"Like what?"

"Long. Chaotic. Disoriented."

She pointed out her car in the lot. "Yes."

Flynn shifted the weight of the stakes slightly, wondering how she managed to carry them back and forth each week. The load wasn't heavy so much as awkward, especially for someone as small as she was.

"You enjoy this." It was more than obvious.

"I enjoy children." She glanced over her shoulder at the field. Michael and Billie were straggling behind, throwing the ball to each other as they walked.

There was love in her eyes, love that suddenly had Flynn yearning to be touched by something like it, to feel the warmth of that kind of all-encompassing feeling. He reminded himself that that kind of love carried stiff penalties with it, penalties he no longer wanted to face. You love, you hurt, it was as simple and as complicated as that.

"How do you feel about adults?" And where the hell had that come from? He sounded as if he was making a pitch when it was the last damn thing on earth he wanted to do. Flynn turned his face away, looking toward her car, hoping she wouldn't say anything.

He might have known better. Susanna was the type, he realized, who could *always* say something.

"I enjoy them, too. Especially brooding poets who grudgingly do good deeds. Right here." She nodded needlessly at her white car.

He realized after a beat that she meant him. He rested the stakes and banner against the side of the car. "I'm not a poet."

"A pity." She couldn't think of an occupation he looked more suited for. "You've got the face for it."

Dropping her knapsack to the ground, she rooted through her purse for the car keys. She liked the slight flush that had come over his face at her comment. She wasn't sure if it was annoyance or embarrassment, but it did become him. Opening her door, she turned to face Flynn. Billie had reached her side and she placed an arm around his shoulders in easy camaraderie.

"Well, thanks again for your help and the conversation." She couldn't help grinning at the last part. "Most people prefer to sit on the sidelines."

And so did he. More than most. He still didn't fully understand why he hadn't gone with his first instincts. "Yeah."

A man of few words, she thought, wishing she knew how to set free what was bottled up inside of him. That it needed to be set free was something she wholeheartedly believed. It didn't matter that she had only known him for an hour and a half. Susanna made up her mind about people quickly. "I enjoyed the company."

She sounded sincere, Flynn thought. She was flirting—and yet, it didn't really seem like it, not if he were honest about his appraisal. There was a kind of innocence to her words. He wondered if that was possible, then shrugged off the thought. Women with seven-year-old boys weren't innocent.

The words, "See you at the game," were on the tip of his tongue, but then Flynn decided he had already said far too much. If he said that, it would sound as if he hoped to see her again. And he didn't. He distinctly hoped that he *wouldn't* see her again. He had more than just a small nagging feeling that for all her good intentions and supposed openness, Susanna Troy spelled trouble. With a capital *T*. And right now, his world was in enough turmoil.

With a curt nod born of a strong sense of self-preservation, Flynn took Michael's hand in his and turned away.

"Bye, Michael!" Billie called after them.

Michael craned his neck as he looked back over his shoulder. "See you at the game, Billie!"

Flynn purposely kept his back to Susanna as he walked toward his own car. And escape.

He would have kept on walking without so much as a backward glance, had the whining not begun. A very persistent, tinny whining. The kind an engine made when it refused to perform, like a petulant child throwing a tantrum. Without wanting to, he listened. She was going to flood the carburetor.

Michael dug his heels into the pavement and tugged Flynn's hand. It was obvious that he wanted to ride to the rescue, even if Flynn didn't. "Their car won't start."

"Yeah." There seemed to be no escaping this. Squaring his shoulders, Flynn turned around and slowly walked over to Susanna's car. He saw her frowning as she turned the key again. "Sounds like engine trouble."

That's what it was, all right, she thought, trying not to let an exasperated sigh escape her lips. "Nothing a good mechanic and three hundred dollars probably can't fix, I'm sure." She gave up trying to turn over the engine and pulled her key out of the ignition.

Flynn marveled at the nonchalant way she had mentioned that amount of money. "You have that kind of money to waste?"

She shook her head, dragging her hand through her hair. "No one has that kind of money to waste." She got out. Billie bounced out of the other side, joining her. "But I need a car. I'm a little old to ride a bike to work." Although, if worse came to worst, she thought, she could make the ten-mile trip.

Susanna leaned into the back seat and dragged her paraphernalia onto the pavement. This wasn't exactly shaping up as one of her better days.

Flynn watched her shorts ride up high on her leg again. He grinned despite himself. "Oh, I don't know. It might be interesting to watch at that."

Susanna turned and he saw the surprised look on her face. Damn, she probably thought he was making a pass at her again. Well, he wasn't. The words had just leaked out. His voice became gruff again.

"Can I give you and Billie a lift home?" He couldn't see her walking home with all that stuff in her arms. Besides, it would be dark soon.

Her sigh of relief was audible. "If you don't mind." She looked down at the banner, stakes and knapsack, not to mention a purse that probably weighed in at slightly less than fifteen pounds. "My arms would be kind of full."

Flynn merely shook his head. The woman needed a keeper. Positioning the banner and stakes against his left shoulder, he picked up her knapsack. "I noticed. The car's right over here." He gestured toward it with the tip of the stakes.

The silver convertible was not the last word in roomy comfort. Flynn deposited her things next to it and unlocked the door. "Hop in."

She eyed it dubiously. The car was small and low-slung. Susanna looked at the boys and then at the car. "Is there room enough in that for all of us?"

Seating four would be a challenge. The car had been an impulse, bought last year, he supposed, by the twenty-six-year-old who was trapped inside him. His daughters had fairly drooled over it, each begging to be allowed to take it for a spin. It was an impractical purchase, to say the least. Still he had to admit that he liked it.

"The boys are small. They can scrunch up in the back." Even as he said it, the two scrambled into the rather crammed space behind the two front seats.

"How about these?" She indicated the banner and stakes.

"They can go in the trunk." He unlocked it and loaded the things in. That was a tight fit, too, even though there was nothing else in there except a jack.

"Good enough." She got in on the passenger side. After almost two hours of cheering the team on, it felt good to sit down again. She watched as Flynn got behind the steering wheel, and then gave him her address. "It's just on the edge of the development," she added.

Flynn started up the engine. They passed her disabled car on their way out. He saw the accusing look she give it. "What about your car?"

"I'll call my mechanic in the morning. He'll send over his tow truck." She closed her eyes, not relishing the bill that this was going to generate.

Flynn glanced at her as he took a corner. The sight of her with her eyes shut like that stirred him. He pictured her head on a pillow next to his, sleeping after a night of—

Damn, what had gotten into him?

"What about work tomorrow?" His voice felt tight in his throat, even as he cursed himself for it.

She shrugged, wondering why his voice had gotten so gruff again. "I'll call someone for a ride."

Was there a special someone she turned to? A man in her life?

All the better for him, Flynn thought quickly. He didn't need to get his life entangled with an overzealous blonde. He knew that. Which was why he was surprised to hear himself asking, "You don't happen to work at Palisades Mutual, do you?" with a strange sense of forboding.

She leaned forward to look at him. "Why don't I? Take that turn there." She pointed to the left.

Too late. He missed it. Muttering under his breath, Flynn did a U-turn. "Then you do?" he asked impatiently.

He was the most reluctant do-gooder she had ever run into. Listening to his tone, one would have thought she had held a gun to his head, ordering him to bring her home. "The payroll department thinks I do. Why?"

Just his luck. "I'm an engineer at Worth Aerospace up the road from Palisades Mutual."

She was familiar with the company. She passed it twice a day, on her way to and from work. "Small world."

Flynn paused. He had expected her to ask for a lift. That would have taken it all out of his hands. *Was* there a man in her life? He wished he'd stop wondering about that. "I suppose I could drop you off tomorrow morning."

The reluctance in his voice had reached a new high. Why was he offering to do it if he didn't want to? Was this some sort of bet he had going? Or one he had lost? She felt confused.

Susanna held her hands up. "You'll notice that I am not twisting your arm here, Flynn." She said his name, although she had a hunch he would have preferred she call him Mr. O'Roarke. She was getting very mixed signals, his wanting to maintain a distance and yet not wanting to at the same time. He couldn't have it both ways. And she knew which way she would have preferred it. She enjoyed getting along with everyone.

"Besides, you don't know what time I have to be in," she pointed out, feeling obligated to give him a way out if he wanted it.

She was saving him from possibly making a mistake and he was grateful. "It was just a thought."

When he saw her smile, he knew that he wasn't saved after all. On the contrary. Somehow he had managed to voluntarily step into a mine field.

Susanna didn't want him to think that she was being ungrateful. Maybe she had only imagined his reluctance. Maybe that was just his way. She realized that she was making a rather hasty judgment about the man, but she had seen the way he was with Billie as well as the way he was with his own son. It was enough to convince her that though Flynn O'Roarke might scowl like an ogre, a warmhearted man lived beneath the brooding exterior.

Besides, she did rather like the brooding exterior.

And a very nice thought it was, too. "I'll make arrangements. For work, I mean," she added quickly when she saw the scowl threaten to return to his face. "You know, for a Good Samaritan, you do an awful lot of scowling."

"I'm not a Good Samaritan," he fairly snapped, his hands tightening on the wheel.

He might be into denial, but she wasn't. "Then what do you call offering your services?"

That was an easy one. "Temporary insanity."

She laughed, tickled. "I don't think so."

She had to be set straight right here and now. There were no hidden messages to his offer and he didn't want her to misunderstand. She'd been nice to Michael and this was just payback, nothing more. "Mrs.—Troy is it?"

His exasperation had taken on a formal tone. "That way," she said, pointing just as he began to head down the wrong street. She leaned back in her seat. "It is, but Susanna is easier."

He threw the car into reverse to regain the turn as the boys cheered on, enjoying the ride. "I wouldn't know about that."

Susanna decided that for the moment, it was better to back off. There would be other times to try to dig at the underlayer Flynn O'Roarke was trying to hide. Tomorrow morning if nothing else. And she had a very strong feeling that it would not be just tomorrow morning. There would be more times than that.

Some things a woman just felt. And she had a feeling about Flynn.

"Well, whatever you want to call your acts of gallantry, I think you've more than earned your merit badge this evening, starting with helping me put up the banner for the game."

"Yeah, well..." His voice trailed off as he shrugged away her thanks, not knowing how to respond. "What time do you need a pick-up tomorrow?"

His voice was harsh, but by now she had decided that keeping her at a distance was one of his defense mechanisms. "What time do you have to be at work?" He pulled up her street. "Last house on the left."

"Seven-thirty." Reaching her house, he turned off the engine.

That was a good half hour before she had to make an appearance at the office. Still, she didn't want to put him out. "What direction will you be coming from?"

"Never mind that." Flynn wasn't about to tell her where he lived. He had already talked too much to her as it was. He wanted to keep his life private. The less she knew about him, the better.

"Okay, you're coming out of thin air, then." The boys giggled at the solemn way she seemed to accept that. "All right." She smiled at Flynn. "Could you drop out of the sky at about seven?"

She was laughing at him. But that was better than her getting under his skin. As long as he remembered that. "That could be arranged."

Billie leaned forward, holding onto the back of his mother's seat. His eyes were large. "Can I watch?"

Flynn turned in his seat to look at the boy. "Watch what?"

"You drop out of the sky."

"You might have noticed that they take everything literally at this age." Susanna fought to keep a straight face. She turned to look at Billie. "It was just a figure of speech, Billie."

Wheat-colored eyebrows knitted together as Billie tried to puzzled that one out. "What's a 'figure of speech'?"

Susanna kept her eyes on Flynn's face as she answered. "Something someone says when they don't want to tell the truth."

"Union Street," Flynn said, damning her, not for this, but for what might come. What would come. "I live on

Union Street. Look, I don't see what the fuss is over an address—''

Hardly hearing him, Susanna did some quick mental calculations. "Then you'll have to backtrack." She shook her head. She really didn't want to put him out. "I don't want—''

"I wouldn't have made the offer if I wasn't willing to go through with it,'' he snapped as he stomped out of the car and opened the trunk. Why in God's name had he ever even opened his mouth?

With a heave that was mightier than warranted, he removed her things from his trunk, as if he was symbolically removing her from his life.

"I have a feeling, Flynn,'' Susanna said softly as she got out of the car, "that you wouldn't do anything you weren't willing to do. Thank you." She accepted the banner and the rest of her belongings as Flynn all but shoved them toward her.

The stakes clattered to the ground and Billie scooped them up, one in each hand.

Eyes the color of the sky over a stormy sea, Flynn thought suddenly, looking down into her face. It was an omen. One he was damn well going to heed.

Right after he picked her up in the morning.

Flynn slammed the trunk shut and got into the car as Michael crawled out of the rear and tumbled into the passenger seat. Susanna managed a wave as he drove away. Flynn didn't wave back.

Willingly. He was doing this willingly. He needed his head x-rayed. And fast.

Maybe, he pondered as he drove home, Michael chattering at his side, there was a twenty-four-hour lunatic asylum he could check into, preferably before tomorrow morning at seven.

Chapter Three

Swimming in a sea of euphoria created by winning the game, Billie burst through the front door just ahead of Susanna. Without looking, he pitched his glove and hat in the general vicinity of the sofa. The articles bounced once against the sofa and tumbled down under the coffee table.

Obviously remembering his mother's oft-repeated instructions Billie turned to see her struggling to open the hall closet door while balancing the banner and stakes and yanked the door open for Susanna. He hung on the doorknob, pivoting on his toes as he leaned back, swaying. "Did you like Michael's dad, Mom?" He watched her face, waiting for an answer.

Susanna knew that tone. She stood the banner and stakes upright in the recesses of the hall closet, securing them with the side of the ironing board. Satisfied that they wouldn't pitch forward the next time she opened the door, she closed the closet and turned to look at her precocious seven-year-old.

Billie had been playing matchmaker for a little more than a year now, fancifully pairing her up with everyone from hockey immortal Wayne Gretzky, who she tactfully pointed out was married, to matching her up with the muscle-bound star of an eight o'clock action-packed series on Saturday nights, who wasn't. At least, not to her knowledge. It appeared that Billie was bringing his efforts closer to home now. Susanna wasn't at all certain that that was an improvement, and it might make for embarrassing situations.

"Yes, I like Michael's dad." Hope sprang into her son's eyes. She went on quickly. "I also like Drew's dad and Chris's dad—"

"Wow."

She could see the possibilities hatching in his very fertile little brain. The boy was seven, going on twenty. And at times she had to hustle to keep up.

Susanna placed her hand on the small shoulder, bending down to be eye to eye with her son. "Put your eyes back in your head, young man. I like everyone, remember?" Or at least she tried, she amended silently. Some people were harder to like than others. Some people, Flynn O'Roarke for instance, didn't seem as if they really wanted to be liked at all.

She looked over Billie's head into the living room. The boy was a positive whirlwind. Two seconds in a room and he turned it into a mess. "What I don't like is seeing things lying all over the place." Straightening, she pointed to the fallen objects.

With a frustrated huff, Billie marched to the sofa and picked up his glove and hat. Billie placed the two items on the first step of the stairs, an indication that he would take them up to his room later.

"If you like everybody so much," Billie said as he followed Susanna into the kitchen, "how come you're not married again?"

He was like a dog trying to get at a bone that was just out of reach, she thought with a sigh. She supposed she really couldn't blame him. It was rough being a boy without a father.

Susanna pulled open the refrigerator door and reached for a carton of milk. "Really cut to the chase, don't you?"

His eyes narrowed as he watched his mother take out a glass from the cupboard overhead and hand it to him. He held the glass in both hands as she poured. "Huh?"

Susanna popped the spout on the container closed again. "I'm not married, my love," she told him patiently as she slipped the carton back on the shelf, "because I've never met anyone who's made that something 'special' happen." No bells, no banjos, she thought fondly. Brett had made all that happen for her.

Billie knew the procedure. He placed his glass on the table and took out a small plate from the dishwasher rack. He held it in his hands as he waited for his mother. "Special?"

Susanna opened the cookie tin and counted out three chocolate chip cookies before she pushed the lid closed again. Taking out a spoon, she reopened the refrigerator and retrieved her own evening snack. Non-fat cherry yogurt. She had to admit that the cookies looked a great deal more tempting.

She smiled as she sat down next to Billie at the small kitchen table. Without its leaf, the table was just big enough for the two of them and Aunt Jane whenever she felt the urge to pop by for breakfast. And that was just the way Susanna liked it. Just the three of them.

She leaned forward in the chair, elbows on the table as she absently stirred the yogurt and let her mind wander back through the years. Her lips curved wistfully as she pulled up

Brett's image. "When I first met your father, something very special happened."

A milk-drenched cookie stuffed in his mouth, Billie cocked his head. He chewed furiously, in a hurry to get the next word out. "Like fireworks?"

Susanna thought of the way she had felt when Brett had looked into her eyes that first day they had bumped into each other in the hall at the university. Brett's sky-blue eyes had rippled directly into her soul. She had known, right from the start, that he was the one. It had been as simple as that.

"Exactly like fireworks."

Billie sank his last cookie in the glass, counting to ten under his breath. He looked at his mother incredulously. "And is that what you're waiting for now? Fireworks?"

Susanna swallowed two spoonfuls of yogurt before answering. She wasn't waiting for anything. She'd had her perfect love and that was enough. She couldn't hope for anything more. Lightning rarely struck twice. "What I am waiting for, young man, is for you to get cleaned up and ready for bed."

"Aw, Mom. It's too early to go to bed." Billie purposely ignored the clock that hung on the wall.

Susanna used the end of her spoon to point to it. Her voice became formal. "It's almost eight. Your game lasted a lot longer tonight than it usually does, William, and you know what time curfew is."

Billie frowned deeply as he bit into the last of his cookies.. When she called him William it meant she was serious.

His face brightened suddenly and Susanna eyed his expression cautiously. What was he up to now? She knew Billie could be devious. His next words were predictable. "Can I stay up another half hour, Mom, please?"

This was well-traveled territory. She knew what he was angling for. She was torn between doing what she knew was right and giving him everything he wanted. There were times when being a parent was no picnic.

"If you get all ready," she said slowly, not wanting him to feel that the battle had been won so easily, "there might be an extra fifteen minutes in it for you."

Billie got up and dutifully rinsed out his glass and washed off his plate. "The Angels are playing the Mets." He gave her his most dazzling smile.

She was raising a con artist. She should have named him Artful Dodger instead of William Brett, she mused. Susanna nodded approvingly at the dish and glass drying on the rack. "You can watch one inning."

He hung his head while raising his eyes. It gave him a hangdog expression. "Just one?"

Susanna had to struggle to keep from laughing. If Billie put this much effort into a future career, the boy was going to make president by the time he turned thirty. "Just one."

He stuck out his chin. "Aw, Mom."

She shook her head, holding firm for his sake, but having a sneaking suspicion that she would give in down the line. But at least she could put up a good front. "And if you whine, it might be just half an inning."

There wasn't another word out of Billie as he dashed up the stairs to get ready.

Susanna sighed and laughed. Looking at the bottom of her container, she scraped the last bit of yogurt out of the corners. This wasn't the easiest job in the world, being both mother and father to Billie, even though it had tremendous rewards. She knew he craved male companionship and she ached for him. She did the best she could to fill in on all those father-son things that kept coming up, but it just wasn't enough. He needed a father.

Still, she couldn't get married just to give him one. That wouldn't be fair to any of them, not to Billie, or to herself and certainly not to the man who would be pulled into the vortex of this bargain. It was hard, very hard being a single mother and raising a son.

She thought about the man who had given her a ride home and smiled to herself. Flynn O'Roarke had no idea how easy he had it, having a child of his own gender to raise. And although she wouldn't have traded Billie for the world, things might have gone a lot easier for her if Billie had been born a girl.

Flynn wished passionately that his daughter had given birth to a girl instead of a boy. At least then he would have had a vague memory as to how to go about things. Being put in charge of a boy was a whole different ball game, one in which he wasn't sure of any of the rules. Things were different with boys than with girls.

He shook his head as he peeked in on Michael in the family room. The boy had made a beeline for the television set as soon as they had walked into the house.

Michael saw Flynn looking in. With nachos clutched in his stubby little fingers, he gestured for his grandfather to come in. "Wanna watch the game, Granddad?" he asked hopefully, in between crunching.

Flynn shook his head, not in answer to the boy's question, but at the way Michael had so effortlessly settled in. Michael was inviting him into the room as if Flynn was the late arrival to the household and not the other way around. Michael was certainly having a lot less trouble adjusting to this situation than he was, Flynn thought.

He took a seat next to his grandson. Michael repositioned the bag of nachos so that they could share them.

Michael was trying very hard to make things easier on him, Flynn thought. He was trying hard to be thought of as an integral part of Flynn's life. Poor little guy, Flynn mused as he looked at the boy's face. Michael needed to be part of a family, needed so many things that Flynn felt ill-equipped to give him.

Still, he had to admire his grandson's courageous approach to the curves life had thrown him so far. Flynn had yet to see Michael cry, even when he had woken up in the hospital to find that he no longer had parents. He had been silent for a long time, so long that Flynn had grown concerned. And then he had asked in a small, still voice, if he could come home with him. It had almost broken Flynn's heart.

The green numbers on the VCR announced the hour. It was after nine. "Shouldn't you be going to bed?" Flynn prompted.

"Not sleepy." Michael stifled a huge yawn that belied his words.

"Oh. I see." Flynn dropped the subject.

Kelly, he remembered, had always been a stickler about bedtime, even when the girls had begged to stay up. Flynn had always thought that was rather a silly rule, making someone go to bed when they weren't tired. But he had never opposed Kelly. She usually knew what was best in the long run.

On his own now, Flynn thought he'd wait Michael out. When the boy was tired, he'd be ready to go to bed.

"So," Flynn said, taking a handful of chips, and eating them one at a time. "Who's winning?"

Michael pointed with his chin, a look of pure disgust on his normally sunny face. "They are."

By Michael's tone, Flynn surmised that "they" were the Mets. He crossed his arms before him and settled back to watch the game. There was no work to catch up on tonight and he could think of nothing else he'd rather do than stay in the company of this complex little being who required so little of him to exist. It was only everything he had to give, Flynn thought with an amused shake of his head.

The whole situation still baffled him.

Rules, structure, things like that belonged on blueprints and designs for space station satellites. He was having trouble finding his way around rules and structure as they applied to everyday life. He had always been a believer in live and let live. It had been Kelly who had administered the rules, Kelly who had seen to the punishments on the rare occasions that they were needed. During all that child rearing, all those years of marriage, Flynn had been, by and large, an innocent bystander.

The roles they had taken on had evolved naturally. He hadn't cared to get bogged down in the details of day-to-day living. He had enough of that to contend with at work. Flynn hadn't wanted to run into it in his home life as well. So Kelly had taken over the budget, the bills, the children, and the myriad minutiae that went along with running a home. Flynn's capacity had been that of a silent backup.

When she died, leaving him so abruptly, everything had come crashing in all at once. The late payment notice from the mortgage company had been his first indication that every nook and cranny of his life was going to have to be overhauled. It had been a tough struggle, but he had managed somehow.

He had just been getting to the point where he could handle the day-to-day annoying details, blessing the powers that be that at least his daughters were full-grown and didn't need constant care, when that midnight call had come about Aimee and Doug.

Suddenly he was not only mired in life, but was instantly thrown into fatherhood all over again. Or perhaps, more accurately, for the first time.

So far, Michael seemed unharmed by his grandfather's inexperience. Michael had proven to be a rather resilient little boy. But still, Flynn felt he was on shaky ground.

He rolled the metaphor around in his head. The ground had really felt shaky under his feet this evening at the field. What had possessed him to offer to take that overly effervescent woman to work tomorrow? He didn't have time to play Good Samaritan. And God knows he certainly didn't have time to—to—

To what?

To feel something? Flynn sighed as the side was retired. Michael flashed him a conspiratorial, albeit sleepy, grin.

Flynn thought of Susanna. Hormones, that's what it was, pure and simple. He had felt a physical reaction to her company. He was certainly old enough to know all about hormones. His had been in suspended animation for the last fifteen months.

He could honestly say that he had been in love with only one woman in his life and he had married her. Sure, he had looked, but he had never wanted, never even fantasized. He'd been too happy, too content. Too busy counting his blessings. When Kelly died, he was so devastated, he was certain that all of him had died from the neck down.

To find that it hadn't was a shock all its own. A shock that didn't really please him. There were far too many complications that went along with this revelation. And too many people to consider. He just had to put the whole thing, the whole evening from his mind.

Yet there was something about Susanna. Something. That was the only way he could describe it. He couldn't put his finger on it, or maybe he just didn't want to give it a name. What he knew was that he didn't want to want to voluntarily see her again.

But he did.

He wondered if senility hit some men at forty-five.

Michael suddenly slumped against Flynn's shoulder, the nachos bag falling to the floor. Flynn leaned slightly to peer into the boy's face. "Hey, Michael, what inning is it?"

Michael didn't even stir.

"Well, that was easy enough," Flynn murmured to himself. Shifting Michael over onto his lap, Flynn rose with the boy in his arms. Funny how something that felt so light could be such a heavy burden, he thought as he headed toward the stairs.

Michael's room was next to his own. The boy had asked for it. It had once been Aimee's. Somehow, it was fitting that Michael should have it.

Flynn tucked Michael into bed, removing just enough from the boy to make sleeping comfortable. He didn't bother with the boy's jeans or shirt. Flynn had long ago discovered that donning pajamas was somehow a signal to his system to stay awake. So when Michael asked to emulate him, Flynn saw no harm in it. Flynn slept in cutoff shorts. Michael usually did, too. But not tonight.

"You played a great game, sport," Flynn whispered to the sleeping boy as he closed the door behind him.

An image of Susanna, her T-shirt flapping in the wind, licking the tops of her thighs rose in Flynn's mind, immediately followed by a spontaneous tightening of his stomach. "But your grandfather is totally out of the game," Flynn added firmly, shaking off the grip of what he was afraid he felt.

He went downstairs to call Susanna and cancel tomorrow's pickup. He was sure someone as resourceful as she would find another way to get to work.

She was unlisted.

It seemed, Flynn thought as he shoved the telephone book back to its place under the phone stand in the hall, that the fates were conspiring against him, obviously determined to throw his life into even further havoc.

He turned toward the stairs again. Still, he absently mused, havoc had never looked quite as attractive as this before.

But attractive or not, Susanna Troy had absolutely no place in his life beyond a passing, friendly gesture. He'd pick her up, drop her off at work and be done with it.

She was standing in front of her house, Billie in tow, waiting for him.

Flynn saw her in the distance as he turned a corner. The mist had burned off early and a breeze was rifling through the newly minted foliage on the trees. The leaves fairly glistened in the morning sun. The daisies on the lawn next door to her house were nodding their white-and-yellow heads in rhythm to the wind. It teased the edges of her flared skirt, sending the navy blue material up way past her knees. For some reason, that seemed even more enticing than the sight of her in shorts.

It was as if he had been given a glimpse of somewhere he wasn't supposed to be.

And he wasn't. What was the matter with him? Was he having a midlife crisis, like Jake Emersol in stats? On Jake's forty-fifth birthday, the portly man had handed in a letter of resignation, left his wife of twenty years and bought himself a one-way ticket to Madrid, Spain.

But he wasn't Jake. He was a grandfather. He had no business feeling blood stir in him like a teenage boy. He had left that part of himself behind years ago, when he had married Kelly.

And Kelly was gone.

He blew out an impatient breath. When he pulled up beside Susanna, his frown was in direct contrast to the sunny expression on her face. He remembered his initial instinct this morning as he had climbed into the car. He had wanted to head the car toward Michael's school and then go to work, completely forgetting about Susanna and his rash offer. Not that Michael would have let him, he thought, glancing at the beaming boy next to him.

"What if I hadn't shown up?" Flynn asked Susanna.

"But you did," she said cheerfully. Her words were almost lost as Billie shouted a loud greeting to Michael. The latter was already scrambling out of his seat in the front and wiggling his way into the cramped, almost nonexistent back seat, dragging his lime-green backpack with him.

Billie clambered in beside him. As before, it was a tight fit. "Do you have another car?" Billie asked Flynn, clutching at the edge of the driver's seat.

Flynn waited, trying not to notice Susanna's legs as she pulled them in and shut the door. This morning, she looked light years away from the woman he had heard shouting encouragement on the field last night. That was a mom. The woman next to him was a very competent-looking professional. While he admired the latter, he found that he rather liked the former better.

He had no business liking either, he reminded himself.

Flynn addressed Billie's question. It was a lot easier than sorting out the cauldron of swirling thoughts and feelings that confused and mystified him even as they caused him concern. "As a matter of fact, I do. Why?"

Billie raised and dropped his shoulders in an exaggerated motion, striving to look innocent to the roots of his hair. "I just thought it'd be more comfortable for all of us."

I don't plan to make a habit of this, Flynn thought and very nearly said aloud.

"I'm afraid you're out of luck." He eased the car out of the development and onto the main street that cut through Bedford. "My daughters are sharing that one."

"You have daughters, too?" Susanna asked, interested.

He glanced at Susanna. She looked much too comfortable next to him. Didn't she feel awkward around strangers? He knew *he* did.

Flynn nodded as he looked back at the road. "Stephanie and Julia. They're away at school. U.C. Santa Barbara," he added.

He looked entirely too young to have college-aged daughters. Susanna looked at him, trying to guess his age. She settled for asking about his daughters. For now. "How old are they?"

"Julia's nineteen, Stephanie's twenty." *And Aimee would have been twenty-four,* he added silently.

Susanna wanted to explore this further, to ask him more questions about his family, but she had the definite impression that a curtain had just gone down around the subject. Maybe his daughters reminded him too much of his wife. Some people, she knew, locked up their grief inside and wouldn't let it out. She had worked through hers by talking, by remembering all the good times. But everyone was different.

"Well, you've certainly spaced out your family," she smiled. "Michael can't be more than seven."

"Six," Michael corrected her. "But I'm going to be seven."

"You sure are," Susanna agreed, aware of the fragility of the masculine ego, no matter how young it was.

"I didn't space out my family," Flynn told her after a beat. He didn't want to talk about it, but it was best to get this all out in the open now, before this woman got any ideas. She was a nester if he ever saw one and he had no intentions of being in a nest, no matter how inviting the plumage.

There were probably several ways to interpret his words, but for the life of her, Susanna couldn't come up with even one. "I'm afraid I don't understand."

"Michael's not my son, he's my grandson."

"Oh." The information threw her for a loop. If ever a man had seemed virile and in top condition, it was Flynn

O'Roarke. There was nothing about him that would suggest he was even remotely up for the role of grandfather.

Susanna recovered quickly, hoping Flynn hadn't noticed her initial confusion. One look at his face as they stopped at a light told her he had. "I'm sorry if I sound flustered, but you're not exactly the way I picture a grandfather."

He couldn't help the amusement that quirked his lips. "And exactly what do you picture?"

"A cane," Billie piped up before she could say anything. "My grandpa's got a cane."

"My father broke his hip last year and he's had to use a cane ever since," Susanna explained.

"Both my hips are fine." He addressed the remark to Billie, but his eyes strayed toward Susanna.

Yes, Susanna thought, they certainly were that. It was one of the first things she had noticed about him yesterday. The jeans he had worn had fit him like a glove. If he was a grandfather, he certainly was the youngest-looking one she had ever met. At least in appearance.

There was something about his manner, though, that contradicted the youth she saw in both his face and his body. His manner was intended, she had a feeling, to be off-putting.

But then, Susanna found that she was never put off by very much.

Chapter Four

The trip to the school that Michael and Billie attended took only five minutes. All too soon for Flynn, the boys were deposited at the front doors. The two dashed off to join their friends, determined to get in some serious playtime before the line-up bell rang.

And then it was just the two of them within the confines of the small car. The two of them and a pervading aura of awkward silence. At least, the silence felt awkward to Flynn.

As he fumbled with the radio dial, the same sensations he'd experienced last night returned. He couldn't help wondering why. This was just an acquaintance he was helping. Yet he couldn't shake the total awareness that this acquaintance was a single, attractive woman.

Which was what bothered him. Among other nameless things that pricked his conscience and played havoc with his nervous system.

A country-and-western song about unrequited love filled the car as he made his way into the stream of traffic heading south. He glanced at her, wondering what she thought of the music. Flynn noticed that Susanna was moving her shoulders ever so slightly, in time to the beat. She seemed to be enjoying it, he thought.

Susanna could spot a case of nerves a mile away, even though this man was doing his damnedest to hide it. When she caught his eye, she flashed a smile, hoping for one in return. She was out of luck. Maybe next time.

She smoothed down her skirt beneath the briefcase she held in her lap. "I really do appreciate the ride, Flynn, but I hope I'm not taking you out of your way."

For a moment, he lost his train of thought. His name, when she uttered it, sounded like music. He told himself it was just the mood created by Eddie Rabbit and his mournful song, nothing more.

"You are," Flynn said, looking at the road again. He shrugged a little too carelessly, as if the mistake was his. "But I volunteered." He took the next turn a bit too sharply.

Susanna caught her briefcase as it began to slide off her lap. What was he running from, she wondered. It couldn't possibly be her. Or could it? "Why?"

Flynn thought he hadn't heard her correctly above the music. "Excuse me?"

She studied his profile. It was a rugged masculine face with just enough lines about his mouth and eyes to make him interesting. He was too young and too good-looking to lock himself away. And some part of him was trying to break out. But not all. "You're obviously uncomfortable about all this." She gestured around the car to indicate the ride he was giving her. "*Why* did you volunteer?"

He shrugged again, wishing she wouldn't press him on this. "It seemed like the thing to do at the time."

It was a lame excuse, but it was all he had. Saying that he had wanted to give her a ride didn't seem right. He couldn't reconcile the desire to be around her with Kelly's memory. Somehow, it made him feel disloyal.

"I see." Susanna paused for a moment, rolling over her next words in her mind, testing them out. She knew that some might say that the next question was none of her business, but Susanna took a keen interest in everyone who crossed her path. And this man merited a stronger interest, a stronger response than most. She leaned toward him, her voice lowering, her tone gentle. "How long has your wife been gone?"

The question surprised him. He felt himself tense, as if his body was fighting off the image that was generated by the word "gone." The long vigil at the hospital. The clergyman droning on at Kelly's grave site. The way the air had felt that day, oppressive and stifling because she wasn't breathing it with him anymore.

"Too long," Flynn snapped without hesitation. His conscience caught up to him after a beat. He hadn't meant to bark at her that way. He sighed, taking the edge from his voice. It was as close as he was going to come to offering an apology. "She died fifteen months ago."

Rather than take affront, Susanna felt for him as empathy flooded her body. She remembered what it was like. Susanna wasn't even aware of the hand she placed on his shoulder. "It gets easier, you know."

There was immense comfort in the small gesture. But he didn't want comfort. He was doing just fine on his own. He had to hang on to that. "Does it?"

His voice had an uncertain tone. It was a mixture of bitter anger and sadness. She withdrew her hand. But not her offer of friendship. That he definitely needed, if she was any judge of things.

"Never easy, but easier." She thought back just enough for the words, but not the pain the memory generated. The pain came anyway. It always did. "Brett died when Billie was a baby. I was sure I was going to fold completely."

"But you didn't." It wasn't a question. Somehow he could have guessed that about her. Knowing her a total of two hours, he would have guessed. Delicate-looking, she still wasn't the collapsing type. The woman had survivor written all over her small appearance. Unless you looked at her eyes, or the set of her mouth. He realized that he had been looking at her mouth a lot.

"No," she said quietly, looking off into space. "You surprise yourself. You have to." She was talking more to herself than to him. Susanna looked at Flynn and smiled. "There are people depending on you, so you go on. One step at a time until you've forged a path. And then a pattern that you can live with."

It was a deceptively simple philosophy that required so much, he thought. He pressed down on the gas pedal as the road stretched upward before him, heading toward the Coast. Time to change the subject. "You have just one son?"

Susanna grinned. There was nothing she liked better than to talk about Billie. "There is no 'just' in front of Billie's name. He's a handful and a half."

The boy seemed to be well behaved from what Flynn had seen of him. "You seem to be bearing up to the job pretty well."

"I love him."

And that, Flynn could tell, said it all for Susanna. She loved and so she coped. Love was obviously the deciding factor for her, the great equalizer. He wondered if that was why he had managed to get as far as he had in this maze he had found himself wandering through in the last fifteen months. He knew it had to be. It was hard for him to show love and far harder to express it verbally. When he came right down to it, Flynn couldn't remember ever saying the words. But he did love his daughters. And Michael.

Flynn glanced at Susanna as the line of cars before him slowed at the next light at the top of the hill. "Your son's a lucky kid."

"It goes both ways," she said mildly.

What would she have ever done without Billie? She wasn't certain she could have managed nearly half as well as if she had been on her own when Brett died. For the longest time, until she got her bearings, Billie had been her reason for living. Her only reason.

She wondered about the little boy Flynn had taken into his home. Was it just for a visit? Where were his parents? Questions popped up, seeing answers. She began cautiously, testing the waters. "Michael seems to be a very well mannered little boy."

Flynn thought of the way the boy had looked up at him from his hospital bed, his arm in a cast, a large bandage slanted over his left eyebrow. He'd been the picture of bravery.

"He's a resilient little guy, considering what he's been through." Flynn pressed his lips together. The words that followed were spoken harshly to hide the emotion that they evoked. "His parents died in a car crash a year ago. His mother was my daughter."

"Oh, Flynn, I'm so sorry." She had just assumed that he was taking care of Michael for a limited time while the boy's parents were elsewhere. She stared at him, compassion in her eyes. He had endured so much in such a short period of time. "It must have been hell for you."

"That's the word for it. Hell," he echoed. Sheer hell.

Flynn stopped, suddenly aware that he was sharing private matters, private pain with a veritable stranger. Someone he had felt awkward with only ten minutes ago. Flynn

shifted gears mentally. It wouldn't do to get too comfortable here. He wasn't one of those men who needed to talk,
to get his feelings out in the open. That was for others, not
him. He didn't need it. He was never going to "need" anything from anyone again.

Searching for something to get her mind off the topic,
Flynn glanced at Susanna and took in the flat gray briefcase on her lap. A tiny purse hung suspended by a thin black
leather strap from her shoulder. Unless her lunch was very
flat, she hadn't brought any with her. "You don't brown-
bag it?"

Susanna shook her head, aware of his diversionary tac-
tic. Maybe she had delved too much. She had a habit of
overdoing. But only because she always became so caught
up. Part of her problem was that she always cared.

"Making Billie's lunch is about all I can stand. I usually
eat in the cafeteria. Or send out."

Flynn brought the car to a stop at the light right before the
spacious mall that spread out to within a quarter of a mile
of the edge of the harbor. He had already driven past his
place of work. Palisades Mutual was just ahead. "Ever tried
the restaurant in the mall?"

The mall was where Susanna did most of her last-minute
shopping, flying from one store to another during her lunch
hour. Except for the rare farewell luncheon thrown by people where she worked, Susanna didn't frequent the restau-
rants in the mall. "Which one?"

"Robert Burns." Deeper and deeper, he thought, unable
to curb his tongue. Was he actually asking this woman out?
No, it couldn't be that. He didn't ask women out. He
wouldn't have the slightest idea how to go about that. The
last date he had had was twenty-six years ago, with Kelly.

Susanna tried to match the name he had given her with a
place and failed. "No."

Drop it here, now. Say something inane about the food and let it go. The words came out anyway. "Would you like to?" Damn, how had that happened?

A slow, intrigued smile curved her mouth as Susanna shifted in her seat, facing him. "Are you asking me out to lunch?"

Flynn cleared his throat. He felt as if his nerves were doing deep knee bends in his stomach. He kept his gaze glued to the road, grateful for the sparse flow of traffic. He wasn't completely sure of his reflexes at this moment. "In a roundabout way, yes, I suppose so."

Was she the first woman he had socialized with since his wife's death? Susanna had a feeling that she might be. The thought warmed her more than she thought possible. "I thought engineers were supposed to be rather direct and abrupt."

"We are." He knew he sounded gruff but he was having trouble justifying his own behavior to himself.

Susanna lifted an eyebrow. "Well, you have the abrupt part down pat, but I'd work on the direct bit if I were you."

She was turning him down. Thank God. It had been an impulsive thought that had absolutely no business even occurring to him. What the hell was going on with him, anyway? "Then it's no?"

She couldn't tell if he was relieved or disappointed. "Whatever gave you that idea?"

Confusion had taken over completely. Confusion at his own actions, and his reactions to this woman. He wanted her to say yes and yet he didn't. In either case, he wasn't sure what her answer was. "Aren't actuaries supposed to be direct, too?"

She grinned. He looked absolutely adorable when he was flustered. She wondered how he would respond to that assessment. Probably frown some more. "I was a changeling."

If that meant that she wasn't the garden-variety type of woman one usually met, she was a changeling all right. "Somehow, I think I can buy that."

She leaned slightly toward the right as he turned down the road that led to the outdoor mall. The surrounding blocks along the mall's outer perimeter were lined with office buildings. Hers was on the far end, closest to the ocean. "Speaking of buying, I am."

He was going to need a road map with this conversation. "You are what?"

"Buying." When his frown didn't dissipate, she took it to mean he had again lost the thread of what they were discussing. "Lunch."

Did she think he was going to ask her to lunch and then not pay for it? He didn't care what the nineties dictated, some things a man just did. "Now hold on a minute—"

His stern voice left her unfazed. She had been on her own far too long to cringe before authority. "I insist. After all, you've gone out of your way for me. It's the least I can do."

No, not really, he thought. The least she could do was to leave him alone.

God knew Flynn didn't want to be attracted to her. He didn't want to take her to lunch. And he certainly didn't want to open up to her. He didn't feel right about any of it. Flynn had been married to Kelly all his adult life, he was too set in his ways, too out of practice to be having lunch with an attractive, unattached woman. And try as he might, he couldn't make himself think of Susanna as just Billie's mother. She was far too female for that title alone. He wondered how it was that she hadn't become involved with someone yet. And why the powers that be had made their paths cross.

"You're passing it," she prompted, pointing toward the circular, four-story building that stood with the ocean at its back. "That's where I work."

Flynn realized that his thoughts were drifting into a fog. Murmuring an unintelligible oath under his breath, he did an abrupt U-turn at the corner. Among other things, Susanna was having a bad effect on his driving skills. Going a little faster than he normally would, he made his way through the parking lot of a thriving department store on the edge of the mall. The wide, squat three-story structure faced the front of Susanna's office.

Flynn stopped the convertible at the curb in front of steps that spread out like a lady's fan, leading up to the glass front doors of Palisades Mutual.

Susanna unbuckled her seat belt, but made no further move to get out. She waited a moment for him to say something else. When he didn't, she took the initiative. Again. It was quickly becoming a habit. "So what time would you like to meet?"

Sunlight bathed the entire area with golden hues. The rays caught in her hair, making it appear even blonder and softer-looking than it was. Like silk, he thought, then struggled to bring his mind back to what she was saying. "For what?"

Susanna shook her head in mild disbelief. He certainly had trouble keeping his mind on the conversation. "Are they all as absent-minded as you in the space program?" she teased.

He liked the smile that flashed across her lips, the dimple that winked at him just above the corner of her mouth. He didn't want to notice it, much less like it. Was determined not to like it. And yet, he knew he did.

"No, I mean—" He dragged an impatient hand through his hair, wondering how the hell he had gotten himself into this mess. "It's been a rather difficult morning."

She glanced at her watch, amused. For a second, she pretended to play along. "It's just started." She raised her eyes to his, compassion highlighting the blue-and-gray irises. She didn't want him to feel that there was no way out. "If you'd rather skip lunch, I understand."

He stared at her, surprised. "Do you?" Flynn could almost believe that she did. That put her one up on him. He wasn't sure that he understood or even knew what was going on inside him. Right now, he felt as if his own thoughts and feelings were jumbled up in a massive hodgepodge that he couldn't begin to make heads or tails of.

"Sure. Maybe another time." Susanna opened the car door and slipped out, three-inch navy heels lightly striking the concrete. "Well, thank you again." With a little shove, she closed the door behind her, and began to hurry away.

He watched her back for a moment, his conscience taking him to task. She was pushy, but she knew just when to strategically retreat. "Wait," he called after her.

Susanna turned around and returned to the car. Someone called out to her as he passed and she waved, but her attention was on Flynn. She leaned into the car.

He caught another heavy whiff of her perfume as he inclined his head toward her.

He had never felt so unsure of himself in his life. "Um, do you have a ride home?" Even his voice sounded hopelessly stilted. It was the same booming voice that had made complex presentations before a roomful of NASA executives and had never once wavered. What had caused the uncertainty in it now?

"No." She glided her fingers slowly along her purse strap. "I thought I'd just call a cab."

"Those are expensive," he lectured. "You shouldn't go throwing your money around."

The gruff voice didn't fool her. He was going to offer to take her home. She wondered if he ever made offers willingly. She shrugged innocently, just the way Billie had last night. Her son came by it naturally, she realized. "Well, my car is out of commission."

He was doing it again, he thought. He was volunteering to help. But he couldn't very well leave her stranded, he reasoned. Sure she could call a cab, but what with the mechanic's bill she was probably facing, she would need all the ready cash that she could gather at her disposal. Flynn refused to look any further into his own motives. "What time do you get off?" He nodded toward the wide, imposing building.

"Four-thirty." She made it a practice never to work overtime. If a project needed extra time put in, she found a way to bring the work home with her. The hours she spent with Billie were precious to her.

Flynn left his second-floor office at four. That gave him a half hour to kill. He supposed there was some extra work he could do to kill time.

He nodded his head, sealing the bargain. "I'll meet you here." He threw the transmission into drive and began to pull away from the curb.

"All right," she called to him. "But on one condition."

His foot slid onto the brake. Flynn turned, looking at her in surprise. "You're setting up conditions?" he asked incredulously.

Susanna nodded as she shifted her briefcase into her other hand and approached the car again. "I want you to smile."

It sounded like a completely off-the-wall request. "When?" he asked archly.

"I'd say anytime the mood hit you, but I'm afraid if I said that, I'd never see one. How about when you pick me up?"

He turned to face the road, shaking his head. She was a strange one, all right. "I'll work on it."

"Please."

The word hung in the air, echoing in his head and mingling with the scent of her perfume in the car as he drove to work.

* * *

Several times during the course of the day, Flynn caught himself inexplicably whistling. Each time he would abruptly stop, mentally chastising himself for acting like an idiot. He was garnering strange looks from the people he worked with. Of late Flynn hadn't exactly been known for his cheerful demeanor.

Lunch came and went and he breathed a sigh of relief, remembering the rash invitation he had extended. Half of him fully expected to get a call from the guard at the front gate, telling him that a blond-haired woman was trying to crash the compound, a picnic basket in her hands. It probably would have been like her.

Like her.

It was hard, he realized, not to like her. But he really didn't have a place in his life for where this could lead. In all probability *would* lead. He had finally gotten to the point where he was independent and he liked it that way. If independence carried the weight of loneliness with it at times, so be it. He had had love in his life. Had treasured it, reveled in it. But it had been snatched away from him and he had found a way to go on living. He had no intention of getting back on the merry-go-round.

That's why his behavior struck him as so illogical. He had no idea why his step felt a little lighter today. Or why he kept whistling. Nothing had changed in his life, except that he was picking up a loquacious woman after work, one who somehow seemed to tap into a hidden vein within him and made him want to talk, as well.

Maybe his talking was just a self-defense mechanism. If he talked, he wouldn't find himself buried under her rhetoric.

But even as he formed the excuse, he knew it rang hollow. He talked because she seemed to draw the words out of him. She made him *want* to talk.

Sitting in front of his computer terminal, he tapped on the keyboard slowly, bringing a three-dimensional design on the monitor around to face another angle.

All in all, Susanna Troy was a very dangerous lady.

He paused, his fingers hovering over the keys, his mind wandering. If she was such an unwanted threat, why was he looking forward to seeing her again?

Flynn had no answers handy, so he blocked the whole thing from his mind. He'd get to it, the way he intended to get to the bills that were piling up on his desk in the study.

Later.

"You're very punctual." Susanna slid into the silver sports car. She had been waiting on the corner of the building's steps for ten minutes, afraid that Flynn might arrive early and, not seeing her, leave without her. There were a lot of people at the office who would have willingly given her a ride, but Susanna wanted to go home with Flynn. Somehow, though she couldn't fully put it into words yet, it was important.

The flow of traffic home was heavier than it had been this morning. Flynn picked his way carefully through the serpentine roads of the mall. "I hate people who are late. It's rude."

He sounded unbending. But she already knew better. "Sometimes, it's unavoidable."

He shrugged. Kelly had never been on time, he recalled, marching to some inner clock all her own. It was one of the few things they had words over. "They have phones for that."

"You won't get an argument out of me." Susanna raised her hands, her palms facing upward. "Even if you do want one," she added quietly. Perhaps, she thought, he might be enjoying her company a little more than he thought he should and that bothered him. That, too, she could understand. She'd been through that herself once, in the beginning.

Flynn looked at her quizzically. The woman was crazy. "Why should I want an argument? I hate arguing."

She saw that he was having trouble with all this. It was easy to see the signs. "Maybe the fact that you're talking to me bothers you."

He let out an annoyed huff. "I think your analyzing mode is in overdrive."

Susanna backed off. Perhaps it was too soon for him to face the truth. "Maybe. Maybe I was wrong."

"Damn straight you were wrong." He glanced at her impassive face. Though she was admitting defeat, he couldn't shake the impression that she had somehow won. "But you don't have to be that agreeable about it."

She could only grin. He sounded like a wounded bear. Had she been like that at first, snapping at everyone because the one she loved was gone? She wasn't sure that had been the case, but that period of her life was a haze, as if she had been sleepwalking through life.

"Sorry, it's in the genes. Agreeableness," Susanna clarified as he raised his eyebrow in silent query. "Will you be at the game on Saturday?"

He shrugged. He hadn't planned on it, but without a housekeeper, he'd have to take Michael there himself. "I suppose so. What time does it begin?"

"Ten-thirty." Now that she thought back, Michael had been attending the games since the season started. "That woman who used to bring Michael—"

He saw the question coming. This one was easy. "She was my housekeeper. Mrs. Henderson."

"Was?"

"She quit."

She tried to picture working for Flynn. It almost made her shiver. "Your sunny disposition got to her?"

"Her husband's promotion and transfer got to her." The last thing he needed was sarcasm, he thought, then looked at Susanna. She was smiling. The woman's facial muscles really got a workout. "What do you mean, my sunny disposition?"

"You haven't smiled yet," she pointed out.

He took a breath, annoyed. "Mrs. Troy—"

Susanna shook her head. "Susanna," she corrected. "If you say it, your lips will curve and you don't even have to say it's a smile. You can call it an involuntary spasm if you like."

The laugh that came was automatic. He couldn't have stopped it if he tried. He had to admit it felt good to laugh. There'd been so little reason to lately. "Always get your way?" He glided the car onto the main thoroughfare that would eventually lead to her house.

"Yes," she said simply. "But then, I don't usually ask for much. Toys to be picked up, a smile, a good mystery to read. Things I know I can attain."

He wondered if she was on the level. She sounded much too idealistic to have suffered through a death and its subsequent upheaval. If she was genuine, he had to admire her.

Another dangerous sentiment, his warning system informed him.

"I want to thank you again for coming to Billie's rescue yesterday."

He shrugged off her words. Gratitude embarrassed him. "I've never seen anyone hit like that before—in slow motion."

"It's something he has to work on. The coaches try but they don't seem to be getting through to him." She thought of the hours they had put in. The tears. She was at her wit's end, really. "I wish I could help him, give him some advice on how to improve his batting style, but I can't hit the broadside of a barn myself."

"I kind of figured that, after watching you throw yesterday." He chuckled, then gave the matter some serious though. "Maybe I could give Billie a few pointers the next time I'm in the neighborhood." The words slipped out before he could stop them.

"How about this Friday, after work?"

He was a man, he thought, determined to orchestrate his own funeral.

Chapter Five

"Friday?" Flynn repeated, as if saying the word would buy him some time.

He searched his mind for an excuse. It produced absolutely nothing he could use. His brain seemed to have suddenly gone completely numb. His job required that he brief management on a regular basis. That meant sharp, probing questions aimed his way, and he had always done well fielding them. Thinking on his feet was second nature to him. Why then, when a slip of a woman, who came up to his shoulder, tendered an invitation that he knew he should refuse, did his mind go utterly blank?

Was it because he wanted to accept? Flynn wasn't about to try to analyze his actions for a baser motive. He had never felt the need for introspection. Life had always been simple. Wife, family, work, in that order. Now that his world had been turned inside out, it seemed that nothing was straightforward anymore.

Susanna got the impression that everything triggered an internal war with him. The man was a great deal more complex than he seemed on the surface. She couldn't help being intrigued.

"You know, the day in the week everyone likes best," she prodded, her eyes bright, amused. "Friday. Tomorrow."

He cleared his throat, trying one more halfhearted attempt at dodging the invitation. "Well, I—"

Maybe he just needed a push. Otherwise, he would have said no immediately. Susanna played her ace card. The only one in her hand that counted to her. "It would really mean a great deal to Billie. I think his inability to bat in front of the others is destroying his confidence."

Flynn could remember what that was like, having your self-esteem blown to smithereens in front of a bunch of superior, smirking seven-year-olds. For Flynn, it had all come to a head with a bully named Seth who, at the time, seemed to be twice Flynn's size and had shown him up in every sport in school. The humiliation had grown to unbearable proportions. And then his Uncle Frank had given him a set of weights for his birthday.

Every morning before school, Flynn would exercise religiously, the image of Seth's sneering face shimmering before him, egging him on, making him work that much harder. Eventually, the skinny little boy disappeared and a teenager emerged, a teenager with a physique that made others treat him with respect before he ever opened his mouth.

With all that in his past, how could he say no to Susanna's request? "All right."

He made it sound as if he had just agreed to visit the dentist for a root canal. "I'll make it worth your while," Susanna promised.

Just how forward had women become while he had been safely bound up in matrimony all those years? Flynn leveled a look at her. "I beg your pardon?"

"Dinner." By the expression on his face, Susanna gathered that the prospect of a meal in exchange for his good deed hadn't crossed his mind. "I make a mean Yankee Pot Roast."

He blew out a breath, relieved. Maybe he was making mountains out of molehills, after all. Maybe Susanna was as genuine as she seemed and was offering him nothing more than friendship in return for a few favors on his part. He mulled over her offer. A home-cooked meal for a change sounded terrific. With Mrs. Henderson gone, dinners lately had consisted of sandwiches and things that he could readily boil in a pouch. Cooking was never something he had had to do for himself before. Michael didn't complain about the makeshift meals, but he knew the boy would have preferred something a little more flavorful to eat once in a while.

Either that, or frequenting a fast-food restaurant every night. He grinned. "I guess you're on."

Score one for the home team, she thought, noting his smile. It made him appear less forbidding. Maybe that was why he didn't smile too often.

Susanna thought of her son. He'd enjoy the company of a man helping him. She knew Billie loved her and Aunt Jane, but he needed a male influence in his life. She looked at Flynn, gratitude in her eyes. "Thank you. Billie will be very excited."

Flynn turned to comment and saw the look in her eyes. Something within him responded. Melted. He searched madly for his resolve and found it raining through his fingers. No, this wasn't going to be a woman he could easily cast off from his mind without a massive effort on his part. He was going to have to start gearing up now.

His grip tightened on the steering wheel. "Hope it's worth it, for him," Flynn muttered in reply, more to himself than to her. It had better be. God knew the effort might cost him more than he was willing to pay.

His thoughts playing bumper pool in his head, Flynn completely forgot about stopping at the day-care center for Michael. It was Susanna who brought the slip to his attention.

Mumbling his thanks, annoyed that he had had to be reminded, Flynn backtracked half a mile. Luckily, the center was closer to her house than he remembered.

Once Michael bounced into the rear seat of the car, Flynn found that the tight feeling in his chest had dissipated. It was a sad state of affairs. Flynn O'Roarke, forty-five-year-old senior design engineer for the space program was using a six-year-old boy as a buffer. He shook his head.

Susanna noticed the distracted look on Flynn's face as he resumed driving. "What's the matter?"

"Nothing." The denial came too quickly to be true, in Susanna's opinion. "Don't we have to pick up your son from someplace?"

He kept changing the subject, she thought. By her count, he had fumbled his way out of three so far today. "No, Aunt Jane picks him up at school for me in the afternoon."

Aunt Jane. Was that the name of her housekeeper? "She lives with you?"

Susanna grinned. She loved the woman dearly, but if ever a person needed her own space, it was Aunt Jane. Jane Carter Hall Caldwell was a financially independent, headstrong woman who could be loved and taken in small doses only. "No, Aunt Jane lives across the street from me. She's really a character, but I don't know what I would have done without her. After Brett died, she took it upon herself to sell her house in San Juan Capistrano and moved up here to help me out. She was a godsend."

"No parents?" He didn't know what made him tactlessly blurt out the question. He didn't want to know all the personal things he already knew about her. So, why was he asking more questions?

She thought of her parents and smiled fondly. "They live in Florida. They wanted me to come live with them, but I just couldn't leave my home. There were too many memories I wasn't ready to give up yet. So Aunt Jane humored me and moved up here."

They pulled up to the cul-de-sac. Billie was attempting to shoot baskets in the driveway of their trim, gray-and-blue two-story house. "That's her house over there." Susanna pointed to a one-story structure with a tall, white fountain in the front yard.

Flynn brought the car to a stop in Susanna's driveway. Billie ran to meet them, hugging the basketball to his chest. His eyes shone. "Hi!" he called out to them. "Wanna play?" he asked Michael eagerly.

Susanna turned toward Flynn. "Would you like to come in for a few minutes?"

That was the last thing he thought he should do. He'd made enough mistakes today. "No, I think we'd better be getting home." He nodded toward the rear. "Michael has homework to do."

"No I don't," Michael piped up, utterly destroying Flynn's one excuse. "Old Miss Fischer was out today. The sub was neat. She didn't give us any work and let us have an extra-long recess."

The exasperated look on Flynn's face had Susanna struggling not to laugh. He looked endearingly flustered. She gathered her briefcase to her, one hand on the door handle. "How about some coffee? I've been fantasizing about real coffee all day."

Flynn had a weakness for home-brewed coffee himself. But he was afraid that another weakness might crop up if he was alone with her. He wanted to get a better rein on himself, one he felt he didn't have at the moment, before he faced that test.

"No, I…" His voice trailed off as he watched a cat streak down the block, then up a tree. That's how he felt. Up a tree.

Susanna saw that Michael was on the edge of his seat, ready to shoot out of the car at a moment's notice. "Flynn."

He turned his head toward her, the lights that played in her eyes surprising him. "What?"

She smiled guilelessly. More melting went on inside him. If he wasn't careful, he was going to turn into a damn puddle soon.

"I don't bite," Susanna assured him.

"Why would you bite?" Michael looked at her, confused, his thin eyebrows knitted together over the bridge of his nose. "People shouldn't bite other people."

"She doesn't," Flynn said gruffly as he tried to ignore Susanna's laughter. With a sigh of resignation, he got out of the car, slamming the door shut. Michael was out of the car ahead of him, dashing up the driveway with Billie. "All right, ten minutes."

The time limit was for both Michael and Susanna. It seemed safe enough. After all, what could happen in ten minutes?

Too late he remembered as he followed her through the front door, that championship games could be lost in less time than that.

The house wasn't what he had expected.

For some reason, he had been prepared to see a lot of clutter, photographs, knickknacks, mementos on every available surface, all vying for attention. She struck him as a saver. Instead, there was space, a feeling of vast space. The vaulted ceiling evident upon entry doubled the illusion of openness.

He liked that.

There was room here, room for a man to stretch out, to get comfortable. To breathe. Susanna's living room, with its green and dusty pink floral sofa and dark rose recliner surrounding a small white marble coffee table seemed almost Spartan in comparison to the clutter of his house. He wondered who had designed this room.

Susanna opened the front window and turned around to look at Flynn's reaction to her home. His face was an open book when he wasn't trying so hard to guard his thoughts. Susanna liked watching his emotions pass over it. "You look a little bemused."

He spread his hands out to either side, encompassing the room with this gesture. "Just taking in the decor."

"Do you like it?"

He rocked back slightly on his heels as he shoved his hands into his pockets. Expressing enthusiasm for things had never been easy for him. "It's all right."

She laughed, delighted. The man didn't give an inch. "Heady praise indeed."

He ignored the teasing comment. "Your husband pick out the furniture?"

"No, I did." Susanna led the way through the dining room to the country kitchen. She could tell her answer surprised him. "I like room when I move around."

That made sense, considering the fact that she seemed to always be moving. "That would keep you from bumping into the furniture as you streak through."

Crossing his arms before him, he leaned against the pale blue wall. The family room that was just beyond the kitchen was an echo of the living room. Except for the small plastic baseball figures that were spread out all over the floor in front of the television set, a testimony to an early game before school this morning.

She glanced at him as she poured water into the glass coffeepot. The corners of her mouth quirked in amusement. "You make me sound like the roadrunner in the Saturday-morning cartoons."

Yes, he supposed he did. But he thought it an apt description of her. "That was the impression I got, watching you on the field yesterday."

She opened the tin of chocolate chip cookies she had made earlier in the week for Billie and placed them on the kitchen table. "You have to move fast to be both mother and father." She nudged the tin toward Flynn, urging him to take one. "You should know that."

There was still a lot of things that he should know, things that he didn't know. He picked up a cookie and bit into it. The deep chocolate flavor exploded on his tongue. "I haven't got the hang of it yet."

She turned from the coffeemaker, a black, intimidating appliance with tubes and switches running over the length of it. One would need a degree in engineering just to turn it on, Flynn thought. He'd used an old dented metal drip pot for the last fifteen years. When he had tried to replace it recently, he found that there were none available in the stores. Not about to try anything new, Flynn contented himself with cleaning out the holes on the strainer with a toothpick when it warranted maintenance.

"Why would it be so difficult to raise a boy?" She had just envied him that last night. "You were one once," she reminded him. Empathy should make the job easier.

He reached for a second cookie. She had laced them with mint and he had a fondness for mint. "Yeah." Flynn nodded. "A hundred years ago."

The man was ridiculously determined to stick to this image of himself as old. "Oh, right." She pulled a dish towel from the rack and dried her hands. "I keep forgetting your advanced age."

She was laughing at him. He didn't appreciate that. "You don't even know how old I am."

She leaned her hip against the gray, tiled counter, studying him. He was, as Aunt Jane might say, very easy on the eyes. "You don't look old."

He shrugged, finishing what he realized was his third cookie. He pushed the tin farther back on the table. "Well, I feel old."

Susanna reached into the cupboard for a paper filter. Securing one, she glanced at him over her shoulder. "We all do at times."

"*And* I am a grandfather." The very word made him feel old.

It wasn't enough of a case for Susanna. "That doesn't automatically make you ready for a rocking chair." She frowned, hand on her hip. "Just how old are you?"

The woman was far too personal for his liking. Flynn almost caught himself about to tell her to mind her own business. But what was the harm in admitting it? "Forty-five."

Susanna dropped the filter on the tile, clutched at her heart and swayed, leaning against the counter. "And you still get around without a cane?" She straightened again, laughter punctuating her words.

He looked at her indignantly. She didn't seem to understand the natural progression of things. Of people. "You think it's a joke?"

"No." She sobered, but only slightly. The man was crying out for help, even if he didn't know it. He needed to lighten up. "But I think forty-five is young. It's all in your perspective, Flynn. Daisy Mae thought she was past her prime at seventeen."

Susanna opened the refrigerator door. Three coffee cans stood lined up one behind the other on the bottom shelf. She bent over to get them. "What's your pleasure?"

He blinked, watching the way her skirt hiked up on her thigh. No doubt about it. They were the best pair of legs he had ever seen. "What?"

Susanna looked over her shoulder. The impish grin on her face told him she had read the unguarded thought that had raced across his mind. "Coffee. I have regular, espresso and cappuccino."

He nodded at the ominous black object on her counter. "That gizmo can make all three?"

"And hum 'Amore Scusami' while it's doing it." Heaven knew it had cost enough. By all rights, it should tap-dance as well.

Strange. The woman was definitely strange. He'd have one cup of coffee and go. Quickly. "What do you normally have?"

"Well, I had espresso this morning. If I have another, I'll be up all night. Regular," she decided.

Because she felt warm, Susanna peeled off her jacket. The thin white cotton shell beneath it did an excellent job of re-affirming the initial impression Flynn had had yesterday. She was exceptionally well built. He had always admired a good figure. It spoke of health and discipline.

But right now, it spoke of other things that he didn't want to hear.

He turned his attention to her question, though it wasn't easy. "Make it two."

Flynn sat down at the table, his large frame making her kitchen appear small. He watched her as she moved about, measuring out the coffee, fishing out two cups and saucers from the cupboard. She moved quickly, fluidly, like the tempo of a fast song. He opened the top button on his shirt, suddenly needing air.

The sound of the boys shouting and laughing came in through the open window. In between the shouts was the jarring thud of the basketball as it missed the hoop and bounced against the garage door.

"Takes the paint off," he observed. When she raised her eyes quizzically to his face, he elaborated. "The basketball against the house."

She shrugged. It didn't faze her. "So does the sun. This way, he's having fun. The house can be repainted," she added philosophically. "He'll only be seven once."

Unable to help himself, Flynn toyed with another cookie. "Seems to me you've got this parenting thing pretty much down pat."

"Thanks. I just try to remember what it was like from the other end." She handed him a napkin and slid the cookie onto it with a grin. He might protest that he was old, but there was still a little of the small boy in him. "That was when I thought my parents knew everything."

The coffee was ready. She poured two cups and set them down on the table. Dragging the chair closer, she sat down next to him. Crowding him somehow. Or maybe it was just the scent of her perfume. Rather than dissipate during the course of the day, it seemed to have grown stronger, more intense. It was filling his head, weakening the resolve that should have remained strong.

She broke off a corner of a cookie, popped the morsel into her mouth and savored it. "Now I lie awake at night, worrying if I did this wrong, or that wrong."

She didn't strike him as the type to worry about anything. Parenting was just something she would instinctively know how to do. All women did. It was part of their genetic makeup. Or so watching Kelly and his daughters had made him feel.

"I'd say you were doing just fine." She took a sip of coffee and he absently followed suit. His eyes opened wider as the hot liquid lodged in his throat like a solid entity.

Susanna bit her lower lip. She had overdone it again. "Too strong?"

He managed to get it down, then coughed. "Depends on what you use it for." He cleared his throat again. "Asphalt comes to mind at the moment."

She flashed him an apologetic grin. "Sorry, Brett got me used to strong coffee." She rose and turned toward the pantry. "I'll get you some sugar."

"Milk." The single word struggled out like a plea and he had to clear his throat again.

She grabbed the half-filled carton of milk from the refrigerator and yanked it out. In her hurry to make amends, Susanna swung around and rammed her hip against Flynn as she placed the milk carton in front of him. The length of her thigh jarred his arm.

Something hot opened, then tightened within him as the outline of her body registered with every nerve ending he had, making anticipation spring to life. The pull was sudden and demanding, almost taking his breath away. It had been a long time since he had physically reacted to a woman. A long time since he had thought of women at all.

He was thinking of one now.

And he wasn't comfortable about it. Not in any way, shape or form.

Susanna looked down at Flynn, another apology on her lips. She wanted to apologize for the coffee, for her clumsiness. Both apologies evaporated on her lips as she saw the look of desire, dark and dangerous, in his eyes. Her mouth went dry, even as the center of her palms began to itch. She took a step back, away from him, rubbing her moist hands against the sides of her skirt.

"Sorry," Susanna mumbled. "I'm not usually this clumsy."

Flynn shook his head, dismissing her words. He didn't like what he was feeling, didn't like feeling at all. It opened up things, wounds, memories. Needs. He wanted none of that. None of them. His life was finally in order and he was finding his way again. What he was feeling now would throw everything back into chaos. He didn't want to redefine himself again. As it was, life was too complicated, too overwhelming just getting through each day.

Why the hell did this have to happen?

He rose quickly, as if backing away from his feelings. The chair tipped behind him as he sprang to his feet. He turned, trying to catch it before it crashed. Susanna reached out quickly, grabbing for the chair. Their hands touched, their bodies collided.

The chair fell, forgotten.

Hiding was something that had never sat well with Flynn. Neither had running away. Flynn had approached everything in his life head on. It was the only way to overcome things, to clear his path. He would have to face this situation that threatened to come into being if he was going to vanquish it. If he frightened her away now, he wouldn't have to deal with the situation, with his feelings any further. It would be out of his hands. He wouldn't be to blame.

Susanna saw it coming, saw the war going on inside of him. She watched first desire, then surprise and finally anger wash over him. She wasn't certain who Flynn was angriest with, her or himself. But right now, she didn't care.

Right now, all she wanted was for Flynn to hold her. To make her feel again. To touch that part of her that had been held in reserve for so very long.

Where had this devastating need come from? Flynn felt his knees almost give out beneath him. An ocean of feelings, all tugging from different directions advanced on him at once, tearing at him, trying to claim him. Guilt, desire, confusion. And need. Need frightened him most of all. He never wanted to need again. And yet, at this moment, he did.

He sank his fingers into her hair, dislodging pins, taking hold of the silkiness, trying to anchor himself to something tangible.

His mouth touched hers even as an oath formed in his head, damning his own weakness, damning her for being here, for being accessible. And for being so incredibly desirable when he had no defenses. He closed his arms around her, pulled her against him, wishing her somewhere else.

Wanting her to be exactly where she was.

Open-mouthed, hungry, needy. It wasn't a gentle kiss. It wasn't meant to be. It was hot and passionate and was intended to make her afraid.

He wasn't expecting passion from her, wasn't expecting the devastating need he discovered within her, within himself.

Most of all, he wasn't expecting to be blown away.

Chapter Six

My God, what had he just done?

Flynn was stunned at his behavior. He had come in, against his better judgement, for a cup of coffee and had wound up holding a strange woman in his arms and kissing her. Worse, he wanted to do it again. He wanted to take that kiss further, to its logical conclusion. If his intentions in kissing her had purely been to frighten her, he had done the job royally on himself instead.

Speechless, confused, Flynn pulled away. He stared down at Susanna's face, bewildered at the incredibly small degree of control he seemed to possess when he was around her. He had never been impulsive before, never. And in the last year, he had prided himself on becoming emotionally independent.

So why had he felt this great need to kiss her? And why was he still feeling it?

He took a step away from her and backed up into the capsized chair that had triggered his downfall. Grateful for something to do, he bent down to pick it up. "I'm sorry," he mumbled to her.

Yes, he would say that. What else could she expect? But even though she had expected it, there still was that small prick of pain that nettled her.

"There's no need to be." Susanna's voice sounded oddly husky to her own ear. She cleared her throat, trying madly to steady herself internally. For a man who now looked as if he hadn't wanted to kiss her, he had certainly done a fantastic job of it. She couldn't remember ever feeling every part of her body vibrate this way, not over a kiss.

Flynn set the chair upright, shoving it under the table so hard it spilled the coffee. Avoiding her eyes, he nodded at the cup that had sloshed dark liquid over its sides. "Must have been your coffee."

Liar. You wanted to kiss me. Why can't you admit it? I can. She forced a smile. "I've got to remember the exact proportions I used."

Flynn dragged a hand through his hair, feeling totally out of place. He should have gone with his instincts and never set foot inside the house.

"I think it was a pound of coffee to six ounces of water." He made himself look at her. He was surprised to see hurt in her eyes. Why? What had he said? "Look, this wasn't supposed to have happened."

Next he'd be putting on a hair shirt to atone for having touched her. "I had no idea we were following a script." She curbed her hurt feelings. The man was stumbling. Sympathy budded. Maybe it was hard for him to accept the fact that he hadn't died along with his wife. That his needs hadn't, either.

Susanna placed a hand on his shoulder. "Flynn," she said softly. "It's all right."

"No, it's not." He lowered his voice. It would do no good to shout at her. It was himself he was angry with, not her. He sighed, shoving his hands into his pockets, wanting to shove himself into some small hole somewhere, far from everything. "I'm sorry. I shouldn't be yelling." He tried to make her understand. He felt he owed it to her. "I haven't touched another woman since Kelly—" The right words wouldn't come. After all, this wasn't about equations or launch patterns. He was out of his element. "Well, since Kelly," he repeated helplessly. "That's over twenty-seven years if you count the time we went together before we were married."

Flynn searched her face to see if she understood and wound up wanting to bury his hands in her hair and drag her back to him. God, he was a mess.

She smiled, wishing there was some guideline she could follow, some way to make him not feel that he had committed a cardinal sin. "I'm honored."

She wasn't supposed to be honored. She was supposed to retreat, to forget about the whole thing. One of them had to.

He began to pace around the kitchen, a bull in a china shop of emotions. "What I'm trying to say is that it's a matter of hormones." And nothing else. He swore that to himself. It was only his hormones overreacting.

Was he trying to insult her? To give her a polite brush-off? No, she didn't think so. His struggle was too obvious for that. Besides, there was something in his kiss, something warm, needy. He had enjoyed kissing her. She was certain she hadn't imagined it. "I'm not a child, Flynn. I know that's the way it usually starts."

He turned to her, anger in his eyes. "There is no start because there's not going to be anything further." There couldn't be. He wouldn't let himself get tangled up inside again. It wasn't fair.

"Flynn. Flynn," she repeated a bit more loudly when he didn't look at her, his expression a mixture of annoyance and disorientation. Did he think she was some desperate female, trying to lay a trap for him? She felt her own anger rise and forced herself to push it aside. Two people arguing wasn't going to solve anything. Especially since she wasn't sure what the problem was. He wasn't the only one who had been knocked for a loop here. "I'm not trying to do anything. *You* kissed *me*, remember?" If ever there was a mule-headed man—

She bit back her temper. "Why don't we just . . . see?"

"See what?" he asked, confused.

She smiled. "What" was the operative word here. "Exactly."

Flynn shook his head. What was she trying to say? "Did I miss a turn here somewhere?"

He would be almost sweet in his confusion, if he wasn't being so difficult. "Probably, but it'll come to you by and by." She thought of his resistance to what they had both experienced. "Have you ever heard the old saying, life is what happens while you're making plans?"

He shrugged absently. Why was she spouting trite sayings at a time like this? "No."

"Don't get around much, do you?" Susanna's eyes shone with amusement.

"My work and Michael keep me pretty busy." Why was he bothering to explain anything to her? He moved toward the living room. "Look, I'd better go."

She gestured toward the front door. Her amusement warred with annoyance because he was trying to make her feel that this was all her fault. That might make their encounter easier for him to accept, but it didn't make it right. Or true. "The door's not locked."

Flynn frowned. She was making it hard for him to blame anyone but himself for what had happened just now. But if she hadn't been there, if she hadn't been so damn desirable, if she had been Billie's father instead of his mother, it wouldn't have happened. So she was partially to blame.

He sighed. He was grasping at straws. It was his fault, and it wouldn't happen again. There was no reason for it to. He turned to leave when he remembered. "You'll need a ride tomorrow?"

Susanna crossed her arms before her as she followed him. She felt suddenly cold, bereft. "The car will be fixed Saturday." She was about to say that she would find a ride, but curiosity got the better of her.

Flynn realized there was no way out, not in good conscience at any rate. He couldn't just abandon her now. It would seem as if he was running. And though he wanted to, it wasn't his way. "I'll be here at seven."

She was about to ask if he was sure, but decided that would just get them into another round of conversation she didn't want to start. Besides, she did want to see him again. She wasn't certain what was happening between them or where it would go from here, but there *was* definitely something.

"I'll be ready," she promised. "Oh, wait." She hurried to the kitchen and wrapped up six cookies in a rose-colored napkin. She returned and thrust them at Flynn. "Here." Their hands touched as she gave him the bundle. This time, she couldn't help noticing the shiver of electricity that danced through her. Yes, definitely something. "Why don't you take these for Michael? They're homemade."

Flynn stared down almost dumbly at the cookies. "Thanks."

"Anytime."

Her tone made him look down at her. He knew she wasn't talking about the cookies.

As far as he was concerned, he had no idea what he was talking about, what he was thinking, or even feeling. Later, he told himself as he shut the last few minutes out of his mind. He'd sort it out later.

With his free hand, Flynn yanked open the front door. "Michael, we're leaving," he announced, stalking out of the house as quickly as he feasibly could.

Susanna followed, keeping a few feet between them. She figured he needed the space.

Michael jumped to attention at Flynn's tone of voice. He passed the basketball to Billie with one bounce and turned toward the sports car.

"Yes, Granddad." He hurried after Flynn and jumped into the front seat just as Flynn turned the ignition on.

Billie ran over to the passenger side, the basketball rakishly carried over to one side, under his arm. He'd seen the big boys do it this way at the schoolyard. His arm was straining to keep the ball in place. "Bye!"

"See you tomorrow," Michael called out over his shoulder as they sped away. The back tires squealed. Michael shifted in his seat to look straight ahead. He sat quietly for a moment, waiting for Flynn to say something.

When Flynn said nothing, Michael shifted restlessly in his seat. He peered at Flynn's face. Flynn saw an almost anxious look on Michael's face as the boy asked, "Why are you mad?"

"Dogs get mad. People get angry." Flynn knew he was nit-picking, but he didn't want to talk about it. He didn't even want to think about it. Which was why there seemed to be nothing else on his mind.

Michael's expression was puzzled but he was willing to agree. "Okay, why are you angry?"

Now he was taking his mood out on Michael. What the hell was wrong with him? "I'm not angry."

"Your face is," Michael pointed out.

And so was the rest of him. Angry at himself for giving in to what he took to be a purely physical reaction. Angry at Kelly for leaving him. Angry at the world at large. Forty-five and he was having an internal tantrum, he thought in disgust.

Michael's wistful voice interrupted his thoughts. "Is it Billie's mom?"

"Is what Billie's mom?" Flynn asked evasively. Did all kids ask this many questions at the wrong time?

"Is she the one who got you mad—angry?" Michael repeated patiently.

He couldn't begin to find the right way to explain this to Michael. He hadn't a clue himself. "It's been a long day, Michael."

"We only stayed there ten minutes, like you said."

That showed him how wrong he could be about how much damage could be done in under a quarter of an hour. The light before Flynn was turning yellow. Flynn stepped on the gas, getting through the intersection before the light turned red. "Sometimes, things happen fast."

Michael looked off, his small face growing solemn. "Yeah, I know."

Flynn heard the pain in the small voice. Guilt built on top of guilt. It had been a hell of an afternoon, all right. Damn, how had he managed to mess up so many things in such a short space of time? He searched for a way to make amends, at least with Michael.

He saw a mini-mall on the next corner. "Say, since you don't have any homework, what d'you say to going out for some pizza?"

Michael turned toward his grandfather. The solemn look dissolved. "At the arcade?"

"Sure, we'll shoot the works."

"Yeah!"

Flynn smiled at the bright, happy face, and felt a little better.

* * *

Susanna watched as the sports car sped down the block and turned, disappearing down the next street.

Coward, she thought.

With a sigh, she turned around. "I want you to start your homework, Billie. Dinner will be ready in half an hour." She passed Billie and echoed, "Aw, Mom," along with him as she ruffled his hair. They both laughed.

Billie followed her inside. She heard the sound of his sneaker-shod feet pounding up the stairs to his room. For a boy who only weighed forty-eight pounds, he sounded like a miniature elephant.

Walking into the kitchen, Susanna began to tick off numbers in her head in a mental countdown. She had gone from ten to three when the front door flew open again.

"Hi, Susie, where are you?"

Susanna smiled. Right on time. She braced herself, waiting for what she knew was going to come. "I'm in the kitchen, Aunt Jane."

On first glance, Jane Carter Hall Caldwell looked like a carbon copy of Susanna, except that she was an inch taller. It was only on closer examination that the small, fine lines about her bright gray-blue eyes and wide, inviting mouth could be detected. Susanna smiled as she thought about her aunt. Laugh lines Jane liked to call them, and then she would laugh to prove that they had been honestly earned. And Jane's laugh was loud and lusty, as was her approach to life. She believed that everyone should have a good time whenever possible. The fact that her niece seemed satisfied to live hers out quietly, closeted with ratebooks, data and dust greatly disturbed her and she didn't hesitate to speak her mind.

Wearing a pink pullover and white short-shorts that did a magnificent job of showing off the legs that she was still very proud of, Jane entered the kitchen.

Susanna was standing next to the stove, distracted, staring into the frying pan in her hand.

Jane joined her, looking over her shoulder. There appeared to be nothing wrong with the pan. "What's the matter?"

Susanna looked up, startled at the sound of her aunt's voice. Just for a moment, her mind had wandered. The sensation of Flynn's mouth pressed hotly against hers had suddenly washed over her. The image had come out of nowhere, and her breath had been snatched away, just as it had when it had actually happened. And then his apology had played itself back in her head.

Susanna roused herself. "Nothing. Why?" She placed the frying pan on the stove and slowly turned toward the refrigerator. She took out a package of skinless chicken breasts. She felt like making something special tonight.

Knowing the procedure, Jane handed her the bread crumbs and oil from the pantry. "You were frowning into your frying pan."

Susanna shrugged, accepting the bottle of oil in one hand, the container of bread crumbs in the other. "Sorry."

"Don't apologize to me." Jane took out an egg from the refrigerator and placed it on the counter next to the bowl Susanna had retrieved from the cupboard. "It's the frying pan's feelings you've hurt." Jane reached up from behind and placed her hands on Susanna's shoulders. Slowly, she massaged the twin knots. "So, is it about a man?"

Susanna almost purred. Jane's fingers kneaded just the right spots. Her aunt probably did it to get her mind off the fact that she was indulging in her favorite habit—prying into Susanna's affairs. But there was no use lying. From her window across the street her aunt missed nothing that went on in the neighborhood, and certainly nothing that transpired in her niece's life. "Yes."

Jane stopped massaging. Moving around to face Susanna, she clapped her hands together, rolled her eyes heavenward and exclaimed, "Finally," much the way Columbus must have when he first sighted the New World.

Jane, Susanna knew, would have liked nothing better than to see her married off. Susanna aimed the frying pan at Jane's midsection as if it were an extension of her hand. "You follow that up with 'hallelujah' and I'm cutting you out of the will."

Jane laughed, then nodded. Disposing of the empty plastic wrapper for her niece, she turned toward Susanna, curiosity flowing from every pore.

"So, what's he like?"

Jane's eagerness made Susanna smile. She had seen Jane peeking out the window and had seen the look she'd given Flynn. If she had been about ten years younger, Jane would have considered Flynn worth any effort.

Susanna thought of Flynn's grunted apology, of the annoyed look on his face. The frying pan went down on the burner a little too forcefully. "Impossible."

Jane's expression grew hopeful. "The most fascinating ones usually are."

Susanna looked at her aunt, swirling the first piece of chicken in the bread crumb mixture. "Is that why you've married so many of them?"

Jane shrugged as she picked up the chicken and placed it in the pan. She waited for the second piece as Susanna worked. "Hey, once the mystery's gone, so am I. But enough about me." She plopped the next piece in. "Tell me about Mr. Johnny-Come-Lately."

Susanna knew that Jane's feelings regarding her marriages ran far deeper than she let on. There had been three. The first had ended when her husband died. The other two had ended in divorces that seemed amicable enough on the surface, but Susanna knew Jane had grieved privately, even though she had been the one to initiate the proceedings. She still got together with her ex-husbands occasionally. Susanna had met both of them and they were a lot friendlier to Jane than Flynn had been to her as he had hurried out.

Flynn. His reluctance, the fact that he seemed to be pushing her away with both hands, as if she were throwing herself at him, irritated Susanna. "Johnny doesn't want to come at all."

Jane moved the chicken around to make room for the last two pieces. "And that's stopping you?"

Susanna looked at her aunt oddly. "Shouldn't it?"

Jane shook her head. "Oh, Susie, Susie, where have I gone wrong?"

Susanna found she wasn't quite in the mood for jokes as she started on the next part of the meal. "I don't want to force him into anything, Aunt Jane. I just wouldn't feel—"

But Jane didn't let her finish. As she cleared away the remainder of the bread crumb mixture, she kept her eyes on her niece. "Hasn't anyone read you the rules of the game? This is for his own good."

Carrots tumbled out of their plastic bag onto the tiled counter. Susanna counted out six. "What is?"

"You." Jane turned and stroked her niece's cheek fondly as she smiled at her. She had no children of her own. Susanna was her older sister's daughter. Susanna knew that Jane had directed all her maternal instincts that had gone begging toward Susanna and Billie.

She took Susanna's hand in her own and held them. "Listen to me, Susie. If anyone was for a man's own good, you are."

It was much too soon to even be thinking of things like that. Susanna drew her hands away and got back to preparing dinner.

"You don't know anything about the situation." She placed the first peeled carrot on the chopping block and diced it quickly. "Or the man. For that matter, I don't know that much."

Jane obviously saw no problems in the future. She scraped another carrot for Susanna. "Facts only get in the way."

"You would say that."

"Yeah, I would." Jane grinned, finished with the carrots. Everyone who knew Jane knew that facts and figures were things she left to her accountant. Jane went for the highlights, the grand picture. She wiped her hands on a nearby towel. "So, what can I do to help?"

Susanna thought for a moment. Everything was almost done. "You can make the salad."

"I mean with Mr. Shoulders-Out-To-Here." Jane spread her hands out wide as she rolled her eyes again.

"Stay out of the way. That's an order." One Susanna had little hope would be obeyed.

Jean read between the lines. "That means he's coming back, doesn't it?"

The woman was hopeless. "Not if you put bear traps out for him."

Jane washed off the chopping block. She looked over her shoulder at Susanna. "A snare?"

"Aunt Jane!" Susanna wouldn't put it past her aunt.

"Only kidding." She wiped dry the chopping block and put it away. "Loosen up, Susie. Life's too short to be serious."

That wasn't anything that Flynn would ever buy into, Susanna thought. "Well, he is. Very." She remembered what he had told her. "And with good reason."

Jane took out three dinner plates from the cupboard and placed them on the table. "Such as?"

"In the last year, his wife died and then his daughter was killed in an accident." Even as Susanna said the words, empathy flooded over her. How must he have felt, getting one blow on top of another? She was surprised he had managed as well as he had. She didn't know what she would do if anything ever happened to Billie.

Jane had heard all that she needed to hear. "He's going to need a lot of comforting."

Flynn would have disagreed. "What he seems to want is a lot of space."

Jane waved her hand at her niece's comment. "Men don't know what they want."

Susanna couldn't help grinning. She turned the heat down as the oil snapped at her, spitting hot trajectories through the air. It reminded her of his kiss. "But you do."

"Absolutely." Jane nodded her head firmly. She reached for the napkins, folding them mechanically and placing them at each setting. "I've had three husbands. And none of them left me," she reminded Susanna proudly. Her voice softened. "Except Kyle, and he didn't have any choice, poor lamb." It was thanks to his fortune that Jane was financially independent, but she owed Kyle a great deal more than that. It was Kyle, with his gentle, caring ways that had Jane firmly hooked on the concept of love and romance.

Susanna eyed the table. "You staying for dinner?"

"Am I invited?" Jane asked innocently, taking out three glasses.

Susanna laughed. "Always." She wavered. She didn't want the conversation at the table to center on Flynn's eligibility. She didn't want Billie getting his hopes up for no reason. "Just don't push this, okay?"

Jane held her hands up in mute surrender. "Okay. Fine. Oh, can I ask just one more question?"

Susanna sighed. She should have known better. "Just one more."

"What's my future nephew-in-law's name?"

Susanna stifled a frustrated scream. "Aunt Jane—" she began warningly.

"No, that's too confusing. We'll have to call him something else." Jane took out the bottle of diet soda and placed it in the center of the table, her hooded eyes dancing mischievously.

Susanna gave up. "His name's Flynn O'Roarke, he's a senior design engineer at Worth Aerospace—"

Jane's head bobbed up and down approvingly at each bit of information. "Sounds good."

"And he's a grandfather."

Jane's eyes narrowed. "A grandfather?"

Susanna nodded, turning the chicken pieces for the last time. "That little boy you saw him with was Michael, his grandson."

"A grandfather?" Jane echoed again incredulously. She eyed Susanna. "Well, if you don't want him—"

"I didn't say that."

Susanna stopped. Had she just said what she thought she had? Up until this very moment, she hadn't really thought about actually wanting the man, wanting him to be in her life.

Susanna raised her eyes to her aunt's face. The older woman was positively glowing.

"I believe the term," Jane said as she began draining the carrots for Susanna, "is 'gotcha!'" She looked very pleased with herself.

Susanna turned off the heat beneath the frying pan, feeling her own rise. "The term is justifiable homicide, Aunt Jane, if you don't drop this subject here and now."

Another innocent look crossed Jane's face. She was well versed in them. It was her, not Susanna, that Billie took after. "Consider it dropped.

"For now," she added softly as she turned away.

Chapter Seven

Flynn couldn't fall asleep that night. He tossed and turned until his sheets were a tangled mess at the foot of the bed. Giving up, he angrily kicked them off onto the floor. For what seemed like hours, he'd been staring at the moving shadow on his wall, cast there by the tree branches outside his window.

Restless, wired and utterly exhausted, Flynn sat up in bed. Frustration fueled his edginess as he stared into the darkness. It was hopeless. He was wide awake.

Normally, he could always sleep, anyplace, anytime. Kelly used to kid him that he could fall asleep standing up in the closet.

But not tonight.

Tonight the vision of blue-gray eyes, wide with surprise and desire, kept him from finding the solace he so desperately sought in sleep. He couldn't sleep because, among other things, his conscience was bothering him. How could he have let his impulses get the better of him; how could he have let himself kiss Susanna? After a lifetime with Kelly, how could he kiss someone else? It seemed wrong, disloyal. His weakness had thrown him into turbulent waters.

And yet—

Flynn rose, hiking up the waistband of his cutoffs that had sunk low on his lean hips. He crossed to the window and opened it. The night air was cool, damp, still. It didn't help to calm him.

There was something that was calling to him, whispering to his senses, stirring him. Something that was within Susanna's power to give him.

He sighed. His mind was wandering. And keeping him awake.

The entire night was a patchwork quilt of insomnia broken only intermittently by small squares of sleep. Rising at six, Flynn felt like hell.

A great way to face Friday, he thought darkly, finding his way into the kitchen. Michael was already up and at the table. Three different boxes of cereal surrounded his bowl. He was making his first decision of the day. When Flynn groped toward his own chair, Michael looked at him for a long moment, then asked Flynn if he was sick.

"No, I couldn't sleep last night."

"Oh," Michael murmured thoughtfully, settling on the box in the middle. "Billie's mom again?"

When Michael had come to live with him, Flynn had promised himself to answer each of the boy's questions truthfully. Honesty was to be the cornerstone of their relationship. "Eat your breakfast. You don't want to be late."

Michael dutifully filled his bowl with multicolored little balls of cereal, then poured an ocean of milk over them until the round balls bobbed precariously close to the top.

There was enough sugar there, Flynn mused, to charge up three children for a week.

Flynn sought his own source of energy. Coffee. Hot and potent. One sip had him thinking that his own was like brown water compared with the coffee Susanna had served him yesterday afternoon.

Coffee, he thought ruefully, taking another long swallow, wasn't the only thing she had served up hot and potent yesterday. If he closed his eyes, he could still feel her mouth, her lips parting beneath his, inviting him to take, offering him what he needed so badly.

Damn, he didn't need anything at all.

Flynn finished his coffee in another two gulps, instructed Michael to hurry along and went upstairs to prepare for his morning ordeal. They had to pick up Susanna at seven.

Susanna and Billie were waiting for him, just as they had been the day before. She wore red today. A two-piece red suit that bespoke power and femininity all in one statement.

As if she needed the color to be noticed, he thought.

It wasn't until after they had dropped off the boys at school that Susanna said anything other than hello to Flynn. Once they were alone, Susanna felt obligated to fill the silence between them. She was relentlessly cheerful. Susanna was determined to act innocently oblivious to the fact that life as they both knew it had been irrevocably changed in her kitchen yesterday.

As tired as she was cheerful, Flynn attempted to ignore her and merely answer in monosyllables whenever she required a response. He found that it was probably easier to ignore a flash flood as it engulfed you than it was to ignore Susanna.

He glared at her as they stopped for a red light. "Are you always this annoyingly cheerful in the morning?"

She was stubbornly determined not to let him ruin anything. Just because he was afraid of being open didn't mean that she was. "It's a beautiful day, it's Friday, and my son is going to get some helpful tips about his batting, which should make him very happy. Why shouldn't I be cheerful?"

The light changed and they were moving again. "Because it's morning."

She had already guessed that he wasn't a morning person after seeing him yesterday. But that didn't seem enough of a reason for him to behave like a bear that had been stung by a bee. "And?"

And you kept me up over half the night. But he knew he couldn't say that.

She leaned forward and saw the dark smudges beneath his eyes. Though there could have been a dozen reasons for their presence there this morning, still Susanna felt heartened. She hadn't slept all that well herself. "Didn't you get any sleep last night?"

"Minimal," he bit off.

"Noisy neighbors?"

Was it his imagination, or was her tone just a little too innocent? Flynn glanced at her, then looked back at the road. "Disruptive neighbors," he amended. It was as far as he would go in admitting the effect she had had on him. He didn't know how to lie believably.

"Oh." Susanna smiled to herself as she rolled his words over in her mind and savored them. She felt vindicated. No matter how much this young grandfather with the age complex protested, yesterday's incident was not something he was going to casually wipe clean from his mind.

Which was good, because neither could she.

Faced with her unmitigating cheerfulness and optimistic viewpoint, Flynn finally began to relax a little by the time they approached her office building.

"See you this afternoon." She made it sound as if they had been doing this everyday for the past month instead of just twice this week. Worse, she had him almost believing it.

"Right," he murmured.

Susanna picked up her briefcase and began to climb out of the car. Impulse seized her. She turned around and surprised both of them by leaning over and kissing Flynn's cheek.

The imprint of her lips was so light, the kiss so fleeting, so unexpected that he hardly felt it at all. And yet it burned itself into his skin.

He splayed his fingers over the spot almost immediately and stared at her back as she slid out. A bittersweet feeling filtered through him no matter how hard he tried to shut it out. "What was that for?"

She wasn't even certain why she had done it. Maybe because she felt so happy. Maybe because she just wanted to share the feeling. She shrugged. "You looked like you needed it."

His eyes darkened. "I don't need anything." And the sooner Susanna realized that, the better off they would both be.

Susanna looked at him. *That's what you think.*

Aunt Jane's words replayed themselves in her head. Men didn't know what they wanted. Aunt Jane, Susanna decided, was a very wise woman.

"Okay, have it your way." She winked at Flynn. "*I* needed it."

He didn't know what to say to that, but then he didn't have to make a comment. Susanna had turned away and was already hurrying up the steps to the building's entrance.

Faster than the speed of light, he thought.

That served to describe both Susanna and the unsettled feeling she seemed to transfer into his veins. The ocean gently lapped at the shore less than a mile away. The breeze that drifted from it flirted with the hem of her flared skirt as she went up the steps. Flynn caught himself looking longer than he was supposed to.

It wasn't that he was afraid of intimacy, he told himself as he backtracked to Worth Aerospace. He just didn't want it in his life. Not the kind she represented. The kind of intimacy that had you looking forward to seeing someone, to letting them slowly infiltrate your life and make you depend on them.

He was determined to depend on nothing and no one but himself.

Parking at the compound was difficult. He knew it would be. Dropping Susanna off had cost him precious minutes, minutes that meant the difference between getting a good parking space by the main building and getting one by the rear gate. For ten minutes he cruised up and down the aisles, looking for an opening. His mood was close to foul by the time he entered his office.

It didn't improve during the course of the day.

The problem, he thought as he got into his car eight hours later, was that part of him was actually looking forward to this. He was looking forward not just to playing with his grandson and helping Susanna's son learn how to bat properly, but to Susanna's company. He muttered under his breath as he jammed his key into the ignition and turned on the engine. It was as if he were at war with himself. Flynn didn't know which made him more uncomfortable: being drawn to the similarities or the differences between Susanna and his late wife.

He had no business, he told himself sternly, being drawn to either. Romance was for the young. He thought of Susanna's assessment of his appearance. The chronologically young, he amended with a slight twist of his lips. He had had his good fortune.

Besides, getting involved with someone meant depending on someone else for his happiness. And that was a trap Flynn was completely committed not to fall into again. Once had almost been fatal. There would be no hope for him the next time around.

She was, Susanna thought as she stood before the tall, imposing glass doors of Palisades Mutual Insurance Company waiting for him, too much of a Good Samaritan. Her mother had always scolded her about that, warning her that she would be hurt more times than not, giving her heart so unconditionally. But Susanna couldn't stand seeing anyone suffer, not even a disgruntled bear of a man.

A disgruntled bear whose one kiss, she thought with a smile, had almost melted every single one of the bones in her body.

"Hi, Susanna, need a lift?"

She turned to see Dave Ackerly walking out. At six-two, with just a hint of gray touching his temples and wearing an expensive suit that would set most people back two weeks' salary, David Ackerly looked as if he belonged between the pages of a fashion magazine. And had the two-dimensional personality to match. Over the last three years, he had tried, unsuccessfully, to ask her out several times. Susanna had found herself totally unmoved and uninterested. She saw no light in his eyes, no spark. Smooth, intelligent, mannerly, with never a hair out of place, he held about as much attraction for her as wax fruit.

Her taste, she thought with a smile, ran to frowns and grudgingly offered good deeds.

"No, I'm waiting for one, thanks."

He took a step closer, as if that would make her change her mind. "Sure I can't take you home?" His smile broadened invitingly. "Your ride doesn't seem to be here."

She found the smell of his cologne stifling. With an inward sigh of relief, she saw Flynn approaching. To the rescue again, she thought.

"No, there's my ride now." She pointed toward the silver convertible. "See you." Gratefully, she ran off as David stood, shaking his head and watching her go.

She all but bounced into his car the way Michael had the day before.

"Friend of yours?" Flynn nodded toward David. He had imagined David trying to put the move on Susanna as he had approached and something possessive had reared its head as temper licked at his insides. If he didn't know any better, he would have said he was jealous. Except that he had never been jealous, not in all the years he could remember. Why would he be jealous now, about a woman he hardly knew?

"David?" This time, she rather liked the way he had growled his question. "No, not really. We work on the same floor. He's an underwriter."

Flynn disliked David on sight. He looked like a mannequin. It was eighty degrees and the man was wearing a jacket. And looked comfortable. Flynn's was slung over the rear seat, with his tie stuffed into the pocket. "Am I supposed to be impressed?"

"No, just informed." She'd caught the note in his voice and smiled to herself. His scowl would break his face if he didn't stop soon. "Hard day?"

"No, nothing out of the ordinary," he answered, careful to look at the road and not her. No, that wasn't true. *She* was out of the ordinary for him.

Susanna settled into the seat, shifting so that she could put her seat belt on. She bit her lower lip as she regarded his expression. It hadn't changed that much from this morning. Maybe he hadn't been jealous just now. Maybe he just growled about everything. "Billie is really looking forward to this afternoon, but if you'd rather not—"

He jerked his head toward her. "Why wouldn't I?"

She shrugged helplessly. The man was impossible to figure out. "Well, for one thing, you're grimacing. I don't want to be accused of forcing you into anything. If there's something else you and Michael would rather be doing, I don't want to stand in your way."

She was offering him a way out. Faced with it, he realized he didn't want one. Not when it meant disappointing a little boy. At least, that was the excuse he gave himself. Digging deep, he tried to sound properly apologetic. "Look, if I'm biting your head off, I'm sorry. It's just been a long day tacked on to a long night."

Apologies always had the same effect on her. Any annoyance Susanna might have been harboring immediately vanished. "Then you're coming over?"

"Yes." A singsong voice in his head chanted, *You'll be sorry, Flynn.*

Susanna let out a relieved sigh. "Good. Otherwise, Billie and I will be eating pot roast sandwiches for at least a week."

He took the turnoff that led toward Michael's day-care center. "Doesn't it take a long time to cook a pot roast?" Flynn vaguely remembered Kelly mentioning something about pot roast taking hours to prepare. He certainly didn't want to stay at Susanna's house for hours. Ten minutes had nearly proven fatal the last time.

This was a mistake.

She glanced at her watch. Dinner should be done within half an hour of their arrival. "Oh, I started it this morning." She saw the quizzical look enter his eyes. "I'm making it in my crock pot."

"Crock pot?" he parroted. What the hell was a crock pot?

She grinned. Flynn said the name as if the appliance was some ancient form of torture. She wondered if he knew what to do with a microwave and what mealtimes must be like at his house. "Never mind. I'll show you when we get home. Dinner'll be ready by the time you feel like taking a break."

Home. She made it seem so natural, Flynn thought. Almost—he quickly stopped that thought and promised to keep a closer guard on his mind.

Michael ran out to meet them, leaving his teacher waving in the background. Conversation immediately switched from pot roasts and crock pots to baseball and the endless weekend that loomed ahead.

Billie was running alongside the car before Flynn could bring it to a full stop in Susanna's driveway. "Hi! I thought you'd never get here!" His greeting was for Flynn. "Oh, hi, Mom."

"I live for these warm, enthusiastic welcomes," she told Flynn with a laugh as she got out of the car. "Hi yourself."

On the far side of the driveway Billie had dragged out every single piece of baseball-related equipment Susanna had bought for him in the last year. Flynn looked at the impressive pile and let out a low whistle. "You've got enough here to outfit a minor-league team."

"He said he needed it all." Susanna kissed the top of Billie's head. He wiggled out of her grasp, embarrassed.

"It's okay," Flynn confided to the boy. "She kissed me, too."

"Yeah?" Billie's eyes grew large and hopeful.

Flynn knew he had made a tactical mistake in his efforts to relieve Billie's discomfort.

"Well, I'll leave you men to your game. Dinner will be ready in a little while," she promised.

Flynn watched her disappear into the house, swinging her briefcase at her side. He could have sworn he heard her humming.

"You gonna stare, or play?" Michael asked impatiently.

Flynn swung around and tossed the ball he had been holding to Michael. "Play!"

Michael jumped and caught the ball. The boys laughed gleefully as they fell upon the mass of gloves, bats and extraneous paraphernalia that went into making up a game. Flynn felt himself beginning to relax as he applied himself to tackling Billie's problem and forgetting about his own.

With Michael serving as catcher, Flynn went back and forth between pitching and showing Billie how to swing. The method was cumbersome at best. But when he attempted to use Michael as a pitcher, things went from bad to worse. As a pitcher, Flynn observed, Michael made a great bowler.

"I think you need a fourth to even things out."

Flynn turned toward the woman who had made the offer. For a moment, he thought Susanna had abandoned her crock pot, whatever that was, and had come out to join them. Though it annoyed him to react this way, a shaft of tension immediately splintered through the lower part of his abdomen.

But if it was Susanna, she was approaching from the wrong direction. This woman was crossing the street, coming from the tidy one-story building Susanna had told him yesterday belonged to her aunt.

As the woman walked toward him, Flynn realized that she was at least several years older than Susanna and a little more shapely. She carried herself well and with pride, as if the years that had advanced on her didn't trouble her one bit.

"Hi, I'm Jane, Susanna's aunt." Jane extended her hand, waiting for Flynn to take it. When he did, she gave him a firm, no-nonsense grip that had him liking her immediately. Hands on her hips, Jane regarded the three men thoughtfully. "Seems to me that you could do with a pitcher."

"Can you pitch?" Flynn asked, amused. He remembered the way Susanna had thrown the ball.

"Can I pitch?" Jane laughed as she picked up a glove from the driveway. Her hands were small, like Susanna's. Still, the glove was a tight fit. She pounded it expertly, making a serviceable indentation in the palm. "Does the sun set in the west?" She grinned at Flynn. "My second husband played in the majors for two years." She positioned herself opposite Billie. "Let's play some ball, handsome."

Flynn got up behind the boy and wrapped his hands around the bat over Billie's. He watched as Jane wound up. If Susanna had an aunt so obviously versed in the game, then why hadn't *she* given Billie the appropriate pointers? He began to smell a rat. Then he realized Jane was holding the ball in her left hand. He supposed it might be difficult for a lefty to correct a problem for a righty.

The ball sailed past him, into Michael's glove.

"Gotta think fast, handsome," Jane said laughing.

The noise from the street had Susanna pushing aside the white nylon curtain and looking out the living-room window. What she saw made her smile as a contented warmth spread all through her. Her aunt, Michael and Flynn were all involved in helping her son attain his heart's desire—a healthy swing. Behind her, on the kitchen counter, the crock pot was coming to the end of its day-long preparation. It wouldn't go anywhere, she thought, opening the front door to watch the practice for a few minutes.

She folded her arms across her chest and stood in the doorway, quietly observing. Billie seemed to be in his element, lapping all this up. A bittersweet feeling shot through her. Her son needed this, needed this kind of male contact. She wished with all her heart that there had been someone for her after Brett, someone she could have loved enough to give Billie the sort of life that a lot of little boys took for granted.

Her eyes strayed to Flynn as he hunched over the boy's small frame, his arms wrapped around the bat, his body poised to stay as clear of Jane's ball as possible. He looked as if he was having fun, as well. Relaxed, the wary, guarded look gone from his face, he looked more like a boy than a senior design engineer with the weight of the world on his broad shoulders. He was handsome, she observed. Very handsome. She wondered if he knew. Probably not. He seemed oblivious to a lot of things.

And stubborn as hell.

Susanna sighed. Just her luck. The first man who made her feel absolutely anything since Brett had left her life and he was hung up on age and probably a whole lot of things she couldn't begin to unscramble.

Leave well enough alone. She eased the front door closed and returned to the kitchen.

She knew it was good, sound advice. And she knew that she wouldn't pay attention to a word of it. It just wasn't in her nature.

Dinner was dynamic. Michael had heartily told her so at least three times, each time he took another helping. He, Billie and Jane had dominated the conversation at the dining table, leaving little leeway for Flynn to say much of anything. He hardly seemed like the same man who had played so energetically with the boys only half an hour ago.

Susanna wondered if it was her, if she made him this uncomfortable. And if that was a good sign.

"Well, who's for dessert?" Aunt Jane asked, pushing her plate back. Two small hands shot up in reply.

The pot roast was gone, as were most of the string beans and baked potatoes. Susanna wondered where any of them would find the room for dessert. "I have some ice cream in the refrigerator," she began, rising.

Jane leaned over and placed her hand over her niece's, stopping her. "That's not any fun." She turned toward the two boys. "We want choices, don't we, boys?"

Two sets of small eyes looked at Jane questioningly.

"How about a ride to the ice-cream parlor?" she suggested, already on her feet. "Over two dozen flavors to choose from."

"Okay," Susanna agreed. The dishes could wait.

"Who invited you?" Jane asked innocently. Susanna looked at her as the boys giggled. Jane winked at them. "I want the exclusive company of two very interesting ball players."

"What's 'clusive?" Billie asked.

"*Ex*clusive," Jane repeated. "You and Michael." She nodded to Susanna. "You and handsome here can have the ice cream in the refrigerator," she instructed cheerfully. "C'mon, boys—" she waved them on to the door "—I have to get my purse."

They began to follow her like mice scampering after the Pied Piper. But Michael stopped at the doorway, one foot over the sill, hesitating. "Is it okay?" he asked Flynn hopefully.

Flynn wanted to say no, it wasn't okay to leave him alone with Susanna. That he needed Michael's small frame as a buffer against his own feelings. But he couldn't very well put any of that into words.

Flynn waved him on. "Go ahead. Just don't get sick." He dug into his pocket to give Jane money, but she shook her head.

"My treat, handsome." She gave a wave to Susanna and left.

Flynn felt like the last one left on the deck of the *Titanic* just before it went under. He told himself he was being foolish. He looked over to see Susanna gathering dishes together. He needed to have something to do, something to talk about. "Need help with that?"

"Sure." She mustered her best encouraging smile. Children and wild, skittish animals responded best to gentleness. "You can help me take these out to the kitchen and stack them in the dishwasher if you like."

He didn't want to say what he'd like. They both knew.

Bland topics were safest. "Dinner was very good." He picked up the remaining dishes she had stacked and followed her to the kitchen.

"Thank you." She nodded toward the counter. He set the pile down next to hers and started scraping them. "I like to cook." She opened the door of the dishwasher and began to place the plates in the rack. "I don't paint or write and I'm not very good with my hands. Cooking is the only creative outlet I have. I don't get to do it nearly often enough though. Most nights it's spaghetti and meat sauce."

He remembered the feel of her hands, soft and light on his shoulders, creating swirls of sensations within him. No, he wouldn't say that she wasn't good with her hands. She was *too* good.

He moved out of the way as she took out the dishwashing detergent from beneath the sink and measured out just enough. Yellow crystals rained into the tiny compartment. "I'm sure Michael welcomed the change from sandwiches." Watching her, Flynn made a mental note to give his dishwasher a try the next time the dishes piled up.

"Is that what you've been living on?"

He nodded. "That, fast food and those little self-contained dinners that you boil."

"Well, you can come by any time you want." She slammed the dishwasher door, turned around and came face-to-face with Flynn. Pulses began to hammer to a new, faster beat. "For dinner," she added haltingly, her breath catching in her throat as she looked at his eyes. They had grown dark again. And pulled her toward him like a magnet. She felt herself losing ground fast. "And someone to talk to, if you'd like." The words dripped from her lips. Why was coherent thought suddenly such a lost art? "I've been through all this, you know. I know what it's like." Her voice lowered to a whisper that feathered along his skin. "I know what you're thinking."

"I don't think you have any idea what I'm thinking," he murmured, threading his arms around her waist, finally surrendering to the craving that had awakened yesterday.

Her mouth felt dry. "Then why don't you tell me?"

Chapter Eight

He brought his mouth down to hers and completely lost his bearings, his way home again.

The sweet taste of her lips, the enticing scent of her breath, the feel of her body as it curved against his heightened Flynn's excitement and magnified his pleasure. It was as if he had terminated a year-long fast and was finally getting his first real taste of food.

He plunged his hands into her hair, cupping the back of her neck as he slanted his mouth over hers again. He needed to feel her, his fingertips sending messages to his brain that she was real, that she was here.

Needs ravaged him, remaining unsatisfied. The more he got, the more he wanted. At each plateau, he went begging, and she was there to meet his demands, which continued to mushroom until he ached.

His head spun.

There were no words to describe how he felt at this moment, no way to relate it to anything that had come before. She was all things to him, shy, eager, giving, taking. Her body felt soft and supple and so sublimely wonderful against his lean, hard frame. Every shred of his being was aware of her, only her. Nothing else existed in the universe beyond this one small woman who had cast him to the depths of agony one moment, the pinnacles of ecstasy the very next.

His hands roamed her back, eagerly pressing her closer, committing each subtle curve to memory. How could someone feel so frail, so delicate and still make such cataclysmic sensations erupt within him?

He held her tighter, closer, afraid that if he loosened his grip those wonderful feelings would fly away, escape, leaving him to return to his world, empty, lonely.

Hunger. Flynn had never known such hunger. He wanted to carry her upstairs to her bedroom and make love to her lyrically, passionately, endlessly. Only the fact that the others would be returning soon stopped him from acting on the overwhelming impulse.

Impulse. Flynn felt like some misguided youth, stumbling into his first romance.

But he wasn't some misguided youth. He was a mature man with an entire life already behind him. How could this be happening now? How could he be at these crossroads again? He wasn't up to it anymore. He didn't want the responsibility of a relationship. Or the pain that inevitably went with it.

And yet, holding Susanna, wanting her, made him feel alive again.

She made him feel alive again.

But this wasn't just happening in a vacuum. If he let go, if he let himself feel, then a whole host of other things would follow as a result. He couldn't divorce himself from that. He couldn't just take and then walk away. He wasn't that kind of man.

Flynn drew away and framed her face in his hands, his eyes searching hers for an answer to his dilemma. All he saw was desire mixed with wonder, anticipation. It was the sort of look small children had on Christmas morning as they stood in front of a tree with a mountain of gifts bursting under it. She was beautiful, and just looking at her made something quicken inside him. He refused to think of it as his heart.

His breathing was far from steady. He heard his own blood roaring in his ears, his own needs hammering through his body, demanding release. It had been so long since he had felt like more than half a man. Too long.

As he trailed his lips along the hollow of her throat, he felt her pulse jump. Her response made him ache to take her, knowing he couldn't. The words seemed to flow out of him on their own, against all reason. "I want to make love to you."

She gripped his forearms, pleased, touched. And filled with the bittersweet ache of desire. She longed to be made to feel totally alive again, to have that special pleasure exploding within her. "With me."

He blinked, confused at her response. "What?"

She smiled, her cheeks brushing against his palms as her smile spread. "These days, you don't make love *to* a woman, you make love *with* her." She placed her hands on top of his as they still framed her face. Her own hands hardly began to cover his. He had large hands, powerful hands. But they felt so gentle against her face, as if he was afraid he'd hurt her. "We share the process. Together."

Something else that had changed, he thought, while he had been safely, comfortably married to Kelly. He was beginning to feel as if the whole world had changed and he was out of step. He didn't belong in this part of life anymore. His path was somewhere farther down the road.

So what was he doing, wandering around like Alice in Wonderland, going from one unique sensation to another, looking for the way home, yet tarrying too long?

"It'd be pretty lonely, doing it by yourself," Susanna murmured when he made no response. She turned her head slightly and brushed a light kiss against his palm.

Fire licked at his loins.

She looked up and saw the war raging within him. "You're going to say you're sorry again, aren't you?" She thought, this time, that her heart would be badly bruised if he did. She didn't want him to be sorry. She wanted him to be glad.

He started to agree, but hesitated. It wasn't the truth and she deserved that at least. He couldn't give her anything else.

"No, I'm not sorry." He moved aside the wisp of hair from her face. "I'm only sorry that this is happening now, instead of at the right time."

Was he trying to say that he wished he had met her first instead of Kelly? She didn't know. But it wasn't an excuse she would accept. Nor let him hide behind, either. "Anytime is the right time when two people care about each other."

He let her assumption go without comment. To deny that he cared would be to lie. It seemed to be a given at this point, however she wanted to define the word "care." Flynn knew he liked her, he knew what he had here had gone a step beyond mere physical attraction, though the pull of that was slowly undoing him. "It isn't as simple as that."

She drew his hands from her face and then linked her fingers with his. "Nothing is completely simple, but it only gets complicated if you let it."

No, she was wrong; it was far too complicated already. "I'm not single."

The words jolted her. Was there someone else, after all? Had he lied when he'd told her yesterday that he hadn't been with anyone else since his wife? No, she didn't really believe that.

Silently she led him into the living room, to the sofa. She sat, urging him down beside her. And waited for him to explain.

He stared at the white marble coffee table and saw a small fissure at one corner. He curbed the urge to trace it, to feel something cool that would smother the burning ardor he felt gripping him. "I have Michael, and Stephanie and Julia to consider."

Susanna let out the breath she had been holding. She could understand commitment. Admire it. It was just one more thing she liked about him. "And I have Billie. It makes for a fuller life."

Why didn't she understand? He had fallen in love with Kelly when there had been nothing else in his life. She had been the beginning of his life. With her, he had faced college, parenthood and the challenges of his career. That was all in its place now. He couldn't begin to reshuffle his life and start over. "It makes for trouble. My plate's already too full."

She took his analogy one step further. "Life is a feast, not a diet."

He turned to her, a rebuttal on his lips. He made the mistake of looking at hers. A feast. Yes, that would be the word to describe what it was that he had found on her lips. A feast. And he had been starving.

"Oh, God, Susanna. What are you doing to me?" His fingers tangled in her hair and he pulled her to him, against his will, against everything that he held as logical. He couldn't operate on two levels this way. Right now, the only level that counted was that he wanted her, that his body vibrated from wanting her.

It was the first time she had heard him say her name. Sunshine spread within her.

Susanna gave her friendship readily, her affection when it was needed and her understanding without reservation. But her body was something that she had given to only one man before. She had given her love and her body freely to only Brett. She had gone to him without hesitation. It had been right. She had known it, felt it.

Just like she knew it now.

She caught her breath as she felt Flynn's hand edge toward her chest. Large hands, striving so hard to be gentle as he cupped her breasts through the silk of her blouse. Trembling, she felt herself shiver at his very touch. Oh, God, it had been so long.

Tears formed in her eyes as she clung to him.

His kisses grew deeper, more demanding, his need almost savage as he tried to harness it, to hold himself back for both their sakes. He felt as if he were free-falling. There was no control, no restraint.

Flynn knew that he could very easily become addicted to this, to her. A veritable prisoner of his own desires, of what she held out to him with both hands. He had never felt this sort of rush before.

Dependent.

The thought ricocheted through his head. His body snapped to rigid attention, as if he had suddenly been thrown headfirst into ice-cold water. One step before the plunge, he slowly, cautiously backed away. That had been close. Too close. He'd have to be very, very careful not to let it happen again. But at what price? The loss that would be his suddenly filled him with a melancholy yearning that left him bereft. God, he hated common sense.

Dazed, on the brink of falling over into a wild, endless abyss whose boundaries were comprised of walls of sheer emotion, Susanna could only stare at Flynn as he pulled away. "What's the matter?"

He held her by her shoulders, held her in place. Held her away from him. "I can't."

She tried to piece together an explanation and ignore the hurt she felt welling up inside. How could he cast her aside so easily? A spark of temper flared.

"Can't what? Kiss me? Hold me? You're already doing all of that. Can't care for me?" Her voice cracked. She struggled for control. This thing between them had happened fast, so fast. Like lightning flashing across a sky that had been bright and peaceful only a moment before. "I think that's out of your hands, too."

He couldn't look at her. If he did, he'd falter. Again. "This is wrong."

"Why?" she demanded. Why couldn't he unlock what was inside? He wanted to. She could feel it. Taste it. Couldn't he?

"Because."

She rose, surprised that her limbs could actually manage to hold her up. Everything felt shaky from her neck down. Well, that certainly explains everything, she thought, but swallowed her sarcastic retort. You learn something about yourself all the time, she thought. She had just learned that she could be hurt, badly. Susanna had believed herself beyond that by now. "Flynn, it's not wrong to open up, to need."

"Yes, it is." He slapped his hands against his thighs as he rose, angry with himself for having let things go too far. He hadn't been fair to her. "And I don't—"

"—Need anything, yes, you already told me." Susanna sighed as she heard a car pull up across the street. That would probably be Jane and the boys. Just as well. She didn't know how much more of an emotional roller coaster ride she could handle tonight. "Well, right now it's a moot point what either one of us needs. Your marines have landed.''

''What?''

She nodded toward the front door as she tucked her blouse into place. ''Unless I miss my guess, Aunt Jane has brought Michael and Billie back.''

The words were no sooner out of her mouth than the door flew open. Jane shepherded the two lively boys before her. Each was wearing globs of several different shades of ice cream on his shirt like badges of combat. The older woman took one look at Susanna and Flynn and her pleased smile widened. Though they had frantically smoothed and patted in an effort to make themselves look presentable, there was no mistaking their slightly mussed appearance, or what it implied.

''I could take them out to the arcade,'' Jane offered, half turning toward the door again.

Susanna shook her head, grabbing Jane's arm before her aunt could be off and running again. ''It's been a long evening, Aunt Jane. I think Flynn would like to go home now.''

''Oh.'' Jane looked from Susanna's face to Flynn's.

Susanna made it sound as if he were running. And he was, Flynn thought. Running to preserve the safe little slice of life that he had managed to carve out in the last fifteen months. But he didn't have to like the way that sounded. ''Let's go, Michael.''

''Aw, do we have to?'' the boy said, pouting, then abruptly stopped, withdrawing.

Susanna saw and wondered at the sudden change.

''It's getting late, Michael,'' Flynn said, placing his hand firmly on the boy's shoulder. Michael turned and walked obediently out of the room in front of his grandfather.

Billie bracketed Flynn's other side. ''Will you be back?'' he asked Flynn hopefully.

It was the look in Billie's eyes and not the demands of his own body, Flynn told himself, that had him agreeing. "I'll be back," he told him.

Billie followed them to the door. Susanna trailed behind. If Flynn wanted space, she'd give the insensitive lout space.

"There's a game tomorrow," Billie reminded Flynn as they reached the door. "If you come early, you could maybe coach me some more. I really learned a lot tonight."

Flynn almost laughed. So had he, he thought ruefully. And then he thought of tomorrow, and of seeing Susanna again. It was too soon. Who could he get to take Michael to the game tomorrow? Perhaps if he—

No, damn it, he had never been a coward before. He wasn't about to start being one now. He had enough fortitude to resist what he knew was bad for him. "We'll see," he told Billie.

Flynn knew he couldn't leave without saying something. Steeling himself, he looked over his shoulder at Susanna. Her chin was raised, but he could see the look in her eyes, the hurt she was trying to hide. "Thanks for the meal and everything." Lord, that sounded so lame.

"At least the meal turned out well," she said with a purposely studied shrug. "The 'everything' we'll just have to work on."

A small, sad smile played on her lips. He felt a twinge of conscience that he was responsible for that. On impulse, Flynn cupped Susanna's chin in one hand and brushed a kiss over her mouth. The smile, he could feel beneath his lips, widened. And grew genuine. He thought he heard something like a little cheer coming from Billie, but he wasn't certain. It was hard to hear anything with that buzzing going on in his ears.

"It all turned out well. It's not you, it's me," Flynn told her quietly, and walked out with Michael.

Susanna watched him go, then closed the door. "No," she whispered to herself. "It's going to be us. Somehow, in some capacity, it's going to be 'us.' You just don't know it yet."

She turned around to see her aunt and her son grinning at each other. For them, it seemed simple. But as Flynn had said earlier, it was a lot more complicated than what it seemed. "I wouldn't break out the champagne just yet, you two."

Billie made a face. "I don't like champagne. How about grape juice?"

Susanna laughed and hugged him to her, grateful that he was in her life.

"Grape juice it is."

Flynn's plan was a simple one. He intended to bring Michael to the playing field, make some sort of excuse about catching up on work he had brought home with him and then leave. He grudgingly conceded that it might be the coward's way out, but in this case, it was the more prudent approach. Besides, lots of parents dropped off their children on the field and then went to run errands. The game would be over by noon and he'd come back in time to pick up Michael.

Michael hadn't protested when he had outlined his plan to the boy in the car. At least, not in words. But it was there in his eyes, in the way he sat rigidly. Michael was disappointed, but resigned.

His six-year-old grandson was acting more of a man then he was, Flynn thought. The plan began to disintegrate. Flynn couldn't make life more difficult for Michael just because he was trying to hang on to his own sanity, on to the frail niche in the world he had carved out in the last year.

He'd just have to find another way to do it, that's all.

Flynn turned down the street behind the playing field. There were a lot more cars parked here today than there had been on Wednesday. Searching for an available space, Flynn eyed Michael's solemn profile. "Well, I guess that maybe I can do the work later."

"You sure?" Michael turned toward Flynn, looking at him warily with eyes that were far older than any six-year-old should possess.

"Yeah," he said grinning at Michael, tugging the boy's cap down over his eyes. "I'm sure."

"All right!" Michael drew the last word out as if it had four syllables.

If you say so, Flynn thought stoically, carefully squeezing his car into a small space between two full-sized vans.

She was already there, her team banner firmly planted in the ground, clipboard in her hand. Flynn walked toward her slowly, his hands shoved deep into his pockets. Why he had nurtured the small hope that she wouldn't be here was beyond him. She'd probably be here even it she were on crutches. She had that kind of dedication, that kind of spirit. Which was admirable, but it also bespoke a stubbornness that wouldn't give way. It indicated a person who was used to doing whatever she felt like doing. Independent. Like him. There was no hope that a relationship between them would work. He knew that. In his head. It was just going to take the rest of him a little while longer to catch up, that's all.

Flynn felt his gut tightening, a small spasm shooting through his right side. The sensation had him catching his breath and holding it a minute before the unpleasant feeling passed. This, he thought, was going to a little too far. Could anticipation, nerves, whatever, create such pain? he wondered.

If so, this attraction between men and women, he told himself, was highly overrated. There was a great deal more pain involved than anything else, both physical and emotional.

He realized that Michael was holding back, matching his steps to Flynn's. The boy was afraid he'd renege, Flynn thought with a pang. A year together and they were still politely skirting each other. When did unconditional acceptance take place? *Did* it take place at all? He didn't know.

He placed his hand on his grandson's shoulder, giving it a squeeze. "C'mon, let's go."

Michael's smile lit up his face. Maybe, Flynn mused, it would take place soon after all.

Billie raced up to them before they got very far onto the field. He hopped from one foot to the other as he looked up at Flynn. As he tilted his head back, his cap tumbled off.

"You came!" Billie scooped up the cap and plopped it back on his head, where it sat slightly off to one side.

Flynn straightened it. "Didn't you think I would?"

This time, Billie held onto his cap as he looked up. It was a long way to Flynn's face. "Mom thought you might have other plans."

Mom, Flynn thought, looking into the distance and catching Susanna's glance, seemed to be able to read his mind. A very dangerous talent.

"Is it okay if we practice?" Billie asked, waving the bat in front of Flynn.

Flynn took hold of it, his eyes on Susanna as she walked toward them, her gait unhurried, the unconscious sway of her hips making him yearn for her. Flynn forced himself to look down at Billie instead of at his mother. "That's why I'm here."

Susanna was within earshot. She was sure that Flynn's assertion was meant more for her than for Billie. He meant to tell her that he wanted to close the door on what had happened between them the last two days. This was his way of saying that he was starting out fresh, with a clean slate.

Susanna only smiled, as if she knew something he didn't.

She probably did, he thought as he went out onto the field with the two boys. And it annoyed the hell out of him.

The baseball game between the Cubs and their challengers of the day, the Giants, got underway within the half hour as the rest of the teams straggled onto the field, their parents hauling blankets and beach chairs behind them.

Flynn found himself falling back to the sidelines near Susanna. With a lot more parents spread out over the field than there had been on Wednesday, Flynn reasoned that it was the only logical place to stand. And he had always been a great believer in logic.

Like Lancelot girding himself for battle, Flynn reached for a shield as he came closer to his doom. "Did I tell you I was applying for a transfer?"

Susanna looked up from the latest batting-order sheet the coach had handed her. "From what?" She half expected Flynn to say, "From life."

"My job." He tried to look casual. "There's an opening in the San Francisco branch."

Though he had been interviewed for the position before he had ever met her, he felt as if he was stuttering some flimsy fabrication. What was it about this woman that reduced him to an errant little boy, even as she made his blood run hot?

Susanna looked at him, her pencil hovering over the third child's name. Was Flynn just making up an excuse to create space between them, or was he really looking into a transfer?

In either case, Susanna felt a pang take hold. Well, true or not, she was determined to look unaffected and pleased. "Will it mean a promotion for you?"

She sounded almost happy. Had he misread all the signals? And if he had, why was he feeling this strange prick of desolation? Wasn't that what he wanted? He was beginning to think he didn't know what he wanted. And it was all her fault.

"Not really." He thought of the job description that had initially caught his eye. He had been restless to try something new, something different in his life. He looked at Susanna, as the sun streaked through her hair. But not this different, he assured himself. "It's a lateral transfer. But the work will be more interesting."

She avoided his eyes. She had never been much of an actress and could only keep up her cheerful front for so long. "When will you leave?"

"Well, it hasn't come through yet and then again—" He began to falter as he looked into her eyes, finding himself getting lost again, just as he had last night. "I'm not sure I'll take it if it does. There are a lot of things to consider."

"I see." Susanna fervently hoped that she might be one of those things. But she made no further comment as she turned her attention to the game.

Chapter Nine

Since Susanna's car was once more among the functioning, and was parked in her driveway, there was no reason for Flynn to see her on a daily basis. No reason, except for one that he tried to ignore. He wanted to.

As Monday's lunchtime approached, he struggled with an intense desire to get into his car and drive to the mall, specifically to the department store that stood facing the Palisades Mutual building. If she had errands to run, he might catch a glimpse of her.

Stop it, he admonished himself. He was acting like a lovestruck teenager, when he was neither a teenager nor lovestruck.

With all the projects he was responsible for at Worth Aerospace, there was more than enough to keep his mind occupied. The week ahead promised to be a hectic one. There were briefing charts to prepare and data to gather for a meeting set up by NASA officials. An entire team of experts was flying in from Houston tomorrow. Their plans were to stay for the remainder of the week. And today, meetings were scheduled from morning until late afternoon.

Flynn hardly had time to draw two breaths in succession, much less think about Susanna. But his mind did wander at noon. Fortunately, he mused, his body was too busy to go with it.

What little time he had to himself was spent at home, being with Michael, trying to restore some order into a life that was post-housekeeper and chaotic to say the least. There hadn't even been time to interview anyone for the position.

At eleven-thirty Tuesday night, down to his last briefs and a pair of mismatched socks, Flynn was forced to have his first meeting with the washing machine that resided in his garage. Muttering under his breath as he tried to unscramble the mysteries of cold and warm loads as detailed on the back of the box of detergent, he sorely missed his daughters.

Flynn embraced the concept of independence when they had returned to college in the fall. He dug himself out from beneath myriad details that threatened to overwhelm him. One of the girls would come down once a month to help out, and of course there had been the housekeeper. Now, with no housekeeper and on an off-weekend with no daughter to help, Flynn felt like Atlas with the entire world on his shoulders.

The washing machine made threatening noises as it went into spin. He eyed it warily and elected to spend the duration of the cycle in the garage, on guard against a possible fire. Past experience with household appliances had taught him anything was possible.

It was after twelve when he threw everything into the dryer and went to bed, wondering why most of his shirts had a pink hue to them and if Michael's red baseball T-shirt had anything to do with it.

By Wednesday, Flynn had nearly talked himself into believing that his reaction to Susanna the previous week had been the results of stress combined with feelings of loneliness. The detailed reasons he cited in his mind were far more complex than the charts he had prepared for the visiting brass from NASA. They all seemed airtight and completely convincing.

And then he saw her.

Her hair was bound up in a ponytail that bounced from side to side as she moved quickly about, rounding up all the little boys into their respective batting order for the day. Wisps of blond hair were escaping at either side of the clasp, making Susanna look like a young girl instead of the thirty-odd-year-old actuary that she was.

He knew he had been lying to himself.

"Hi, stranger!" Susanna waved to Flynn, the effervescent feeling within her rising another notch as she watched him approach. She could feel a smile spreading through her. She'd been afraid he wouldn't come.

Billie broke formation, running to Flynn before Susanna had a chance to say anything further, but she understood. After all, Billie had missed him, as well.

Susanna smiled to herself. Funny how quickly children formed attachments to people. The smile became rueful as she looked away. In some cases, she mused, stopping to tie long, flowing shoelaces for one of the younger boys, that held true for adults, as well.

Look at her, she mused.

She rose, brushing her palms against the seat of her denim shorts, feeling a combination of shyness mixed with elated anticipation as Flynn came up to her. Billie dutifully returned to the line, wedging in between two boys and Michael followed. She nodded her approval, then turned to Flynn.

"How have you been?" Now there was an exciting question. She was becoming as scintillating a conversationalist as he was.

"Fine." No, not fine, he thought, allowing himself a moment of truth. He had missed seeing her. Missed her more than he should have missed someone he had known for such a short period of time.

Absently, he rubbed the dull ache in his side. He had come to the conclusion that she wasn't the source of his momentary light jabs of pain. Considering all the factors that were taking place in his life, he was probably working his way toward an ulcer.

The man was never going to be accused of dominating a conversation. She distributed the four batting helmets and stepped back as the first player took his position in the batting cage. Stubbornly, he hefted a wooden bat. Susanna frowned, picked up the lightest one the coach had packed and walked up to the little boy. "This one'll get you a hit, Drew," she promised.

He looked doubtful as he took it from her and stiffly struck a position, bat raised high, his little rear end sticking up just as rigidly in the opposite direction.

Returning to Flynn, Susanna leaned the bat against the back of the batting cage. "Billie asked about you. He wanted me to take the car back to the mechanic so that he'd have an excuse to see you."

The sound of a ball making contact with the bat echoed for a minute and Susanna turned to cheer Drew on to first base. With a nod from her, Michael went up to take his turn.

Flynn cleared his throat, uncomfortable in his omission, though he hadn't a clue why. It wasn't as if time had exactly hung heavily on his hands. "Billie doesn't need an excuse to see me."

"He's rather small to drive over himself," she pointed out. "His foot doesn't reach the gas pedal."

He shrugged, annoyed with himself for feeling guilty. "I've been busy." He raked a hand through his hair. Why did that sound so lame? It was true.

In one glance, she had looked him over from head to toe. "I can tell." He must have come directly from the office. He was the only man on the field in dress pants and a button-down shirt. Her eyes narrowed as she took a closer look. The shirt was wrinkled, not to mention that in the late-afternoon light, it appeared a little pinkish. He didn't strike her as the kind of man who would be comfortable wearing the color pink.

"Who does your ironing?" she asked.

He looked over his shoulder, trying to see what it was that she was looking at so intently. "I do."

"I see."

The woman would have made one hell of a lawyer. She had the most defensive-creating "I see" Flynn had ever heard. "What?"

"You missed a spot." Why not tell him the whole truth. "Actually, you missed a whole side."

He turned so that his back was away from her. "I'll get the hang of it."

She hadn't meant to make him go on the defensive. "Still no housekeeper?" she asked sympathetically. Another little boy marched up to bat, his cap pulled low over his eyes. He'd left his batting helmet on the ground behind him. Seeing it, Susanna grabbed the helmet and dashed out to him before he had a chance to swing.

She seemed to worry about each of the boys as if they were her own. How did she find the energy? And where could he get some? Susanna half turned toward him as she kept one eye on the field, waiting for him to continue. "I don't even have the time to interview one. I've been in meetings all day and swamped with preparations every evening.''

He sounded as if he needed to kick back a little. Overwork had been Brett's main failing, as well, she thought fondly. ''Up to a home-cooked meal?'' She slanted a casual look his way.

Michael ran toward them, tossing his batting helmet to the ground. He had been tagged out at second. He had walked right into the invitation. The frown turned into a broad grin. ''Boy, are we ever.''

Susanna picked up the helmet and handed it to the next child in line. She grinned at Michael. ''You were robbed,'' she said of the play that had cost him the base. Michael's face was shining with love and excitement. His adoration embarrassed her. She turned to Flynn and flushed slightly. He was studying her in that way he had that made her feel as if she had just walked three feet off a cliff and hadn't noticed that there was nothing under her feet yet. ''What's your pleasure?''

The answer was on the tip of his tongue, but he let it go. A Little League baseball field was not the place to tell a woman she was slowly driving him crazy with desire, utterly against his will. ''You keep asking me that.''

And I'll keep doing it until you get it right. ''Maybe I just haven't heard the right answer yet.'' Susanna's eyes twinkled just before she turned them toward the batting cage.

Twinkled, for heaven's sake. Eyes didn't twinkle. Lights on Christmas trees, *they* twinkled. Eyes didn't twinkle, Flynn silently insisted, annoyed with his own foolishness.

Yet he would have sworn on a stack of bibles that hers seemed to.

Michael had been waiting for his grandfather to answer Susanna. When he didn't, Michael took it upon himself to answer for him. He tugged on the hem of her T-shirt until she looked at him. ''Lasagna.''

Had she missed something? She looked down at the small, intent face. "What?"

A small tongue darted over his lips nervously, hope shining in his deep-brown eyes. "Can you make lasagna? My mom used to, for special times."

The sad note that entered his voice created a tightness in Susanna's throat. She dropped to one knee so that she and Michael were at eye level. "Lasagna it is, Michael. If you can't get the big guy to drive you—" she nodded at Flynn "—I'll come for you myself."

Michael's broad smile was all she needed.

It would have been all Flynn needed, as well, except for one thing. She was taking charge and he didn't like that. Didn't want that. He gave Susanna his hand as she rose to her feet. The tug was less than gentle. "Take right over, don't you?"

"Sorry, single parents get used to doing that." She picked up her clipboard again, trying to ignore the annoyed note in his voice. Now what was wrong? "Comes with the territory. There's never anyone else to consult with."

And that, he thought, summarized their problem in a nutshell. They were both too independent to ever make a go of it. There was no need to worry about complications arising again, as long as he kept that in mind. He and Michael would come over for a simple meal and nothing would go any further than he wanted it to go.

Which meant it wasn't going to go anywhere because Michael, he promised himself, wasn't going to go on any ice-cream runs no matter what Susanna's pushy aunt had in mind.

Feeling a little more in control, he turned toward Susanna as the Cubs got their third out. A mad scramble for caps and gloves and they were flooding back onto the field. "What time?" he asked Susanna.

The catcher was having a hard time with his getup. Susanna sighed as she beckoned the small boy over. "What time is convenient for you?"

The twelfth of never. "One o'clock?"

She was back on her knees, adjusting knee pads for a little boy who was having a hard time standing still. Dressing a moving target was a skill that was hard to master. "Perfect," she murmured to Flynn.

He had his doubts about that.

The sound of the doorbell caught Susanna off guard. Hurrying to the door, an open box of lasagna noodles in her hand, she was surprised to see Flynn and Michael standing on her doorstep. She glanced at her watch. Twelve o'clock. Had she gotten the time confused? She opened the door wider. "You're early."

"Blame it on your son." Confident, Flynn could afford to be cheerful. He had the rest of the afternoon mapped out and it didn't include one unattended moment spent with Susanna. He'd play with Michael and Billie, eat and then take the boys out for dessert. Perhaps he'd even take Susanna along. But today was definitely going to be a group affair. Flynn was feeling rather cocky about the whole thing and not a little relieved.

"Billie?" Susanna turned to look at her son as he flew down the stairs in answer to the doorbell, baseball equipment dripping from his arms and littering the stairs in his wake. "What does he have to do with it?"

"Are they here? Are they here?" Billie cried before he got to the bottom.

Flynn stepped into the house, moving past Susanna to give Billie a hand. Michael silently picked up two of the fallen articles. "He called me," Flynn told Susanna.

Susanna's eyes narrowed as she regarded Billie. Where did he get Flynn's phone number? "How did you—?"

Billie was too excited to let his mother finish. He was fairly hopping from foot to foot. "The team roster, Mom, remember? It's got everyone's phone number on it. Michael's, Nikky's, even the coach's."

And she had posted it on the bulletin board in his room. Well, that cleared up one mystery. Still, she had to make Billie accountable for his actions. "Why did you call Mr. O'Roarke?"

Billie shifted and a glove fell at his mother's feet. Susanna scooped it up and plopped it on the pile that Flynn already had in his hands. She noticed that he winced slightly and wondered why. The load certainly wasn't very heavy, just cumbersome.

"So we could have more time to play." It all seemed very logical to Billie. "He said okay," Billie pointed out, forestalling any lecture his mother might feel obligated to deliver. Billie turned his eyes toward Flynn. "Ready?" he asked eagerly.

He found the adulation in the boy's face hard to resist. "Let's play some ball, champ."

"Is your aunt going to play, too?" Michael asked Susanna. She was surprised to hear the hopeful note in his voice. *He's hungry for a family,* she thought with a pang.

"If I know Aunt Jane, nothing could keep her away." She looked down at the box of noodles in her hand. "Take your time, you guys, dinner won't be ready for another hour or so."

An hour was probably all he could handle today, Flynn thought. The dull ache in his side had been progressively growing stronger. He had actually been debating calling this afternoon off but then Billie had telephoned. Between Billie's eager request and the look on Michael's face, he had found himself being roped in.

"I should be good and tired by then."

She let her eyes skim down Flynn's hard, muscular frame. You didn't get that physique by being an armchair athlete. "I'll see if I can't have the easy chair ready," she promised with a grin.

She wasn't taking this age thing seriously, he thought grudgingly. The woman had a Peter Pan complex. He rubbed the ache in his side, wishing it would just go away. It seemed to him that it had begun on the afternoon he first met her.

Susanna stopped. There was a great deal of discomfort evident on his face. "Anything wrong?"

He shook his head. The last thing he wanted was her concern. "I think I'm probably working on an ulcer." Given the nature of his work, it was understandable.

She knew when she was being dismissed. She turned toward the kitchen. The water would be boiling by now. "Well then, stop working on it."

"Easy for you to say," he muttered at her back. *You're part of the reason the ache is there.*

He had no more time to debate the matter any further. Billie and Michael were pulling him, one on each side, urging him outside.

Just as Susanna had predicted, it wasn't long before Jane joined their ranks. Less than five minutes. Flynn had vowed to maintain his distance from the older woman. He didn't want to give her any false impression as to why he was here. He had come only in the capacity of Michael's grandfather and a coach for Billie. Nothing more. He didn't want to encourage any fantasies she might be harboring about Susanna and him. People like Jane, he believed, were born encouraged. Just like her niece.

By the time Susanna walked outside and announced that dinner was ready, Flynn was exhausted. Far more exhausted than he believed he should be.

Susanna noted his gray pallor, but made no comment about it. He'd probably bite her head off if she did, she thought, following him inside.

Dinner was being served in the dining room. He realized that he was taking the same seat he had taken last week. Flynn promised himself that this would be the last time he'd come over for dinner for a while. He didn't want to establish a pattern. That would undoubtedly make Susanna believe that they were having a relationship. And they weren't.

He didn't lower himself into the chair, he collapsed into it. An uncomfortable, ill feeling beginning to take a firm grip on him. He attributed it to the game. Just a stitch in his side. "I'm getting too old for this."

Susanna raised her eyes toward him as she cut the first piece of lasagna for Michael. "Got your plot all picked out at Forest Lawn and everything, do you?" Lifting the piece, she placed it on Michael's plate.

Flynn failed to see the humor in the situation. "Age is not something you can ignore."

Susanna nodded to Billie to move his plate closer to the pan. "It's not something you give in to, either." She gave Billie his portion and began to cut a third. "And you agree with me."

"I can cut my own," he told her, taking the knife from her.

She lifted her shoulders and let them fall, wondering why it was that she should happen to care for such a pigheaded man.

"Mind reading a hobby with you, or a sideline?" he asked, referring to her comment.

"Neither." She turned the pan toward her aunt and offered her a choice of ends. "You wouldn't work out if you believed that you should just throw up your hands and let time ravage you."

The small piece he had sampled was excellent, but his appetite had suddenly vanished. The ill feeling was becoming insistent. What the hell was wrong? He tried to divorce his mind from the way he felt and concentrate on what she was saying. "How do you know I work out?"

He was fishing for compliments, she thought, taking her own slice. "That would be your male ego asking, wouldn't it?" She leaned over and tapped his biceps with her fingertip. It was like tapping a rock. "As far as I know, this isn't regulation issue at birth." Her smile faded as she saw a line of perspiration along his forehead. The room wasn't warm. Glancing at the boys, she saw that they were perfectly comfortable. Something was wrong.

Another hot poker of pain had jabbed at his side. Flynn tried his best not to let it show, but his eyes gave him away.

Susanna dropped the debate, concerned. "How long has that been going on?"

"What?" Flynn looked down at his plate, pretending to eat. But the very idea made him want to gag. He was beginning to feel sick to his stomach. He shifted in his seat, trying to get comfortable. It was like trying to find a cool spot on top of a layer of hot coals.

She placed a hand on his. "Pain," she clarified. "How long have you been in pain?"

He pulled his hand away, aware that all conversation at the table had stopped. Michael was looking at him with large, frightened eyes. "I'm not in pain."

Enough of this macho nonsense. "Flynn, you scowl at me and I'm getting used to that, but you don't usually look as if I were trying to skin you with a dull knife."

He bit his lip. It would pass. Any second now, it would pass. Just like all the other times. "Colorful."

"Observant," she corrected. He had her so frustrated, she wanted to scram. "Mothers learn to look for telltale signs from uncooperative children."

"I'm not your child, Susanna." He threw his napkin onto the plate. It would have been more forceful if he hadn't suddenly grabbed at his side.

Out of the corner of her eye, she saw her aunt rising. Susanna waved her back. "Then don't act like one. Where's the pain?"

He mustered the darkest look he could. "Sitting opposite me."

She gritted her teeth together. "The one in your body," she said clearly and slowly. "Lower right quadrant?"

Maybe she did read minds. He hoped she hadn't been at it for too long. "How did you know?"

The situation was really serious, if he had to ask. "That's where your hand is." Only one thing came to mind. "Do you still have your appendix?"

"And my tonsils," he put in stubbornly. He wasn't about to let her start playing doctor, although that might have some merit when he was feeling more up to it. He realized that his mind was beginning to drift.

He was wasting time. "Your throat doesn't seem to be giving you any trouble."

"No, but you are." The sick feeling continued, but the pain subsided somewhat. Enough to have him rallying against her. "Look, maybe we'd better make this some other time."

Flynn began to rise. Perspiration drenched him. He sank back onto the chair, amazed at how weak he felt.

It was all she had to see. "Billie, bring me my purse." She looked sternly at Flynn. "You're going to see a doctor."

He gripped the sides of the table, as if that would help him stave off the weakness. She wasn't going to order him around. "Not unless there's one on television."

Susanna completely ignored him as Billie ran up with her purse. She slung it onto one shoulder. "Aunt Jane, can you look after the boys?"

She nodded, looking at Flynn. "Don't give it another thought."

Susanna positioned herself on one side of Flynn's chair. "Help me with him, will you?"

She was acting as if he couldn't hear or speak for himself. Worse, as she and Jane each took an arm and slung it over their shoulders, they were acting as if he was completely incompetent. "What do you think you're doing?" he demanded weakly. Flynn tried to pull away, but he felt too sick to make the effort. In only a matter of minutes, he had turned into a bowl of mush.

As Billie opened the front door, Susanna and Jane walked slowly outside with Flynn between them. "I'm going to take you to the emergency room."

"The hell you are. It's probably just something I ate."

Susanna nodded toward the car. Jane maneuvered down the walk as best she could. Leaning Flynn against the car, Susanna tugged open the passenger door with her free hand. "I may not be the world's greatest cook, but I've never lost a dinner guest yet. This is something more serious. You were grimacing when you got here."

He shook his head. The effort made him dizzy. He struggled to keep the world in focus. "I'll just go home and—"

"Crawl under a table and die? No, I don't think so." Too late, she realized her choice of words.

Michael stood before them, tears shining in his eyes. "You're not going to die, are you?" he asked Flynn, his voice quaking.

Her heart ached for the boy. "He's going to be fine, Michael, as long as he listens to me." She turned to Flynn. "Now, you're going to the hospital if I have to tie you to the roof of the car, is that clear?"

He was too weak to fight, but he wasn't going to be agreeable about it. "Like giving orders, don't you?"

"I live for it. Now shut up and get into the car."

"But—"

"That's the part that goes into the seat, yes. Now put yours into it." She pulled the seat belt back to give him room. "That's a direct order."

The stricken look on Michael's face had him doing as Susanna directed. The effort completely drained him. "If I wasn't feeling so lousy, you wouldn't be getting away with this, you know."

"If you weren't feeling so lousy," she snapped, buckling his belt, then closing the door on him, "we wouldn't have to be doing this." She stopped only long enough to offer Michael a reassuring smile and pat his shoulder. "I'll call you as soon as I know anything, Michael." She got behind the wheel, Jane and the boys closing ranks around her. "In the meantime, why don't the three of you finish eating and then watch some television? Billie's got three thousand videotapes for you to choose from." She turned the key and the engine started.

"Always given to exaggeration?" Flynn wanted to know, his voice growing farther and farther away as he strained to hear it.

"I find it keeps people guessing. Now hang on, Flynn. You're in for the ride of your life."

His mind was beginning to grow fuzzy as he leaned back against the seat. The pain almost seemed inviting as it surrounded him on all sides. Flynn felt as if he were sinking into a dark abyss. "I had a feeling about that the minute I met you."

Susanna covered his hand with her own and tore out of the driveway, steering with one hand.

Chapter Ten

Impatience clawed at Susanna as she pressed hard on the gas pedal. Switching from lane to lane, she bypassed slower-moving vehicles on the freeway. She was filled with a sense of urgency.

"Trying to set a new record?" Flynn asked as she swerved to the right, narrowly missing the nose of the car behind them. They wouldn't need the hospital by the time she was finished, he thought. They'd need the morgue.

"Trying to get you to the hospital before something horrible happens. I have a feeling about this." She glanced in her rearview mirror. Where were the police when you needed them? she wondered, frustrated. They could be making much better time with a policeman leading them in.

She looked at Flynn. His complexion had turned completely gray, despite the shot of bravado he was stubbornly clinging to.

"'Feeling.'" She could hear him trying to raise a sneer. "Nothing's going to go wrong."

He wished he could put some sort of strong conviction into his words. The dull, sick feeling that was gnawing away at him was sapping not only his strength, but his breath, as well. "I hate hospitals," he told her vehemently. After the last time, he had vowed never to set foot in one again.

"Fine," she agreed. "I'll tell them you won't be moving in."

Seeing an opening, she swung into the right lane. For some reason, Susanna couldn't shake the feeling that she was trying to outrace time. It was a premonition. Superstition was something she normally scoffed at. That was for people who believed in reading tea leaves, or for those who trusted the prophecies of fortune tellers. But she couldn't deny that she felt something urging her on, something she couldn't shut her eyes to. It was a matter of preferring to be proven wrong later, with a speeding ticket in her hand, than to ignore it now and be eternally sorry.

As the freeway came to an end on a surface street, Flynn debated getting out of the car. It got no further than a nebulous wish. He hadn't the strength for it. "I'm not sick," he insisted, though he felt just that. Right up to the roots of his hair.

She wondered if he thought he *had* to go through this elaborate protest. "I've seen less pained looks in the movies, on the faces of Freddie Kreuger's victims."

He had no idea what she was talking about, but that was becoming par for the course. "Susanna, I want to go home."

She set her mouth hard. He certainly wasn't making this easy. Part of her felt that she should just turn around and go home. After all, he was a grown man, up to making his own decisions. But one look at him overruled objectivity. The man needed a doctor. "Too bad, O'Roarke. I'm driving."

He tried to sit up straighter. It was hard to sound forceful slumped in his seat. The effort was too great. "I'm serious."

She didn't even bother looking at him. "You're weak and in pain and we're going to find out why." Her voice softened. Maybe he was afraid to find out that something really was wrong. "I'm doing this for your own good."

He shook his head, trying to muster annoyance. "You sound like a mother."

Susanna smiled as she raced through a yellow light. The hospital became visible in the distance. One more light to go. "I've had practice."

He gave intimidation one last shot, though he was feeling less than up to it. "I'm forty-five years old. I have two degrees from UCLA. I am a senior design engineer in the aerospace program. Don't you think I know whether or not I need a doctor?"

She made a right, into the side street that fed into the emergency room parking lot. A security guard eyed the car curiously as she drove in. "In a word, no."

Another pain speared through his side and he paused to keep from gasping out loud. Okay, maybe there was something wrong. But he hated admitting it. "And you do know?"

She stopped the car in the space closest to the entrance and ran around to his side. Opening the door, she unfastened his seat belt. "I'm psychic that way."

Sweat trickled down his back as he contemplated the walk into the building. He resigned himself to her managing ways. "You know, you're getting to be very annoying." But there was a slight smile on his lips as he said it.

Bracing herself, Susanna helped him out. With his arm over her shoulder, she guided him toward the entrance. Flynn tried to take his weight himself to make it easy as he could for her. The automatic doors leaped open as they approached. She caught the attention of a passing orderly and the man hurried over to help.

Susanna let out a sigh as the load lightened considerably. "You can tell me all about it once the doctor gives you a clean bill of health."

The emergency room was mercifully empty. All the chairs before the registration desks were unoccupied. The orderly helped Flynn into the one closest to the door.

She all but sank into the chair next to Flynn's. The man might be all muscle, but muscle weighed a lot. "Looks like they've had a spate of good health around here. The doctor will probably see you right away."

He hated hospitals. They smelled of death. Kelly had succumbed to pancreatic cancer in a hospital. He wanted to go home. But his legs wouldn't obey. He turned toward Susanna, trying to keep the world from tilting as he did so. "Don't count on it."

"You know, you're positively surly." She saw a young woman approaching the desks from the rear of the room, coffee cup in hand. The woman nodded toward them and began walking quickly. "How does Michael put up with you?"

"Why are you putting up with me?" He'd tried everything possible, he realized, to drive her away in the last half hour. Why was she still here? He wouldn't have been.

"I enjoy being kind to dumb animals," she answered. The administrative assistant sat down behind the computer terminal, ready to take the pertinent insurance information. Susanna looked at Flynn. She could see the beads of perspiration on his forehead. "Want me to register you?"

A wave of pain was beginning to suck him in. "No." Flynn gritted his teeth. "I can handle it." He leaned forward, trying to grasp his wallet in his back pocket. Even that took too much effort.

The room grew hotter and smaller.

* * *

When Flynn opened his eyes again, he realized that he was horizontal. The surface he was lying on felt too soft to be the floor. There were curtains around him and the smell of antiseptic mixing with the scent of wildflowers. Someone was holding his hand, gently rubbing his knuckles. Struggling against another wave of pain, he focused on the shape in front of him. Susanna. Her delicate face was no longer sunny. It was outlined in solemn concern.

She saw confusion in his eyes. He tried to rise and she lightly touched his shoulder, pushing him back down. It wasn't difficult. "Hi, welcome back."

His head hurt. He probed it gingerly. There was a small bump over his temple. "What happened?"

"You hit your head when you passed out." Her fingers feathered along the bump. "Lucky thing you've got such a hard head."

He frowned. "I didn't pass out."

She shrugged, biting back her impatience. He was far and away the most difficult man she had ever known. For some reason, maintaining this strong, invulnerable image was important to him. The big idiot. "Have it your way—you decided to do an intensified study of the hospital floor and got a little carried away." Susanna's frown softened as her annoyance gave way to concern. "How do you feel?"

"Like hell," he admitted. And being here wasn't helping any. He felt agitated, and frustrated that he was too weak to do anything about it.

She tried to remember the other symptoms that went along with appendicitis. Her cousin Jennifer had had an attack when they were sixteen. It had happened during a slumber party. The party had ended up in the emergency room for Jennifer, while her older brother Kurt had driven everyone else home at one in the morning. "Do you have a burning sensation?"

Flynn nodded. Stubborn, he still refused to concede the round. "It's just an ulcer."

Maybe it was. She looked around, wishing someone would come. The doctor and nurse had taken all of Flynn's vital signs while he was unconscious. The nurse had also drawn some blood to run standard tests. Then they had left, promising to return "soon." She supposed everyone had their own definition of the word. "They'll tell us if it is."

For a moment, the pain abated. Savoring the reprieve, Flynn looked at Susanna. She looked tired. "You don't have to stay here."

Her hand tightened on his. "Like hell I don't." The look she gave him told Flynn she was in for the duration. He didn't say it, *couldn't* say it, but he was grateful.

His eyes widened as he remembered. "Michael—"

This much she could do for him. She could assure him that his grandson was being taken care of. "—Is going to spend the night at my house. Aunt Jane is with the boys now." She glanced at her watch. Michael was probably frantic by now. "Since you're conscious, I'm going to call and tell them it's going to be a while longer."

There was no clock on the wall. He'd lost track of time. "How long was I out?"

She made her voice sound casual. "Hardly any time at all."

He glanced down. Obviously long enough for someone to have undressed him. Instead of the pullover and jeans he had worn to Susanna's house, he had on a thin blue-and-white floral hospital gown. He felt beneath the blanket that was thrown over him and found that the gown was incredibly short. Whoever manufactured these things believed in economy. "What happened to my clothes?"

The look in his eyes made her think he was contemplating leaping off the bed in search of his things. "I decided to see if those muscles of yours were real. Then I had my way with you." She raised her brows so high, they disappeared into her bangs. "Was it good for you?"

He couldn't help it. He laughed, then clutched at his side. "You're crazy."

"Yes, but at least you're smiling." Susanna moved toward the foot of his bed. "Where there's a smile, there's hope."

Despite the pain, he felt a fondness slip over him. She really was rather unique. Having seen what she had of life, she still managed to be optimistic. "Learn that from Mr. Rogers?"

"I was a permanent resident of his neighborhood for the longest time. I'll go phone Michael. And as for you, you stay put," she warned. "Or I swear I'll hunt you down."

She was just persistent enough to do it, too, he thought, watching her walk away.

Susanna hurried to the nearest pay phone she could find. She fed the phone some change, then dialed her own number. It barely had a chance to ring before the receiver was snatched up.

"How is he?" Jane asked without preamble.

"Demanding to go home." She leaned against the wall, suddenly feeling very tired. "The doctor should be with him any minute. I just wanted to tell Michael that everything was under control. Put him on, will you?"

Using her brightest, most positive voice, Susanna told Michael that his grandfather was with the doctor and everything was going to be fine. The doctor would make him feel better.

Michael listened quietly and thanked her. Even over the telephone, she could tell he was trying very hard to be brave. Promising to call again very soon, she hung up.

Susanna shook hear head and hurried back to the emergency room only to find that the cubicle where she had left

Flynn was curtained off. Taking a deep breath, she stood off to the side and waited.

She heard a deep male voice asking Flynn if "this" hurt. "This" obviously did as she heard Flynn emit a hiss of air before answering affirmatively.

Probably biting on a bullet, she thought. The doctor's next words had her snapping to attention.

"We're going to have to operate, Mr. O'Roarke. I would recommend immediately. I'll send someone in with the proper papers and I'll have the nurse start your IV."

The air backed up in Susanna's throat. She told herself that she was panicking needlessly. After all, lots of people were operated on everyday. Operations were routine. Still, she felt her heart hammering in her chest.

This was childish. She had to get herself under control. There was nothing to worry about, she told herself fiercely. Nothing.

By the time the curtain was drawn back, she had a smile fixed into place. It only felt tight around the edges. She nodded at the doctor as he passed her. "So, they're going to operate," she said to Flynn. She couldn't think of anything else to say.

"He looks too young to know what he's doing," Flynn muttered as Susanna moved to his side. He made up his mind. The doctor was wrong. He'd get better on his own. "Get me my pants." He would have pointed if only he knew where they were.

Susanna glanced at the dark green plastic shopping bag the orderly had stuffed all his belongings into. It was tucked under the wheels of the bed. "If I do, it'll be to tear them into strips and tie you to the bed." Didn't he know this was past the time for games? If the doctor wanted to operate, that meant Flynn's condition was serious, very serious. When would he get it through his thick skull?

He saw her concern and tried not to let it affect him. Flynn tried to smile. "You really get kinky when you get angry."

She let her anger go. It served no purpose. "Remember that. Now be a good boy and let them do what they have to do in order to save your hide." Flynn merely nodded, finally accepting the inevitable.

The same administrative assistant who had registered Flynn came by with release forms for him to sign. He had just finished when the nurse arrived with his starting IV.

It was all happening fast, too fast. Flynn felt himself losing what little control he thought he had. Something potent and warm began to fill his system. He began to drift, float. Each time he tried to hold on, his grasp weakened a little more.

She was still standing there. Susanna. Looking small and lost and worried. She refused to leave him. He wondered why.

Affection washed over Flynn. He was too tired to be on guard, too tired to try to reach for the control that had, up until a few moments ago, been so very important to him. He tried to keep her in focus, but that was getting more difficult with each passing moment. "Have I told you thanks?"

"No." She smiled, surprised and touched. "But it'll come to you."

She stepped out of the way as two husky orderlies arrived with a gurney. The small cubicle was getting very crowded. The nurse moved the IV bottle and its stand aside, waiting for the two men to shift Flynn from his bed to the gurney in order to transport him to the operating room.

The shorter of the two men looked Flynn over and shook his head. "You're sure a big guy." Positioning himself at Flynn's knees, the man let the other orderly handle Flynn's upper torso.

"Yeah," Flynn muttered disparagingly as he was rolled from one bed to the other. "The bigger they are, the harder they fall."

Susanna grabbed at Flynn's blanket as it began to slide off. She moved it over him, trying her best to leave him his dignity. "You're not falling, Flynn, you're just leaning a little." Taking the plastic bag with his clothes, she moved to the side opposite the IV stand.

Leaning. It was just what he didn't want to do, but he couldn't remember why. He felt the rolling motion and began to feel sick. Except it didn't really seem to matter. The drug was blotting it all out. Instinctively, he fought for consciousness and realized that they were wheeling toward the door. He wasn't moving, the bed was.

"Susanna?" His fingers groped along the bedclothes, though he felt as if he were searching for her everywhere. He didn't want to lose her.

"Right here." She gripped his hand as the orderlies guided the gurney quickly from the emergency room to the long corridor.

Flynn opened his eyes, his mind feeling full of cotton. And swirling colors. She was still there. "Thanks."

He probably wouldn't remember any of this later. Susanna savored it anyway. "See, I told you you'd get around to saying it."

The distracted, vacant smile on Flynn's face told her that he was no longer hearing anything she said. The sedative had done its work. At least he wasn't feeling any pain, she thought.

"You'll have to wait out here, ma'am," the taller of the two orderlies informed her gently. "The doctor'll be out to tell you when it's all over."

She nodded slowly and loosened her fingers from Flynn's lax hand. Susanna suddenly felt cold. She moved her hands up and down her arms and stepped back. The doors swung closed behind Flynn, shutting her out, leaving her alone to wait.

"You're not the only one who hates hospitals, Flynn," she murmured, wishing the fear wouldn't come.

But it did.

Six years ago, she had been standing in this very corridor, as she was now. Except that six years ago, she had watched the doors close on Brett. They'd never opened again. The hernia he had refused to pay attention to had become strangulated. By the time he had reached the operating table, it had been too late.

Oh God, don't let it be too late now.

Susanna passed her hands over her face and shuddered. The memory of that night was one she tried very hard to keep at bay, far away from her conscious mind, but being here brought it all back.

It was going to be all right, she told herself.

She walked slowly to the cheerfully decorated room just a few feet down the hall. It was set aside for the friends and relatives of the people being operated on. There was no one there now. The room was as empty as she felt inside. Susanna sat stiffly. The light coffee-colored vinyl whooshed quietly around her. There was nothing left to do except to mark the passing of incredibly slow minutes. And wait.

It was taking too long, she thought, twisting her fingers together. Much too long. Her cousin's appendectomy had only taken forty-five minutes. The doctor had told the family that an hour was standard. Flynn had been in the operating room for almost two hours. Terrible thoughts were crowding Susanna's mind.

What if something went wrong? What if—?

How would she ever face Michael if something happened to his grandfather?

And how could a man be taken away from her just when she had finally found one she could care about?

It wasn't fair.

Restless, worried, Susanna rose and began to pace. Life, she knew, wasn't fair. It didn't work that way. There were no checks and balances to adhere to. It hadn't been fair that Brett had died before he could see Billie grow up, not fair that Michael had had to deal with pain so early in life.

She turned and looked accusingly down the hall. It wasn't fair that the big lummox should suffer any consequences because she hadn't bullied him into coming here sooner. She should have, she told herself. She had noticed his discomfort earlier. Hell, she had noticed it on Wednesday, when he had talked to her. He had been massaging his side then. She had thought it was because she was making him nervous.

She smiled ruefully. And now she was paying for her vanity.

"Mrs. O'Roarke?"

Susanna jumped as she swung around. The surgeon Flynn had claimed was too young to operate was standing behind her, still dressed in his green gown, his surgical mask dangling about his neck.

Dear heavens. He looked so solemn, so drained. Was he going to tell her—

Susanna's heart began to throb in her throat, nearly cutting off her air. "Yes?"

The doctor paused for a moment before he spoke. "It was touch and go for a while, but he's one lucky man. If you hadn't brought him in when you did, quite possibly you'd be making funeral arrangements by now."

No drama, right? she thought, her bones instantly turning to water. She collapsed onto the sofa. He was all right, she thought, almost giddy. He was going to be all right.

The doctor sat down next to her, obviously quite proud of the work he had just done. "His appendix burst as soon as

I touched it, but we managed to drain the area. We got all the poison out. Dr. Moyres assisted."

Susanna stared at him, trying to gather her wits together into some semblance of order. The name of the assistant surgeon was familiar. But something didn't make sense. There had to be two of them.

"Carla Moyres?" When he nodded, her surprise dissolved into a relieved giggle. Dr. Carla Moyres was her gynecologist.

The doctor looked a tad uncomfortable about the revelation. "Yes, she's a very competent doctor."

"I know. She's mine." Susanna couldn't help the smile that emerged. "You had a gynecologist assisting?" Wait until Flynn heard this one. This certainly put the cap on a very long, difficult day.

The doctor shrugged a little helplessly. "It's Sunday. We're not overstocked with doctors at the hospital on Sundays. It was a slow day until your husband arrived."

She had to correct him before things got any more complicated. "I'm not Mrs. O'Roarke."

The surgeon nodded as he rose to his feet. "Well, even if you're not, according to some ancient cultures, his life is yours, since you were instrumental in saving it."

And wouldn't Flynn just love to hear that one? she thought, feeling suddenly buoyant. She rose with the doctor, picking up Flynn's belongings. "When can I see him?"

"He'll be in his room in about an hour." He nodded at the bag. "You can bring those up there then. Admissions can tell you which room. In the meantime, I suggest you get something to eat. You look as if you need it." He grinned. "No charge for the advice."

Susanna could only nod. Relief was a wonderful thing. You never appreciated it fully until you didn't have it. "Thank you, Doctor."

Humming, Susanna went to call Michael.

*   *   *

An hour later, fortified with a bacon, lettuce and tomato sandwich from the hospital cafeteria, Susanna slipped into Flynn's individual care unit. She found him asleep. There was an IV in either arm and he was still very pale. But for a man who had been on the brink of death, he looked damn good, she thought. Even in a blue-and-white floral hospital gown.

She closed the door behind her and put away his clothes in the small closet on the side. Then she stood at the foot of his bed, content to just look at him. Content to know he was alive. Michael had asked her twice if she was certain that Flynn was all right. It felt wonderful to assure the small boy that he was.

There was someone in the room. He could feel it. Flynn fought his way to the surface, struggling with heavy blankets that threatened to smother him. His eyelids felt as if they weighed ten pounds apiece. And there was pain, oceans of pain, radiating from his side, washing over him each time he tried to take a deep breath.

Somehow he managed to open his eyes.

The images before him swam until the three women merged into one. Susanna. He might have known. He tried to say something but the words wouldn't get past his throat. He tried again. "Where are my pants?" he rasped.

His pants again. Didn't this man ever give up? Susanna found herself smiling. Right now, even his bad mood was encouraging. "The nurses had a raffle."

Flynn tried to swallow. His Adam's apple felt stuck. He coughed, then narrowed his eyes as he looked at her. "Is that humor?"

"A very poor attempt." She moved closer. "I brought all your clothes up." She nodded toward her right. "They're in the closet."

He turned his head. The room shimmered. The closet looked a hundred miles away. The effort in turning his head cost him. He felt weak. He hated feeling weak. "What's all this?" He tried to raise his tethered arms and couldn't manage it.

"That one's whiskey," Susanna pointed to the left one, "That one's Scotch, take your pick." She blinked, suddenly realizing that there were tears in her eyes. Now that it was all over, now that he was conscious, there were tears threatening to fall. Talk about timing, she thought, annoyed as she brushed one away. "One's to feed you," she said seriously. "The other's in case of infection. The nurses told me."

He had to know. "Was it my appendix?"

She nodded. "According to the doctor, it exploded like an overblown balloon."

He didn't like the image, or the fact that he was in debt to her. "I guess I should thank you."

She wondered what it had cost him to say those words. "You already did."

He couldn't remember. "When?"

Susanna perched on the arm of the lone chair that was next to his bed. "When they wheeled you in to the operating room."

He searched for the memory. It eluded him. "I don't remember."

"I know."

He felt so tired, as if he could sleep forever. He struggled to stay awake. "Michael—"

She was one step ahead of him. "—Is all taken care of."

What else was there? Oh, now he remembered. "My daughters should be informed."

She had made a list while sitting in the cafeteria. "I already made note of that. I'll talk to them tonight."

He looked at her, puzzled. "How?"

She smiled, wishing he would stop talking and get some rest. "By telephone."

"You don't have their number."

"They're at the campus at Santa Barbara right? Information will do the rest. Now go to sleep."

He wanted to, yet fought it because it was what she wanted him to do. Couldn't have her winning every round. "Thought of everything, haven't you?"

"I try."

He should be grateful. She was just being helpful. And he was grateful, dammit, but in the midst of all that, he felt hemmed in. And too damn tired and weak to do anything about it.

"Susanna?" he whispered as he felt himself drifting back to sleep.

She lowered her head next to Flynn's mouth in order to hear him. "Yes?"

"Don't try too hard."

She knew that it was wrong to want to hit a man just out of surgery, but she was sorely tempted.

Chapter Eleven

By nine-thirty the next morning, Susanna felt as if she had packed three days of living into one. After leaving her telephone number at the nurses' station with the nurse who was taking care of Flynn, Susanna had gone home to comfort Michael and let him know in person that everything was fine.

Because she thought that familiar surroundings might help, she took Michael with her to Flynn's house. It took almost an hour to gather together the essentials for Flynn's stay at the hospital and Michael's stay at her house. Once that was accomplished, she asked Michael to help her find his grandfather's telephone book so that she could copy down the personal and business numbers she needed.

She returned home and put both boys to bed. Fighting off exhaustion, Susanna sat down and braced herself for the task of calling Flynn's daughters.

There was no easy way to break the news to two girls who had already had their share of emergency phone calls. After introducing herself, Susanna prefaced her information with "Your father's fine now" and then in a quick and straightforward manner, raced into an explanation of what had happened.

It went a lot easier than she thought it would. It took only a few minutes of conversation to discover that the girls' personalities seemed to be light years away from their father's. Stephanie and Julia were grateful to her for calling and for having taken it upon herself to handle the details. When they began to make plans to drive down immediately, Susanna assured them that at this point speed was no longer the essence. The morning would do just fine.

By the time Susanna finally crawled into bed, it was close to two a.m.

Four hours later, she was up, making sandwiches for Billie and Michael and mentally listing the calls she had to make and things she had to do before she went to see Flynn at the hospital.

The first order of business was calling in to work and informing her superior that she was taking a few days off. She had amassed more than her share of vacation days, but James Harper, the senior actuary who was collaborating with her on the ratebook revisions for the whole life policies saw her leave as nothing short of desertion. The new ratebook figures were due by the end of the month. This was no time, he told her, to take off on a whim. Susanna made her apologies, but remained firm. Some things, she thought as she dialed the next number, took precedence over ratebook figures.

Flynn's boss, she discovered to her relief, was a great deal more compassionate than Harper had been. He told her to inform Flynn that if there was anything he needed, he shouldn't hesitate to call and that he himself would initiate the paperwork for a six-week medical leave of absence for Flynn.

Some people, Susanna thought, hanging up the phone, were just basically nice. She wondered if Flynn knew that.

Stopping only for toast and an extra-strong cup of coffee to keep her going, Susanna packed up the items she had selected for Flynn last night and drove to the hospital. On an impulse, she stopped at a florist and landscaping shop, which specialized in the unusual. She thought that summed up Flynn quite neatly.

Susanna had no trouble selecting a gift for Flynn. She knew the plant was meant for him the second she saw it. If sweets were for the sweet, she mused as she paid for the gift, then the same could be applied to the term prickly.

She grinned at her own analogy as she hefted the unwieldy plant into the car.

Her grin had faded slightly around the edges by the time she walked to the bank of elevators in the rear of the hospital. The plant was growing steadily heavier. Still, it would be worth it to see the expression on Flynn's face.

She hoped he was still doing all right and that nothing unforeseen had happened during the night. No, she thought, drawing on her overabundant supply of optimism, they would have called if anything had gone wrong. Everything, consequently, was fine.

The elevator doors opened and she did her best to hurry to Flynn's room. With the plant before her, Susanna nearly crashed into Flynn's attending physician as he left Flynn's room.

The man grabbed the tottering plant by the only accessible place, the base, as he eyed it with the healthy respect it deserved.

"Sorry." Susanna took a moment to get her bearings. "Thank you, Doctor." She nodded toward the closed door behind him. "How is he?"

The young physician was clearly pleased. "The man has the most marvelous constitution I've ever come across. Better than a man half his age. Most men are lying in bed and calling for painkillers this soon after surgery. Your Mr. O'Roarke is asking for solid foods and the nearest escape route."

She laughed, shifting the plant slightly. That would be Flynn all right. Except that he wasn't *her* Mr. O'Roarke, not if he had anything to say about it. But now at least they would have time to work on that prospect.

Susanna asked the question that she knew Flynn would confront her with as soon as she walked through the door. "When *can* he go home?"

The doctor checked the chart he had under his arm and shook his head again in amazement. He flipped the metal cover back over the pages and looked at Susanna. "If no complications set in, I see no reason to keep him here longer than Thursday."

By then Flynn would probably be tying sheets together and planning to lower himself out the window on them, but not before alienating every nurse within a forty-mile radius. Good looks and an incredible body went only so far. "Believe me, you won't."

The doctor looked at her a little oddly. Perhaps the two did deserve each other. "Here, let me get that for you," he offered as she began to struggle with the door handle.

Balancing the plant before her, Susanna tottered in. If she didn't set it down soon, her arms were going to break. It hadn't been heavy at first, but after ten minutes, it felt like it weighed a ton.

Flynn was sitting up in bed, frowning at the IV that was still attached to his arm. He was down to one but it was still one too many as far as he was concerned. He wanted to get up and test his legs. How was he going to get around with this thing tethered to his arm?

He turned when he heard her enter and stared at the large flat dished plant she set down on his windowsill. "What's that?"

Susanna let out a sigh of relief. It felt wonderful to get rid of the plant. Her arms felt so light, she momentarily forgot about the shopping bag she had dangling from her wrist.

"I brought you a little gift." She turned the plant so that the bright yellow bow faced Flynn instead of the pigeons on the ledge outside. "I thought a cactus was more appropriate than flowers." She smiled at the tall, single dark green column, spines as sharp as needles covering every available inch. "It seemed to suit your personality a lot better than carnations."

Flynn eyed the cactus. It had to be just about the ugliest thing he had ever seen. And yet somehow it was oddly pleasing in its ugliness.

"Very funny." He picked at the bedclothes, uncomfortable. She was doing entirely too much for him. It made him remember things. And yearn for a life that he had shut the door on. "Aren't you going to say it?"

"Say what?" She moved closer to him. The room was small, but airy. Flynn probably thought of it as a cage. "How are you?"

"No." She was playing games. "That you were right and I was wrong."

He hated being wrong, she thought. Probably hated it more than anything, except being confined. Susanna shrugged casually. "I think that part went without saying." She looked at him innocently. "And I'm not the type to gloat."

She didn't have to. It was there, in her eyes. She was smug about all this. About saving his life. He owed his life to an over-efficient woman who looked like a Barbie Doll come to life, he thought grudgingly. He nodded at the shopping bag she had brought. "What do you have there?"

Susanna glanced down at it. "Oh." She set the bag on the bed next to his leg. "I stopped at your house and got some things I thought you might want." She left it for him to open. "Michael helped me."

He left the bag where it was. He wanted something explained first. "How did you get in?"

How did he think she got in? Actuaries didn't learn how to pick locks as a sideline. "With your keys."

"My keys?" he repeated. He hadn't given her his keys.

Oh-h, she had undoubtedly trespassed. She smiled soothingly, knowing it did no good. "I picked your pocket," she explained simply. "You didn't look as if you'd be driving anywhere last night."

Regardless of that fact, she hadn't asked if she could go through his pockets. He didn't like being treated as if he had no say in anything, no wishes of his own to be observed. "Aren't you taking a little too much upon yourself?"

She wasn't going to get angry at him, she wasn't. Susanna fisted her hands at her sides. "No, I don't think so. After all, your life is mine."

Now what was she talking about? "What?"

She laughed at his confused expression. "Just a little custom the surgeon told me about." She leaned toward him, patting his hand the way she would a child's. "Now behave yourself or I'll tell everyone the assistant surgeon was a gynecologist."

He stared at her as if she had lost her mind.

"That's right," she said mildly. "They needed another surgeon right away and it just so happened that the doctor who delivered Billie was on call at the hospital."

"And he came?" That sounded a little unorthodox to Flynn.

"No." Susanna had to admit she was enjoying this. "*She* came."

Flynn blanched, then recovered. The woman had a weird sense of humor. "You're making this up." His eyes dared her to contradict him.

Susanna sat on the edge of the bed, her arms folded before her. "I don't need to. You'll believe me when you get her bill." She'd tortured him enough, she decided, changing the subject. "So, how are you feeling?"

"Lousy." He fairly growled the word.

"Ah, nothing's changed."

She didn't deserve to have him take his frustration out on her. It wasn't her fault his appendix had decided to give up the ghost. "I'm sorry I snapped at you. I don't like not having control over things."

She could identify with that. Still, she couldn't help teasing him. "You could have fooled me." Idly, she toyed with the side of the shopping bag, dropping the wordplay. "Everyone needs to be taken care of sometime, Flynn. Sometimes, you can't help it."

Perhaps it was the near meeting with death that had him wanting her to understand. "I spent most of my life being taken care of, Susanna. I didn't know it until it wasn't happening anymore. I *don't* want to be dependent again."

She waved her hand around the room. "This is only temporary."

"Yes, I know." His tone made her feel that he wasn't referring to the operation or his subsequent hospital stay. Lord, he made her angry. "How's Michael taking this?"

Nice safe ground, she thought. For the moment, she'd retreat. "I calmed him down and assured him you were all right. He's staying with me. By the way, I called Mr. Ecklund. He's a nice man."

His supervisor? What was she doing calling him? "Why did you call him?"

"To let him know what happened and that you weren't playing hooky. He's putting you down for a six-week medical leave and says to call if you need anything."

Was there any part of his life she hadn't invaded? he wondered. It was bad enough that she had haunted him all through the operation. It had taken him several hours, after the drugs began to wear off, to realize that he had dreamed of fairies and mermaids and all sorts of creatures he had never believed in as a child. And they had all had her face. It bothered him that he had tried to capture every one of them. But then, a man couldn't be held accountable for what he did in his sleep.

He swallowed his ill temper. She was just trying to help. It wasn't her fault that it made him feel threatened. "I guess I should thank you."

She rose. Being close to him this way was affecting her. She kept remembering that she had almost lost him. The realization made her emotions raw. "Not unless you want to."

He looked at her, wishing she could understand. Wishing he knew why it was so hard for him to say. "I do. It's just that—"

"You don't want to be in the position to have to, yes, I figured that part out. You don't have to." *Yes, you do,* she thought, *but I'm not going to drag it out of you. Maybe I can wait you out.* "In the meantime..." She upended the shopping bag and a black bathrobe along with various toiletries came tumbling out onto the off-white blanket. "I believe that this is what the well-dressed patient is wearing and using these days." She folded the robe in half and slung it over the foot of his bed. "I couldn't find any pajamas."

"That's because I don't own any."

She nodded, pretending that the image of him that generated hadn't made her palms suddenly grow damp.

"That's what Michael said. He pointed out these." She drew his cutoffs out of the pile and held them up. Looking them over, she shook her head. "You wear this and the nurses are going to think you're going surfing." *Not to mention the fact that their bones will probably turn to mush.*

He took the shorts from her. "It's a lot better than what they have me in now."

"Oh, I don't know." She stood back and cocked her head, pretending to study him. "Blue's your color."

He glanced down at the lightly starched, washed-out gown. A network of daisies covered the entire field. "Flowers aren't."

She placed the other items, his razor, toothbrush, comb, one by one on the small table. "Maybe they can scrounge up a hospital gown with a cactus on it." Moving the table within his reach, she turned to brush back the lock of hair that had fallen into his eyes. He caught her hand, stopping her. She was surprised at how much strength he had. He certainly did recover quickly.

"I'm a toucher, Flynn," she said softly. "You're going to have to get used to that."

"Why?" It wasn't a challenge. Maybe he wanted to hear something that would force him to change his mind. Maybe he was still a little groggy from the medication. He wasn't sure of anything anymore.

"Because."

"If you can't do any better than that—" he muttered, echoing words she had said to him.

"Oh, I can." She leaned over his bed, bracing her hands on either side of him. "I can." She lightly brushed her lips over his. The flash of fire came. It didn't take much. She leaned her forehead against his. "God, you scared me, Flynn."

He sifted her hair through his fingers, then framed her face. Just this once, he'd allow himself to savor, to feel, knowing that once he was on his feet again, back in control, things would return to what they had been. As they should. "It wasn't exactly a picnic on this end, either," he admitted.

Despite his weakened state, he felt the strong pull of desire course through his veins, demanding one more taste, just one more. Flynn brought her lips to his.

Was it his imagination, or did her mouth taste sweeter than it had before? Lost in the heady sensations she always generated with him, Flynn wasn't aware of the door to his room opening until he heard Stephanie's amused voice. "Pop?"

Surprised, embarrassed, Flynn dropped his hands from Susanna's face.

Slightly dazed, Susanna took a step back. The operation hadn't affected his ability to scramble all her pulses, that was for damn sure.

Flynn looked at the two young women who, looking clearly confused and somewhat amazed, were standing behind Susanna. "Stephanie, Julia, what are you doing here?"

Stephanie, the older of the two by eleven months, assessed the situation quickly and grinned. "Coming to see if you were all right." Her eyes flicked over Susanna and apparently liked what they saw. "Obviously, you are."

"Hi. You must be Stephanie." Michael had pointed out pictures to her when they had stopped over at his house last night. There was no confusing the two sisters. Pleased at their arrival, Susanna shook the tall, vibrant brunette's hand. She looked like Flynn, the coloring, the mouth, everything. Except that she was smiling. "I'm Susanna. We spoke on the phone last night."

Julia was always quick to forge a place for herself. The youngest of three very out-going girls, Julia had always had to nudge her sisters aside to be noticed. It had become second nature to her. She grasped Susanna's hand as soon as Stephanie released it. "And I'm Julia."

Julia, Susanna decided, took after Kelly. There was hardly a trace of Flynn about her, except in the slight slant of her eyes. She was as fair as Stephanie was dark, with long blond hair that fell in deep curls almost to her waist. Night and day, Susanna thought, as she appraised Flynn's handiwork.

"I'm very pleased to meet you both." Time to withdraw, Susanna thought, sliding her purse from the bed. The reunion would be more relaxed for Flynn without her here. "Well, I'd better leave the three of you alone."

Stephanie was quick to take hold of her elbow. Flynn realized with an inward groan that now that there was someone in her father's life, his daughter didn't want to take the chance on the woman slipping away. "Oh, please don't leave on our account."

It wasn't on their account that she was leaving. She didn't want to crowd Flynn. "No, in this case, four's a crowd. Besides," she nodded toward Flynn, "let him snap your head off for a while. I've had my quota for the morning." She grinned at him, relief still fresh in her veins. "I'll be back later tonight, Flynn, whether you like it or not."

Stephanie claimed the chair by right of seniority, making herself comfortable. She glanced toward the door as it closed, then at her father. "I like your lady, Pop."

It was a hard thing to deny, after what they had seen as they'd walked in, but he tried. "She's not my lady."

Stephanie laughed and shook her head. "Oh, that's right, it was your appendix, not your stubborn streak they removed."

His eyes narrowed. When under siege, man an offensive. "Why aren't you two in school?"

Julia, sitting at his feet, reached over and placed her hand on top of his. "School can wait. We can make up assignments."

He didn't like the fact that they had come down all this way. It was a one hundred fifty mile trip from Santa Barbara. They'd probably driven half the night. "Did she tell you to come?"

Neither daughter missed the tone of voice he'd used. They knew him well enough to know that he was trying to hide his feelings. Fat chance.

"*She* gave us a very detailed report and let us know how well you were doing," Stephanie told him. She smiled with relief. "But you know us, we have to see for ourselves. We also wanted to check her out."

It was a conspiracy. There was no other term for it. "There's no need."

"I think," Julia told him, "there's more of a need than you think." She exchanged looks with her older sister. "Personally, we're very relieved."

Flynn raised his eyebrow. "Relieved about what?"

"That Susanna's here to look after you," Stephanie said, completing her sister's thought. "We felt pretty guilty, leaving you like that in September."

Why did everyone think he couldn't manage? He was a man. Men always manage. Besides, he was their father. "I'm not a toddler," he reminded them impatiently.

"No, you're a pop." Julia leaned over and kissed his cheek. "And you're ours and we love you. We want you to be happy."

"I am happy."

Stephanie crossed her arms before her chest and eyed Flynn. "Maybe it's the scowl that fooled us."

Julia joined ranks with her sister. They stood on either side of him, twin smiles of approval on their faces. "Definitely," she said to Stephanie.

Flynn suppressed a laugh. "Stop talking over me as if I were dead."

Stephanie sprawled boneless in the chair. She took his hand and held it in both of hers, her young face serious. "That's just it, Pop, you're not dead. And we want you to enjoy life, like you used to. With someone at your side."

He didn't want to risk the hurt that was out there. Didn't want to ever be bereft again. Not like that. "I have Michael."

Stephanie gave his hand a tug. "Somebody a little taller and closer to your own age," she amended.

Flynn sighed. "You women are in cahoots, you know that?"

Laughter met his ears from both sides. Stephanie and Julia each kissed a cheek as they prepared to leave. "We have to be, you men are so hopelessly stubborn," Julia said. Stephanie nodded in agreement. "We're going to check in on Michael and then come back. Need anything?"

He said the first thing that came to mind. "Freedom."

Stephanie was undaunted. "Prisons are created in your mind, Pop."

He tried to look stern but the effort was getting to him. He loved each of his daughters equally, but there was a special bond between Stephanie and him that went back to the time she had lamented about being the middle child and neglected. He had told her that the middle of a sandwich was the best part. "Is that what I'm paying for? Philosophy?"

"No, that's a freebie," she said fondly.

A nurse walked into the room with a plastic basin in her hands. Towels were slung casually over her forearm. Stephanie and Julia took the opportunity to withdraw. "See you, Pop."

"Bye." The girls grinned as they pointed to the basin.

The small, heavyset nurse gave Flynn a no-nonsense nod. "It's time for your sponge bath, Mr. O'Roarke."

He drew himself up as tall as he could, given the fact that he was sitting. It was enough. Flynn O'Roarke cast an intimidating shadow. "Not on your life. Leave the bowl. I can do it myself."

"I'd listen to him if I were you, Nurse," Julia told the older woman solemnly. "He bites."

Stephanie pointed toward the windowsill. "I like the cactus, Pop."

Flynn glanced at the specimen. It was growing on him. "Susanna brought it. It's her idea of a joke."

Stephanie nodded her approval. "I think it suits you."

Flynn frowned. The nurse left the basin and towels, then shuffled out, wisely following the girls' advice. "That's what she said."

Stephanie was the last to leave. She smiled fondly at her father. "Just remember, even a cactus needs a little water once in a while."

When she returned to the hospital that evening, Susanna brought Michael and Billie with her. She thought that Michael needed to see Flynn for himself. He had seemed satisfied, but there was a wary look in his eyes when she had told him that Flynn was recovering quickly and would be home soon. Even the sight of his aunts hadn't settled him completely. Obviously, he needed visual proof. Billie had wanted to tag along. She saw no reason to make him stay home with Jane.

Flynn's room was empty.

Nothing short of panic entered Michael's eyes as he looked around. He grabbed hold of Susanna's arm. "They took him!"

Though her own heart lurched, she managed to calm herself down. Doing the same for Michael was another matter. "I'm sure there's an explanation, honey." She searched her brain for one. They didn't do tests at this hour unless something was wrong. But he had seemed so healthy this morning.

Desperate for a way to reassure Michael, she opened the closet. "Look." She pointed to the jeans that were neatly hung. "His things are still here. He couldn't have gone very far." She closed the metal door, then looked down at Michael. "Maybe he escaped."

The dark brows knitted together in confusion. "Escaped?"

She nodded solemnly. "He told me this morning he wanted to break out of here. He doesn't like being in the hospital."

Michael struggled manfully with his feelings. "Maybe."

She took the small hand firmly in hers. "Let's go ask the nurse."

They didn't have to.

As Susanna turned the corner to the nurses' station with Billie and Michael in tow, she heard an odd clanging noise. It was the sound of glass tapping against metal. And then she saw Flynn, his robe draped around his body, one hand on the IV stand as he pushed it before him.

Susanna didn't know whether to laugh or cry. The man put a new spin on the word *stubborn*. She hurried over to him, wanting to punch him for frightening her and Michael so much. Wanting to hug him because he was all right.

She looked Flynn over. He looked winded, but there was no missing the stubborn set of his chin. "Is it alms for the poor you're collecting, or trying out for the part of the Hunchback of Notre Dame?"

"Hi, Michael, Billie," he murmured to the boys. Susanna merited a nod. He gritted his teeth. When he had started this walk down the corridor, it had seemed a good idea. It didn't any longer, but he was too proud to say so. "I'm trying to get some exercise."

"You're trying to open your stitches," she contradicted. Two could play at this stubborn game.

He took another step, focusing on the handle of the last room down the hall. If he didn't, he'd fall over. "You're not a doctor."

She wanted to hold him, but fought back the desire. She knew he wouldn't let her. *Please don't let the big jerk fall.* "And neither are you. Aren't you supposed to be in bed?"

How had the damn hall become so long? It hadn't been this long when he had walked in the opposite direction. All he had wanted to do was to make it once around the corridor by himself. Just once. Was that asking too much? "I'm supposed to be where I am."

"Are you okay, Granddad?"

Michael's small, awestruck voice brought Flynn around. He felt chagrined at his show of temper in front of the boys. "I'm fine, Michael." He looked at Susanna. "A hospital's no place for them. Why did you bring them?"

"To show them how well you looked. And how stubborn you could be." Pride or no pride, she couldn't just stand here and watch him struggle. "C'mon, Jesse Owens, let's get you back into bed so these little guys can talk to you."

"We'll help with this," Billie offered, wrapping his hands around the slim metal column before them. Michael placed his hands below Billie's and they pushed together, each eager to help.

Susanna watched the IV bottle sway. She steadied it quickly. "Not too fast, boys, Mr. O'Roarke's racing days are temporarily on hold for now."

Flynn would have protested both her assumption and her help if he had had the strength. "So how was school today, Michael?" he asked.

The sound of Michael's voice soothed him as Flynn made his way back to his room.

Chapter Twelve

Flynn stretched his legs out gingerly before him in the car as it sped down Jeffrey Road. It felt wonderful to be out of the hospital. It had annoyed him that he had had to make the trip from his room to the hospital's entrance in a wheelchair, as per hospital policy. What annoyed him more was that just being in the open air seemed to sap his strength.

He wanted to be well now, this instant. It frustrated him that he had to wait.

But he was on his way home, which was what counted. He glanced to his left at Susanna. She had arrived on the heels of the discharging physician, informing him that she was taking him home.

Flynn had already made arrangements. "I have a cab coming."

He would, she thought, rather than ask her to pick him up. When would he learn to accept the smallest favors?

"That's all right, we'll cancel." She was already picking up the phone, waiting for him to supply the number.

Since he was anxious to leave as soon as possible, he didn't argue with her.

Still, he thought as they drove home, he didn't want to give up too much ground. After all, she hadn't bothered to consult him about this, either. "You didn't have to come to the hospital to pick me up."

It was too much to hope for a simple thank you, she supposed. She passed a large open field. In the distance, there were cows grazing. It was a sharp contrast to the shopping center to her left. Soon all the fields would be gone. It made her feel sad. "No trouble. Besides, I didn't like picturing you rattling around in the back seat of a cab in your condition."

He wished she'd stop making him sound like an invalid. He'd had appendicitis not a fatal heart attack. "My condition is fine."

"So you keep telling me." She was going to stay cheerful if it killed her. Mentally counting to ten, she calmed herself down. "The doctor is absolutely amazed at your speedy recovery. Said he wouldn't have expected it of a man half your age."

She had an incredible collection of euphemisms, he thought. "You mean a young man."

She blew out a breath, losing her temper, forgetting her vow. "Nice to see that some things don't change." She passed a row of towering eucalyptus trees, straggly branches raking the sky, their bark peeling in the sun. "Everyone's got someone around who's half their age, Flynn, even newborns." She looked at him as she slowed, then stopped at a four-way stop sign. "I wish you'd rid yourself of this attitude that your life is on the decline. You've just been given a new chance to live." She took her foot off the brake and pressed too hard on the gas. The car jerked forward. "Use it."

There was truth in what she said, at least the last part. He had been given a second chance. He just didn't want to get carried away with it. There were penalties for recklessness.

Flynn stared at the road, seeing it for the first time. "This isn't the way to my house."

"No," she said slowly. "If you recall, it's the way to mine." She waited for the explosion, knowing it would come even though this was the only sensible option open to him.

He looked at Susanna suspiciously. "Are we picking up Michael?"

"No, we're setting *you* down." She took a breath, then plunged ahead. "The girls and I decided you're staying at my house for a few days until you're stronger." She hadn't said anything earlier because she knew he'd argue with her. But it *was* the only sensible way to proceed. She slanted him a look when the explosion didn't come. He really *was* weak.

"I am stronger," he insisted. She had no right to keep making decisions for him. He hadn't abdicated control over his life. Just who did she think she was?

Susanna licked her lips. Why couldn't he just accept things instead of always making them difficult? Why wasn't he just grateful that she cared? "Let me rephrase that." She slowed the car so that she could look at him. "Until you can bench press your own body weight."

It didn't make any sense to him. Why was she putting herself out like this? She hardly knew him. "Why are you taking me in? I'm basically a stranger."

Yes, you would think that, even after what they had gone through together. Even after the kiss they had shared. She felt as if she were hitting her head against a stone wall. But two could be stubborn.

"Maybe, but a weak one." She reached for humor. It had seen her through a lot before. She regarded the tall, strapping man next to her. "I could probably throw you to the ground before you had a chance to try anything funny."

Though he had meant that when he'd asked, he didn't like her thinking that he actually was someone she should fear. "I wouldn't try anything funny."

Yes, she knew that, too. "A woman can dream, can't she?"

She had lost him completely now. "Really, I don't think—"

It was the lead-in she needed. "Fine, don't think. Do us both a favor and just heal, okay?" She took on the same tone as she used with Billie when he was being stubborn. "You're in no condition to take care of yourself and Michael." Her voice softened as she approached her street. "Let me live out a fantasy. I'll make you chicken soup, you'll get well, then fold up your tent and slip into the night." When he made no answer, she looked at him.

He was studying her, a look of pure amazement on his face. "Are you always like this?"

She grinned. "Only when I get mad."

"Angry," he corrected out of habit, then wondered if she would be annoyed. He might have known better. That kind of thing didn't seem to bother her.

"That, too. Settled?"

Right, as if he had a chance to debate this. Besides, he supposed it did make sense. If only she had asked instead of told. "Do I have a choice?"

"No."

He shrugged. He'd concede this one time. For Michael's sake. "Then it's settled."

Michael had sat, waiting, in the driveway since Jane had brought the boys home from school. When Susanna had turned the corner onto the block he jumped to his feet, his expression changing from pensive to excited.

He dashed toward the car as Susanna pulled up, then ran next to the passenger side until she cut off the engine. Flynn's window was down and Michael reached in to put his hand on his grandfather's shoulder, touching him for reassurance. His chocolate eyes danced as a grin threatened to split his face. "Hi!"

"Hi, yourself." Emotions ran through Flynn, surprising him. He hadn't realized how much he had missed seeing Michael everyday. Susanna came around the hood to his side of the car. "Mrs. Troy taking good care of you?"

Michael's head bobbed up and down, his eyes never leaving Flynn's face. "Real good. She lets me call her Susanna. Are you gonna stay?" Michael asked hopefully.

Flynn eyed Susanna as she opened the door. "So my warden tells me."

Susanna paused, one hand on the door. "Tell me something, Michael." She leaned over to the boy, then asked in an audible whisper. "Is he always this cranky?"

Michael shook his head.

Susanna sighed dramatically, her mouth curving. "Then it must be me."

"Must be," Michael agreed solemnly, responding to the laughter in Susanna's voice.

Susanna leaned in to help Flynn out.

Flynn moved her hand aside with his own and swung out his legs, albeit a lot slower than he would have liked. Where had this wave of weakness come from? And when would he finally feel like himself again? "I can do it myself."

She was tempted to let him try, but he was just stubborn enough to do it. As annoying as he could be, she didn't want him falling. It would hurt his pride, not to mention everything else. "I'm sure you can."

As he rose on shaky legs, Susanna took his arm and forcibly rested it across her shoulders. She was a lot stronger, he thought, than she looked.

She smiled up at him. "Humor me. I like having big strong men pretend to lean on me. It feeds my ego."

He had a comment about her and her ego, but he kept it to himself. Michael pulled out Flynn's belongings from the back seat.

"Leave the plant," she warned. "I'll take it in later." The last thing she needed was for eager, helpful little hands to wrap themselves around a cactus.

Michael struggled to the front door with the bag, three steps ahead of them. "He's here!" he announced, yelling to Billie. Seconds later, Billie met them in the foyer, his eyes as vibrant as Susanna's as he greeted Flynn.

It almost felt as if he was actually home. Almost. He told himself not to let his emotions get the best of him.

He tried to support his own weight, but it was getting difficult. He looked at Susanna, embarrassed that he would have to lean on her, impatient with the frail state of his own body. He could feel her other hand along his back, holding him, her fingers pressing along his spine. He could probably be dead and still aware of everything about her, the smell of her hair, the feel of her hip against his. This wasn't a good sign, he told himself.

Susanna nodded to the left as she directed him. "Your daughters will be here on the weekend to see how you're doing."

Here. She meant her house. "I'll be home by then."

He made it sound like a mandate. "We'll see," she answered, annoying the hell out of him.

How could someone who filled him with desire one moment make him want to commit justifiable homicide the next? Flynn had no answer for that. He chalked it up to her just being Susanna.

"I've given you the downstairs bedroom," she told him as she turned right. "It's close to the refrigerator in case you get hungry and want to forage for food." Walking into the

small bedroom, she nodded for Michael to place the suit-
case next to the table.

He wanted to sink down on the bed, but forced himself to
take the chair instead. It was a matter of pride. "Is that
some kind of crack?"

"You figure it out." She turned her attention to more
important things than sparring with him. "C'mon boys,
let's get the man settled."

Billie and Michael scrambled to obey.

It was, Flynn thought, watching her put his things away,
what she was used to. Giving orders and being obeyed. Independent. And stubborn as all get out.

Flynn had meant to be gone by Saturday, he really did. He
was mending quickly, just as the physician had foreseen.
Just as he himself willed.

But something made him linger at Susanna's house a little longer. He told himself it was for Michael's sake. The
boy had changed during their forced encampment at Susanna's. For one thing, he laughed a lot more. And he
played. He and Billie pounded up and down the stairs,
playing space invaders, just being little boys. It made
Flynn's heart glad to hear the ruckus.

When he had collected Michael from the hospital in San
Francisco and brought him home to live with him, there had
been something almost too adult about the child. Having
lived through a tragedy, Michael acted far older than his
years. Now Flynn was seeing the small boy in Michael
emerge.

Because of Susanna.

Flynn was fair enough to give credit where it was due and
human enough to wish that he could have done more for his
grandson himself.

True to Susanna's prediction, Stephanie and Julia swept
in midafternoon on Saturday, bringing their exuberance

with them. The house rang with noise, laughter and the opening and closing of a refrigerator that never seemed to get empty. The whole thing left him feeling slightly in awe, slightly out of step.

It would have been so easy, he thought, to get swept away himself, but he hung on, determined that what was happening now wouldn't undermine his basic resolve to handle things for himself, to keep his life untangled. Separate from hers.

When the girls began to leave for home, Susanna talked them out of it. They stayed up and watched an old movie on TV. Susanna made popcorn for everyone, then found places to put them up. No matter what she confronted, Susanna found a way to manage. She seemed to thrive on the challenge. She gave new meaning to the word *independence*.

And she was, he thought late that night as he got ready for bed, impinging on his.

When he heard the noise at his door, Flynn thought that one of the girls had come down to have a late-night talk with him. The subject probably revolved around his needing a wife. He had his answers prepared, pat.

"Come in."

He was surprised to see Michael standing in the shadows of the doorway, looking at him uncertainly. The hour was far too late for the boy to still be up. Maybe he had had a nightmare. Flynn could remember sitting up with his daughters when they were small, assuring them that there were no monsters lurking in their closet.

"Hi, champ." He beckoned the boy forward. "What's on your mind?"

Looking small and frail in a pair of faded cutoffs he loved, Michael hesitated, then walked slowly in. "I was just checking on you."

Flynn patted the space next to him on the bed and Mi
chael scrambled up, then sat very straight, his legs jutting
out, parallel to the floor.

"Checking?" Flynn asked. It seemed an odd thing to do

Michael looked down at his folded hands. "To see if you
were okay."

"I appreciate that." Flynn placed his arm around the
small shoulders and pulled his grandson closer. "Michael
I'm going to be okay for a long time to come."

Aimee's eyes looked up at him as Michael tilted his head
back. "Promise?"

Flynn thought of all the honest things he could say, things
all grounded in reality. But Michael had had too much
reality, far more than a six-year-old should have. Flynn
squeezed the narrow shoulders. "Promise."

Michael nodded, as if digesting the word. Suddenly, he
turned and threw his arms around Flynn's neck, his small
body shaking with sobs. All the tears that had been stored
up, all the tears that hadn't been shed when he had discov
ered he was orphaned, poured out now. He clung to his
grandfather and cried.

Flynn sat for a moment, stunned in the face of so much
emotion, so much grief. He didn't know what to do, what
to say. Michael had always seemed confident and amaz
ingly in control. Flynn thought of his own feelings, of the
emptiness that lived outside the perimeter of his life. He
gathered the boy to him, then held him tightly. He felt his
own eyes sting.

With his cheek against Michael's head, he murmured
"Hey, it's okay, champ. It's okay."

Michael hiccuped, his face buried in Flynn's chest. "I was
so scared that you'd go away, too, and leave me. Then I'd
be all alone."

Flynn thought of how frightening that thought would
have been for a boy. How frightened he had been when Kelly

died. He drew Michael back, holding him by the shoulders. "You'd never be alone, Michael." He enunciated each word clearly to make the boy understand. To make him feel more secure. "You have Stephanie and Julia."

Michael nodded, brushing his tears away, obviously embarrassed that he had been caught crying. "Um, can I ask you something?"

"Sure." Flynn wondered what was going on in that little head of his. He hadn't a clue. It occurred to Flynn that he didn't know what a lot of people were thinking. Maybe he hadn't been paying close enough attention.

Michael rocked nervously. "Could I maybe call you 'Pop' like they do? Stephanie and Julia, I mean. So that you could love me the same as them."

What kind of signals had he been giving off? Flynn wondered. How could Michael doubt the strength of his love? "You don't have to call me anything special for me to love you, Michael." He kissed the top of the boy's head, his heart brimming. "I always have."

Michael twisted in the circle of Flynn's arms, his face hopeful. "I'd kind of like it, though."

Flynn laughed. "Then you can call me 'Pop.'"

Michael wiggled off the bed, ready to resume his role as a fledgling man. He sauntered over to the door. Flynn couldn't help wondering if Michael was trying to imitate him and if he actually swaggered when he walked. "See you in the morning, Pop." He beamed as his tongue rolled around the name.

"You bet."

Mealtime the next day was a circus of sounds and voices competing for center stage. Flynn sat back and watched as his daughters and grandson merged with Susanna, her aunt and son, in a cacophony of syncopated movement.

He shook his head. It looked like the set of *The Brady Bunch Revisited,* he thought, but there was a contentment moving through him that he couldn't deny.

Removed, he had to stay removed, no matter what his feelings were to the contrary. Flynn knew he had to be careful not to slip and allow this contentment to sabotage his guard. This feeling was only temporary. Life could never again be allowed to fall into a pattern where he would just let it pull him along. If he did, it would dash him against the rocks of reality when he was least prepared. And this time, most probably, crush him.

But for a few days, at least, he could pretend that life was actually the wonderful thing that Susanna seemed to believe it was.

He caught her eye over the quiche lorraine she was slicing and for a moment, everything else faded. Desire, hot and demanding, suddenly pulsed through him, here, in the midst of all this. Perhaps because of it.

It appeared that he was getting a whole lot better than he thought, Flynn mused. Happiness, or some reasonable facsimile thereof, made for strong medicine.

The week that stretched ahead found him alone for the better part of each day. He mended and grumbled to himself, finding small odd jobs around the house with which to keep himself occupied. He owed it to her. Flynn O'Roarke stayed in no one's debt and though he knew it was but a small repayment, at least it was something. He fixed her broken screen in the bathroom, rewired the frayed cord on her iron and got a discarded tape recorder operational again.

Mostly, he spent the day thinking about her and trying not to think about her. At that, he was a miserable failure. But a man wasn't accountable, he reasoned, for his thoughts. As long as they went no further than that.

Susanna had returned to work and the boys were in school for six hours of the day. Jane looked in on him from time to time to see if he needed anything.

He never did.

"You know, handsome," Jane said, regarding him thoughtfully as she paused at the front door, "it doesn't hurt your stature as a man to need once in a while."

He shook his head. The woman meant well, she just didn't know. "You're wrong there, Jane. It does. It hurts a lot."

Jane pursed her lips. "It hurts more being alone. Trust me, I know." She began to leave, then turned around, remembering. "Oh, I'll be picking the boys up from school and taking them straight today."

The entire family talked in riddles. If he wasn't careful, he would, too. "Straight?"

"To the jamboree," she explained patiently. "The Cub Scouts are having a camp-out tonight, since tomorrow's a holiday." The smile she gave him as she closed the door spoke volumes.

It was time, Flynn decided, to go home.

He was still there when Susanna arrived home from work. Somehow, he couldn't make himself leave. Not yet. There was time enough, he thought, after dinner.

But after dinner, there was a movie she wanted to see. Somehow, with very little effort, he found himself talked into watching it with her.

"It's no fun watching a movie alone," she insisted.

He was inclined to agree with her. Except that he was watching her more than the movie, the way her face tilted slightly to the left when she laughed, the way the corners of her mouth always seemed to lift upward. The way she smelled, fresh and tempting at the same time. It amazed him how much pleasure he derived from just being near her, a bowl of popcorn between them.

Comfortable. He was getting too comfortable, dammit. Her mouth was far too enticing and his resistance was getting far too low. It seemed to be decreasing in direct proportion to his healing. He was overwhelmed with the desire to make love to her, here, on this small sofa.

He should have gone home. But it was too late for that. But it wasn't too late to retreat. Fast.

Stiffly he rose as the credits began to roll down the screen. "I'd better get to bed."

She nodded, staying where she was. She had felt the hum of electricity between them, the same as he had. She had refrained from acting on it for another reason. She didn't want to start something that he was too weak to finish.

But she was tempted.

He stopped for a moment by the bay window and glanced out. He thought of Michael. Such a little boy. Such a large wilderness. He glanced at Susanna. "Think they'll be all right?"

It was nice to know he was concerned. It reinforced her feelings about him. "Sure. They're with a whole camp full of Cub Scouts. What could go wrong?"

He would have said the same thing about coming over to her house for Sunday dinner two weeks ago and look what had happened.

His mind humming, his body restless, Flynn found himself unable to court sleep for the second time since he had met Susanna. With a huff, he threw off the covers and sat up. Maybe he'd feel better if he got up for a while. With all those cable stations, there had to be something on TV that would take his mind off Michael. And Susanna.

When he walked into the family room, he found her there, standing by the same window he had passed on his way to bed. She was staring out, lost in thought.

Flynn's thoughts weren't lost to him. Moonlight was streaming in, casting beams of light into the room, bathing her body in a silvery hue. She had on a long robe with a matching nightgown beneath it. Both were made of a smoky blue gauze material that allowed him to see enough to make his palms itch, reminding him just how much he missed the intimacy between a man and woman.

He tried to ignore the fact that his blood pressure had gone up several numbers on the scale. She looked worried. "Can't sleep?"

She turned, startled. She hadn't heard him approach. Her nerves were jangled. The warm glass of milk had done nothing to help. Neither did the cutoffs he was wearing. He looked magnificently male in the dim light. She felt her mouth go dry.

"No, I can't." She smiled ruefully, caught. "I lied before."

He took a step toward her, a step toward his destiny. "Oh?"

"I am worried." She knew she was being silly, but she couldn't help it. "Sure he's with a bunch of other boys, but boys wander off. They take dares. They get lost." She sighed. Because she had no pockets to shove her hands into, she made do with folding them across her chest. "I suppose I'm just being overprotective, but if anything ever happened to Billie, I don't know what I'd do."

Moonlight wove its way through her hair, making him want to touch it, to see if it felt as silvery as it seemed. "Nothing's going to happen to him."

"Can I have that in writing?"

She made him think of Michael and the promise he had asked for. "Sure, I'll even have it notarized for you." *I'd even do it now, if I could only draw myself away.*

She turned, a smile on her lips. "When I was a little girl, if my father or mother promised that something would or wouldn't happen, I believed them. Even when I grew older, somehow it seemed to help to have the words to cling to." She shrugged at her own foolishness. "Like a talisman, I guess. Pretty silly, huh?"

Her admission surprised him. It made her seem vulnerable. "I didn't think you needed that."

"Why? Because I do everything on my own? That's because I have to." She realized it probably sounded as if she was complaining. "Oh, I don't mind being needed. I *like* being needed; but once in a while—" her voice grew wistful "—I'd give anything just to lean."

It was a side of her he had never seen before, a side he knew he shouldn't have seen. It upset the balance of things the way he had arranged them in his mind. She had a habit of doing that, he thought, throwing him off balance.

He saw a pad and pencil one of the boys had left, forgotten, on the coffee table. Picking the pad up, Flynn scribbled something on the first sheet.

She tried to see what he was writing. "What are you doing?"

"Here." He tore off the sheet and handed it to her. "Here's your written guarantee. 'I promise nothing is going to happen to Billie.'"

She held it to her and laughed. Flynn probably hadn't a clue how sweet he had just been.

But then her laughter slowly faded as she saw the look that had entered his eyes. They had darkened ever so slightly. A flash of desire penetrated her. Without thinking, she took hold of his arm to steady herself.

Anticipation slammed through her as he lowered his mouth to hers.

Her body melted against his, seeking the warmth, seeking the heat. The note he had written fluttered to the coffee table as she slipped her hands into his hair, giving herself to him so completely in that one kiss that it staggered him.

"We're alone," he murmured against her mouth. He knew it was dangerous to think, yet he couldn't help thinking. It was dangerous to want, yet he couldn't help wanting.

"No," she whispered against his mouth. "We're together." For tonight, they would be together, two souls reaching out to one another. Tonight, they wouldn't be alone.

Chapter Thirteen

It had been so long since she had been touched like this, so long since she had felt the way a woman could with a man. She had almost forgotten what it was like to yearn for that special feeling. When he kissed her, when he held her this way, a hunger consumed her, devouring the morsels cast her way, wanting more, needing more.

As she clung to him, her head spinning, her points of orientation dissolving, as he took her to places she wanted so desperately to revisit, Susanna felt sunshine bursting through her veins.

Yes, oh God, yes.

He had tried so hard to avoid exactly this. And yet, it seemed that every step he had taken, every path he had followed somehow had led him to this point in time. Had led him to her. She felt so good in his arms, like quicksilver he had managed to capture for just a moment. Fingers glided along the soft gauzelike material of her robe, he felt Susanna's skin heat to his touch, heard her soft intake of breath as he brushed along the curve of her spine.

His desire threatened to overwhelm him.

In a fiery haze, Susanna felt his body mold itself against hers. She felt his desire, hard and demanding. Shivering from the thrill of knowing that he wanted her, a rush seized her. Susanna prayed the feeling would never leave.

And yet, she was afraid. Physically, this might be too soon for him. She felt she'd be ripped apart if he stopped now, but Susanna moved back, her hands braced on Flynn's bare chest.

"Flynn—" His name tumbled from her lips as her breath escaped her.

With effort, Flynn steadied his own breathing. She was completely destroying his equilibrium, not to mention scrambling his emotions. Had she had a change of heart at the last moment? He wouldn't force himself on her, but oh Lord, after he had allowed himself to come this far, it would cost him.

Unable to release her, he kept his arms around her, savoring her supple softness. "Woman, this isn't the time for conversation."

No, it was a time for loving. But at what price? She couldn't have that on her conscience. "Do you think you should?"

No, he thought he shouldn't, but it was past the time for warnings, past the time for common sense. His fingers grazed her face lightly, barely making contact. It was enough to make him want her again. "No, but it's happening anyway."

He didn't understand. She could see it in his eyes. She wouldn't forgive herself is something happened to him because of her. "You were just operated on."

"Two weeks ago." His fingers slowly slid along the planes of her cheeks, memorizing the curve there, the way her mouth lifted in a smile. Excitement thundered through his veins. "A lifetime ago. When I thought I had a life."

Now, he knew he hadn't. What he had had was an existence. Life, that vital, exciting force, was in the palm of her hand. And she was offering it to him. Though that wouldn't be acceptable in the light of day, for now, in the shadow of night, he could pretend that it was all right.

Pretend? Hell, right now he *needed* to be all right. He needed her. He *needed* her. The simple phrase held him prisoner, pinning him as surely as a butterfly was pinned against a mounting board.

Her eyes searched his face. She felt herself melting as his touch floated along her lips, her forehead. In another moment, she wouldn't be able to think straight at all. "Flynn, I don't think it's good for you."

He laughed softly. Even now, she was giving orders. She was incorrigible. In an odd way, he found that exciting. He found everything about her exciting. "You have no idea what's good for me." He brushed a kiss against her forehead and heard her sigh. "*I* have no idea what's good for me. I just know I want you."

Her eyes were beginning to flutter closed as she gave herself up to the drugging effect of his mouth. It was dissolving her senses, common and otherwise. "But—" The word slipped between lips that were barely moving.

"Susanna?"

She felt his breath feather along her face and it made her want to cry out, a mixture of anticipation and impatience tugging for equal attention. "Yes?"

"Shut up and let me make love to you—with you," he amended, remembering the words she had used. Things in the world had changed. And they were taking him with them. Not entirely against his will in this instance.

Susanna felt tears gather as she nodded her head in reply. She couldn't resist both him and herself any longer. She needed this as much as she had ever needed anything. More. She curved her fingers along his shoulders, the sensation of his bare, lightly haired chest sending incredible tremors through her.

Amusement quirked the corners of his mouth. She was giving permission. "No more arguments? You're sure?"

There was no amusement in her eyes when she looked up at him. Only desire. "I've been sure a lot longer than you."

She rose on her toes, slipping her hands to his face, bringing his mouth to hers. Words, concerns, everything evaporated.

He had never known it could be so intense, that desire could be this overpowering, this demanding. This sweet and gentle even as it raked through his soul with both hands. He wanted her. Sweet Lord, he wanted her more than he wanted life itself. Just kissing her, being kissed by her, was churning up his insides, making alarms go off in his head while the rest of him got ready for meltdown.

It was, he realized, as if he had just been apprenticing all those years, preparing for this moment. Preparing for her. He was in total awe. Always before, he had felt in control, the one who set the pace. This time, neither set it. It was more like a duet. Susanna not only received, she gave, gave back more than he thought it possible to give. Lovemaking had become a totally new experience for him.

Susanna splayed her hands over his chest. Hard ridges met her touch. The man was a veritable rock. Was his heart just as hard? What would it take to break through and touch him there, too? She knew she had his passion. For tonight, it was enough. But tomorrow, she would want more, so much more. Would he be able to give it to her?

She wanted his love. She wanted the part of his heart that was reserved for the woman in his life. Maybe she had wanted this from the very beginning, but it hadn't been clear to her until she had sat alone in the hospital, waiting to find out if he would live or die. She had wanted him to live for Michael, for his daughters. And for her.

That he was alive and well and desired her filled her with gratitude.

But she wanted more.

Susanna wanted him to want her long after the embers of desire died down to a peaceful glow on the hearth. Long after hunger had been sated. She wanted him to want her at his side.

She wanted, she knew, the moon. But he was offering her the stars and she was determined that in time, she'd have it all. She was just going to have to show him, she thought, that he couldn't live without her.

Flynn hadn't thought that the first time he made love to her would be here, in the middle of the family room. As the thought flashed through his mind, he realized that he had anticipated a first time, that he *had* thought about it. More than he would have even admitted to himself. The dream during the operation had shown him the way. He had thought of slipping her clothes from her body slowly and making love to her inch by agonizing inch, bathing her body in soft, moist kisses.

He had fantasized about taking her quickly, plunging himself into her and spiraling to the heights.

He had thought about it.

He felt her shiver as he pushed her robe from her shoulders, his lips teasing the hollow of her throat. Arousing her. Inflaming himself.

Trouble, he was asking for trouble. But he could handle it, he swore to himself. He could handle it.

Desire twisted, raw and biting, within his belly. He moved back, needing to see her, needing to watch the look in her eyes as he slowly slipped the straps of her nightgown from shoulders that gleamed alabaster white in the moonlight. He caught his breath as the blue cloud slipped to her breasts, the swollen tips clinging to the material for a heartbeat. He tugged just a little more, feeling his blood sizzle through his loins. The thin material whispered to the tiled floor, a pool of gauze and dreams about her small bare feet.

He felt clumsy, his hands feeling much too large to touch her. But he had to. He had to worship her with his hands. "You're beautiful," Flynn whispered.

Her eyes held him prisoner as she moved closer. She pressed her body, her flesh hot, demanding, against his as she fumbled with the catch on his cutoffs. She was going to break it in her eagerness, she admonished herself, feeling impatience surge through her.

He covered her fingers with his own and helped her. The very act made his breath back up in his lungs.

Her irises had grown huge as she watched his face, her cool, long fingers sliding the shorts from his hips until they fell to the floor, joining her discarded nightgown.

It was as if someone had put a torch to her body. Heat suffused her, surrounded her as Flynn pulled her to him.

Unable to hold back any longer, he cupped her face and brought his mouth to hers in one fierce movement, wanting to have her now, here. Wanting to make love all night.

Wanting. Needing. Needing when he had sworn not to. But he couldn't have walked away now even if his life had depended on it.

If that was the price for this one night of ecstasy, so be it.

Susanna arched against him, loving the way his hands roamed her body possessively, as if she had always been his. Loving the heat she felt from his. She moaned his name, then forced herself to move back before she had no will to do anything but be with him.

He looked at her, bewildered.

Almost shyly, Susanna took his hand and turned toward his room. Her own bed was larger, but that was upstairs and she couldn't wait that long. "We'll save the tile for the next time," she murmured.

Next time. He didn't know if he could survive a next time. But he knew there had to be a now. He curved his fingers around hers and followed, never once thinking that she was setting the terms again.

The small bedroom turned into a little piece of paradise as they tumbled onto the gray-and-pink comforter, delighting each other the way young lovers did on the brink of first love.

She made him feel like springtime. It was as if the life he had lived before had never happened, had only existed in a dream. Only this was real. Lost in the fragrance of her body, in the way she drugged his senses, he could almost believe that everything was good and pure, the way she painted it.

Because he was with her.

With practiced skill, he showed her his gratitude for the precious moments she had given him. He explored all the secret places of her body where pleasure hid, his for the taking. He memorized the soft curves with his hands, with his lips, leaving her trembling and nearly frenzied, gasping for him.

Susanna heard the hoarse, dazed gasp and only vaguely thought that it sounded like her voice as Flynn found another, far more volatile erotic area and teased it to explosion with his tongue, bringing her up and over the first crest. She shuddered, a powerful, delicious sensation ripping through her as she arched her back, clinging to him. Pleasure and exquisite agony filled her, exhausting her, making her want more.

When he did it again, she fought back to a level of consciousness, her heart pounding, her body vibrating. She needed to give him ecstasy in kind.

She took her pleasure by giving it to him.

In a movement more agile than she thought herself capable of right now, she reversed their positions until she was on top of him. When he tried to rise, she pushed against his chest with the flat of her hand, her thighs cradling his. She heard him groan.

"The doctor said to take it easy."

This was a hell of a time to bring that up, he thought. "The doctor didn't see you in a nightgown made out of blue cellophane." But he lay back, savoring the feeling of her body over his. "Just what is it you have in mind?"

She didn't answer. She showed him.

With movements that came instinctively, driven on by her desire to pleasure, and be pleasured, Susanna made love with him as he had never had it made before. Following the pattern he had set forth, she drove him crazy with desire as she darted her tongue along the length of his body, pausing at strategic places, making his pulse leap, bringing him to the very edge. Only sheer self-control had him hanging on and kept him from scaling upward and then plummeting without her.

When he had taken all that he could possibly bear, he reached for her. "Come here, Susanna," he rasped, his throat hoarse, desire closing it.

She surprised him by rolling on top. When he tried to move her, she resisted. Taking him to her, she sheathed him and began to slowly rock, breaking through his resolve and old-fashioned notions.

The protest he would have uttered died, forgotten, burning in the flames she fanned. Without realizing what he was doing, he held onto her firm hips and began to move her in a primal rhythm that was as old as Time, as new as tomorrow's sunrise. Susanna gripped his shoulders and rode him.

When they reached the end of the journey, they arrived at the summit together. He groaned her name, pulling her down to him as his mouth covered hers.

A century later, he opened his eyes. She was still lying across him, her body limp, lazily curled like a well-fed kitten stretched out before a warm fire. He could feel the curve of her lips against his chest. She was smiling.

So was everything else, he thought, savoring the afterglow. His hand felt heavy as he raised it to stroke her hair. It was fanned out along his chest, a curtain of spun gold.

Susanna raised her head and looked at him. She loved him, but she bit back the declaration. No use frightening him. Yet. "Did I hurt you?" she asked. Now that the raw flame of passion had abated a little, common sense pricked her conscience. She should have had more self-control than this.

He sifted her hair through his fingers and watched in fascination as golden rain fell. No, there had been no physical pain. But there would be other wounds to reckon with, other scars that would be formed. "More than you could possibly guess."

She knew it. This was too much for him. She had tried to be careful. Obviously, she hadn't succeeded. She started to move from him, ready to investigate his scar, afraid of the damage she would find. His hands slid down to her hips in a fluid movement, igniting a flame that wasn't thoroughly banked.

"Not yet," he told her. "Not yet." Amazing as it seemed to him, he hadn't had his fill of her. If anything, he was even hungrier than before. It was an interesting thing to discover about himself at this point in his life. He grinned, shaking his head.

Susanna traced the outline of his mouth with the tip of her forefinger and watched his lips quirk. "What?"

"I've never had a woman on top before." In all the times he and Kelly had made love, it had always been a sweet, gentle expression of their feelings. This searing passion was something entirely new to him.

She bracketed his body with her hands, shifting her weight. "Am I too heavy?" She searched his face, concerned. He wouldn't tell her. She'd see her answer in his eyes.

"Depends on your perspective." Slowly, he began to massage her hips and she began to move rhythmically. He felt himself responding. "You don't weigh much in pounds." But what she wanted from him was heavy. Perhaps too heavy for him to offer.

Susanna didn't want him taking the thought any further. If he had regrets and voiced them, something was going to die within her. "You realize, of course, that if you say you're sorry you're going to die."

The laughter bubbled up in his chest. They could both feel it before he finally let it free. "No, I'm not sorry. Not for this."

But for other things, she thought. Things that would come. But those could be faced later. One step at a time, she promised herself, on step at a time. She wasn't looking for major miracles, just pieces of one.

"Not about anything," she promised, hoping that she could make good on it.

The feel of her breasts gently moving against him as she breathed distracted him. He struggled to focus on his thoughts. He didn't want her to believe, in the end, that he had just been using her to satisfy himself. He wanted her to know that there were reasons for what was to come. "Susanna, it's a little hard, after you've been cut off at the knees, to learn how to dance again."

She couldn't accept that. She had to make him see that he shouldn't, either. "You weren't cut off, you were wounded. We all are in one way or another."

She had the right to say that. She had been through it too, he thought. And yet, he couldn't understand how she *could* say it. "How do you manage?"

She shrugged, her hair falling over her shoulder. He pushed it back, his hand closing over her breast. It just filled his hand. The way her lovemaking had filled his soul.

"I just do. I don't think about it much." In the early stages, after Brett died, to think would have been her undoing. Now, it was easier. "The way I see it, you have two choices. You let life run you over, or you run with it. Maybe even a step ahead of it at times."

He wanted to lose himself in her philosophy. In her. But he couldn't. He was too much of a realist for that. "You really believe that, don't you?"

She nodded solemnly. "With all my heart." She only wished she could make him believe it, as well.

She didn't seem real. This whole evening didn't seem real. Yet she was here, her body still pressed against his, still one with him. He wished he could tap into her source, but wishes were for fools who didn't know about life. "You really are incredible, you know."

She smiled, sliding her fingers along his lips, willing a smile into place. She shivered, surprised, as he licked the tip of one finger. Desire came, hard and wanting. "Tell me more. You're on a roll, Flynn."

"No," he contradicted, shifting so that she could take him in farther. His need for her magic was growing again. "I'm on a roller coaster and I'm about to plunge down."

She grinned broadly, wickedly. "Then hang on, I'm coming with you."

She brought her mouth down to his.

When Susanna awoke the next morning, she found the bed empty. Her pulse quickened and she forced herself to take a breath, then let it out slowly. He had probably just woken up early. He wasn't gone. He wouldn't leave without telling her.

Was she so sure?

No, she wasn't sure about anything when it came to Flynn, except how she felt about him. The other side of the coin was a mystery to her. She only *thought* he had felt something last night, too. But she wasn't sure.

She pulled the sheet to her as she sat up. Where was he? Flynn's robe was lying bunched up on the floor. She slid out of bed and quickly yanked the robe on, pushing her arms through the large sleeves as she hurried into the hall.

The smell of burnt coffee had her running into the kitchen. The string of muttered, colorful oaths had her slowing down again. He was still here.

Flynn swore he could smell her as she entered the room. The fragrance of wildflowers mingling with the scent that lovemaking left on her skin. It drifted to him, teasing his senses, even as he stood, puzzling over an incomprehensible piece of machinery. She had got to him, he thought, not at all happy about the matter.

He turned and looked at her accusingly. "How do you get this damn thing to work?"

"Not by hurting its feelings." Pulling the sash of the robe tight, she headed toward the refrigerator. So this was how the morning after was going to go. In warfare. She braced herself. "Sit down, I'll make coffee," she offered. "Do you want breakfast?"

"No." He snapped out the word.

Susanna turned to look at him. Barefoot, wearing only his jeans, he appeared no different than he had the other day. Actually, he looked more annoyed if that was possible. Seeing him this way hurt. She had expected, oh, she didn't know, something. A mellowing perhaps. Just something to indicate that they had gone up another plateau. Instead, she had the sinking feeling that they had returned to square one.

Worse, they were back in the box, before the game had even begun. The lid was shut tight.

She wet her lips. Crying would be stupid. So would hitting him with the frying pan, but of the two options, it was the more tempting. "What do you want?"

To make love to you until I die. To have my life back in order. But I can't have it both ways. "I think Michael and I will be going home this afternoon." He couldn't look at her, couldn't bear to see the hurt. "I'm certainly well enough. I think last night proved it."

Her voice was low, even, when she spoke. Without a strong control it would have broke. "Last night wasn't about physical endurance, Flynn."

"Last night—" he helplessly searched for words, "—was very nice."

"Nice?" she echoed in disbelief, her temper flaring. She moved around the table and poked an accusing finger at his chest. "A passing report card is 'nice.' A hit at bat is 'nice.' A glass of soda is 'nice.'"

He grabbed her hand. She was making a hole in his chest. "What's your point?"

She yanked her hand away, furious. "The point isn't mine, it's at the top of your head."

He supposed he deserved her anger and a lot more. He shouldn't have let last night happen, for both their sakes. "Susanna, last night, things got out of hand."

"Yes, they did. You forgot to put the stopper on your feelings." He made her so mad, she wanted to scream. What did it take to make him open up? She hadn't expected last night to be a religious experience for him, but she had hoped that he would open up just a little. She had glimpsed his soul in that small bedroom. Why did he insist on burying it?

It was better to hurt her a little now than to hurt her more later. "There are no feelings. I'm a man. That sort of thing can happen without any feelings being involved at all."

She wasn't buying that. It was a stupid, mindless argument. Men felt. *He* felt, she knew he did. "Then act like a man and stop running." She brought her hand to her mouth, trying to calm down. What was she doing, tossing out insults like that? She had always been so reasonable. "I'm sorry."

"No, I deserve that." *That, and more, he thought if I hurt you.*

She strove for patience. It wasn't easy. "What you deserve is a frying pan across your head, but I'm too much of a lady to do that." *Maybe.* "Now sit down, I'll make you breakfast and then you can plan your escape. Like you said, you proved last night that you're certainly well enough to take care of yourself and Michael."

He was standing behind her. She saw his reflection in the upper oven. He moved to place his hands on her shoulders, then let them drop. *Mustn't have physical contact,* she thought bitterly.

"About last night—I didn't mean to hurt you." The words felt awkward in his mouth.

"You didn't. Last night." She blinked back her tears, keeping her face turned from his as she reached into the refrigerator. "Orange juice?"

"I can get it." He brushed her aside and took out the carton himself. Getting a glass from the dish rack, he poured without knowing why.

"Nobody ever said you couldn't," she muttered. *Love,* she thought as she filled the coffeemaker, certainly didn't account for taste. She closed the lid on the machine, then turned toward him. "I'll help you pack."

He set the glass of orange juice on the table untouched. He wasn't hungry. Not for food. But he couldn't allow himself to indulge. Not again. "I can do that."

Yes, he could do everything. Pour juice. Pack. Bend steel with his bare hands. He didn't need her for anything. She watched as he walked out. "Flynn?"

He stopped, but didn't turn around. Tension knotted at the back of his neck. "What?"

"There's a difference between being independent and being mule-headed. Maybe you should learn it."

He was going to answer, then thought better of it. He knew if he got into a debate with her, he'd lose.

Technically, he already had. He kept on walking, reminding himself that it was better to hurt her a little now than a lot later.

Chapter Fourteen

Damn that woman. Damn her for invading his life, invading his mind and throwing what limited order he had attained into complete chaos again.

Flynn tossed aside the newspaper he had been unsuccessfully trying to read for the last ten minutes and rose from the kitchen table. Steam rising from the small pot told him his water was boiling. He took the lid off the dented drip coffeepot and poured the water in.

When would the order return?

He'd been home for three days. Three days now and he felt more like a stranger here than he had at Susanna's house. He looked around and took a deep breath. There was no subliminal scent of flowers everywhere, no hint of her wafting to him.

Dust, actually, was what he detected. The musty smell reminded Flynn that he had yet to hire a housekeeper. Now would be the perfect time to interview one, when he had nothing else to do.

Except go stir-crazy. Thinking. Wishing his life was back to normal. Wishing she were here.

He returned to the newspaper and paged through the sections until he found the Classifieds. Somehow, he couldn't get himself organized. Even the other times, when life had struck him such a horrible low blow, he had found a way to rally. It had been slow-going, but his basic sense of order had come to his aid. It had all but deserted him now. He found himself wandering from room to room, flipping through books, staring at the TV screen without seeing for whole blocks of time.

It was all her fault, he thought grudgingly, pouring a cup of coffee. All he could think about was his desire for her, the way her body had felt against his, the soft murmuring sound she had made as they had found that timeless, special place that lovers inhabit and make their own.

He took a sip of his coffee and pushed it aside. Maybe he had had too much coffee and was just wired. He should cut down. On coffee, on thoughts of her. The coffee would be the easy part.

She had come by today. Susanna buzzed by each morning, picking Michael up and taking him to school. She did it to spare Flynn the trouble of making arrangements. Yet unintentionally, she caused him more difficulties.

Or maybe it wasn't so unintentional. He wouldn't put it past her. He saw just enough of her to make him remember how much he missed seeing her. How much he missed being with her. Touching her. She appeared just long enough to ruin him for anything else the rest of the day.

No, he thought as he absently took another sip of coffee, he sincerely doubted that it was unintentional. He had no doubt that she was the more resilient one. She seemed to be able to cheerfully bounce back from anything. It wasn't like that for him.

By the beginning of his fourth week on disability, Flynn had restored a little order into his life. He was using this time to get a new perspective and a stronger grasp on things. Applying himself to the task diligently, he had interviewed twelve housekeepers before he had found Mrs. Duffy. She came with glowing references. The maternal-looking woman had had to leave her last position because the family she worked for was being transferred to Puerto Rico. Though they had offered her twice her pay to come with them, Mrs. Duffy had remained regretful, but firm. Puerto Rico was much too far away from her grandchildren. She was very sorry, but she couldn't go. Family meant everything to Mrs. Duffy. She slipped into Flynn's scheme of things very easily. Michael liked her.

"But not," he told Flynn in confidence, making sure that the older woman didn't overhear, "as much as Susanna." They walked outside to the car. When Flynn made no comment, Michael prodded, "How about you?"

Flynn got into the sports car and waited until Michael had buckled up. "How about me what?"

Michael peered into Flynn's face intently. "Do you like Susanna more?"

The kid had the makings of a lawyer, Flynn thought. This came under the heading of badgering the witness. Flynn turned on the ignition, then pulled out of the driveway. "It's too soon to tell."

"Not for me."

No, not for him, either, Flynn thought. That was just the trouble. Flynn turned on the radio, searching for something to take his mind off the topic.

"Can she come with us?" Michael raised his voice hopefully over the music.

"Who?"

"Susanna." Michael let out a sigh. "Aren't you listening?"

Yes, but he wasn't hearing, Flynn thought ruefully. His mind was drifting, as it usually did these days. What he needed, he was convinced, was to get back to work, to occupy his mind with facts and figures—figures other than hers.

Flynn turned down Susanna's street, annoyed at the feeling of homecoming that washed over him.

"Where would you like her to come?" he asked Michael patiently.

That was easy. "To the space 'zibt." They were picking Billie up to take him along with them.

"Exhibit," Flynn corrected. He slowed the car. "She might be busy." At least, he fervently hoped so, knowing where this was leading.

"I'll ask her!" Michael volunteered, jumping out of the car as soon as Flynn pulled up the hand brake. He didn't even wait for Flynn to shut off the engine.

She wasn't too busy.

When Flynn had initially suggested taking Billie with him and Michael to the annual space exhibit Worth Aerospace was holding that weekend, Susanna had been disappointed that Flynn hadn't included her in his invitation. The omission had stung. He had been so reticent, so distant each time she saw him since the night they had made love, she had felt as if that had been the end of everything instead of just the beginning.

Michael's eagerly extended invitation had her hoping that perhaps Flynn had had something to do with it. But she was afraid to ask. If she was uncertain, she could hope, pretend that perhaps Flynn was just being shy. Thinking back to their evening together, she realized that she was stretching hope to its limits.

She walked out to the car. "Hi."

"Hi," Flynn answered stiffly.

Was it just her, or did he look uncomfortable again? Why? They had made love, not declared war. She pretended not to notice. "Thanks for the invitation. I'll be glad to come."

She wasn't wearing any makeup and she looked terrific. How was that possible? "Um, don't you have to change or something?"

Susanna looked down at what she was wearing, jeans and a bright red silky T-shirt that made him think of roses in the spring.

"Why? Something wrong with this?" she asked innocently. She didn't see anything wrong, but it was hard to second-guess him.

"No, no." He shook his head quickly. Most women seemed to take a long time. Life with four girls in the house had taught him that. And even Kelly, who was marvelously organized about everything, had never been able to get ready at a moment's notice. She had required a half day's warning before they went anywhere. Spontaneity had never been a part of their lives even before the children were born. He wasn't used to the idea of a woman being ready so quickly.

Michael and Billie came up behind her, impatient to leave. "You look great," Michael told Susanna.

"Great," Flynn echoed.

A recycled compliment was better than none at all, Susanna thought. She would take what she could get. At least she knew he wasn't given to empty flattery. She cupped Michael's chin and smiled at him, then at Flynn.

"I'll take that as a four-star rating. Just let me grab my purse and I'm ready."

Flynn wished like hell that he was. But no preparation would ever make him ready for Susanna. Each time he saw her, he felt anticipation tingling along his skin, knotting his stomach. This time, there was no appendix to blame it on. She was the cause.

Susanna had taken over his life. Yet he hadn't surrendered it to her. It almost seemed like a dream, all of it leaving him confused. His feelings these last few weeks had gone through drastic changes. It was difficult to come to grips with all the emotions he was experiencing. Flynn sighed. He could understand complicated mathematical concepts, but human behavior, even his own, baffled him. It was almost as if he had no choice but to feel what he was feeling, go in the direction he was going.

No, dammit, Flynn thought as Susanna got into the car, the boys scrambling into the back seat. He *did* have a choice in this matter.

He'd just exercise it tomorrow. Today, the boys deserved an outing.

At least his motive sounded noble.

The compound had been turned into something akin to a fairground. There was even a booth where free hot dogs and sodas were being dispensed. The line for that, Flynn noted, was twice as long as the one snaking into the main building, where the space station mock-ups were being housed.

"We'll eat later," he promised the boys as he herded them toward the main building. As they passed the entrance, a man in a silver space suit handed the boys balloons.

"Now there's a way to lose weight," Susanna commented. "Standing out in the broiling sun wrapped in aluminum foil." She shook her head as she gave the man in the space suit a sympathetic smile.

For a minute, Flynn thought Susanna was going to double back and get the man something to drink. She had the capacity, he thought, to feel empathy for everything and everyone. It was hard to keep someone like that at arm's

length, but he was going to have to try if he wanted to hang
on to his identity. More than try, he was going to have to
succeed. The odds, he was beginning to feel, were strongly
against him.

To keep Susanna from acting on impulse, Flynn took her
arm. "This way, Pearl Pureheart."

Susanna just flashed him a grin and came along quietly.
It was a first, Flynn thought.

At the exhibit, Flynn ran into several people he knew.
Hearty greetings came, coupled with words of concern
about his health. He shrugged the concern off, saying he'd
be back at work soon. More than a couple of people commented that he looked a lot haler than he had of late, then
eyed Susanna as if she were the reason for the improvement.

"Just how long a leave are you taking?" Howard Black,
a slight-built man with a fringe of red hair surrounding a
perfectly shaped head, asked. He peered at Susanna over the
tops of his rimless glasses.

"Until he's well," Susanna spoke up before Flynn could
answer. He glared at her. Now she was taking it upon herself to speak for him, as well.

Susanna bit her tongue. She had a habit of talking for
others when their words failed to materialize at the right
speed. She flashed Flynn a look of apology.

Howard chuckled as he moved on, his children demanding his attention. "Just don't tire him out too much," he
told Susanna. "We need him back in Design." He turned
toward Flynn and said, "Lucky devil," over his shoulder
before he was yanked away.

Flynn made no comment and shepherded the boys to the
next station, where they could walk through the tiny quar-
ters that were meant to house the astronauts for weeks at a
time.

"That tiny space?" Billie marveled. "Are they using midgets?"

Flynn laughed and launched into an explanation. At least here he was on familiar ground, not the way he felt when he was with Susanna. There nothing was familiar, not anymore.

Working with the minute details that went into constructing such a huge project as the space shuttle had given Flynn tunnel vision. He had lost sight of the overall picture, the breathtaking creations that a marriage between science and technology could accomplish. Seeing it through the eyes of two little boys brought it all back to him, making him remember why he had gone into the space program to begin with.

"Wow, and what's this?" Billie grabbed Flynn's hand and dragged him toward an actual space module.

Moments later, Michael was pulling him toward the long bulletin board that had a series of photographs tacked to it, documenting the project's progress. Flynn laughed in protest, but let himself be dragged off. He began to feel like a giant wishbone. A giant, satisfied wishbone.

He looked over his shoulder to see if Susanna was keeping up. She was watching him, amused. She probably thought all this was funny, he mused. Yet there was no denying that it felt right. The whole day felt right. Just the way she had in his arms.

He pushed the thought from his head.

It wasn't going to happen. He wasn't going to allow himself to slip into it. He'd been through all this once, raised his family, moved on to the next level of life. He couldn't start all over again. Because he knew exactly what there was at the end of the exhilarating roller coaster ride. A solid wall of emptiness. He'd worked his way through it before, he wasn't going to go through it again. *Couldn't* go through it again. A man could only endure so much before he folded.

If he didn't depend on anything outside himself for his happiness, for *anything* at all, he would never again know the devastation of suddenly not having it there.

Of suddenly not having *her* there.

Doggedly, Flynn cleared his mind and focused it on answering the boys' questions.

Susanna watched Flynn, watched the contentment take hold, then watched another emotion fight for possession of him. And, from the look in his eyes, she saw it temporarily win.

What sort of devils did he have, she wondered. She knew him intimately, knew some of what he probably felt, had felt it herself. And yet, there was a place he wouldn't let her into, a space he wouldn't share at all. And she didn't know how long she could put up with that. Above all, Susanna needed to share. She needed trust, and while she wanted someone in her life to do all those things with, she also needed to be needed.

Flynn didn't want that, didn't want her help, her support, didn't seem to want anything. He had made it clear that while he might enjoy her company, he didn't need her, wouldn't let himself need her. She couldn't go on like that forever.

For now, she would just enjoy the outing.

She laced her arms about Billie's shoulders, stood behind him and listened to Flynn's explanation. A small rumbling sound coming from Billie's stomach punctuated Flynn's final statement. The boys broke into giggles.

"Lunch?" she suggested pleasantly to Flynn.

He was about to suggest that himself. The fact that she had beat him to it irritated him even when he told himself he was being unreasonable. But the woman was always one step ahead of him.

"Sure." They had seen everything that there was to see at the exhibit. He pointed toward the exit. They made their way past another line leading to the space module. "How about that restaurant I mentioned the first day I took you to work?"

Susanna blinked as they walked out. The exhibit had been moderately lit. Outside, the sunlight seemed almost blinding for a moment. Getting accustomed to it, Susanna turned to make sure everyone was out.

Flynn's suggestion sounded divine. It would have sounded even better had she been wearing long, teardrop earrings, a simple, understated black dress and could look at him over candlelight. Two hungry, squirming little boys didn't seem to fit the picture.

"I'd love to," she told him wistfully. "But I think Hamburger Heaven might be more their style." She glanced at the two boys.

"Yeah!" Billie grinned from ear to ear.

Michael looked at Flynn, waiting. "Could we, Pop?"

"Sounds like a good idea to me," Flynn agreed, taking Susanna by the elbow. A woman who put children's pleasure before her own was not an easy woman to turn his back on. Flynn felt his resistance lowering another notch.

After lunch, Billie and Michael talked Flynn into allowing them to spend some time wandering around the sprawling outdoor mall. With the homing instincts little boys were born with, they zeroed in on the pet shop and dragged Flynn in their wake.

Susanna was just as enchanted as the boys were. To Flynn's surprise, she didn't recoil at the snakes and even expressed a fondness for the mice.

"Aren't girls supposed to find those things icky or gross or whatever the popular term these days is?" Flynn asked her as they stood by a tank filled with straw-and-white rodents.

She laughed. "I don't know. I haven't been reading my girl handbook lately. I'm too busy trying to raise a boy."

And doing more than an adequate job of it, Flynn thought. Every which way he turned, her total competence assaulted him. He admired her for it, yet he would have been lying to himself if he pretended that he didn't wish she were just a little less capable. It would be nice, he mused, if she needed him once in a while.

"Hey, Pop, look at this!"

Michael and Billie were circling a topless, wire-rimmed cage that was placed out in the middle of the floor. The dalmatian puppy inside was madly shredding the paper on the floor. The dog barked and ran back and forth, trying to get at the little boys. He wanted to play.

"Oh, isn't he an adorable puppy?" Susanna reached over the barrier and let the dog sniff her hand, then petted it.

Flynn had never had a pet. He'd grown up in an apartment and dogs had not been allowed. His daughters had never wanted anything larger than a hamster. Warily he eyed the large dog with its over-sized paws. "That's a puppy?"

"It sure is!" Michael exclaimed, his eyes dancing. "Could we buy him, Pop?"

"No, I don't think so." Flynn placed a hand on the boy's shoulder. "Owning a dog is a big commitment, Michael. We're going to have to think about it carefully and discuss it."

Michael nodded, subdued. Disappointed.

Flynn felt bad. A boy needed a dog, he thought. But then, a boy needed a mother, as well, and he wasn't running out to get one of those, either. Each step in life needed to be carefully thought out; otherwise, the consequences could be overwhelming. He slanted a look at Susanna.

Billie turned pleading eyes on his mother. "Could we get him, Mom? Could we? Then Michael and I could share him."

How could she possibly squelch a burst of generosity? And, after all, she *had* promised him a dog for his next birthday. The dog licked her fingers and added his two cents worth. She was a goner. "Okay."

The boys let out a cheer.

Flynn stared at her as Susanna beckoned to a salesgirl. "You're buying a dog?"

"Yes." The pet shop attendant looked at Susanna questioningly. "We'd like this dog, please."

Flynn couldn't believe it. "Just like that?"

Susanna pulled her wallet out and flipped through the compartments for her charge card. "How would you like me to do it?"

Was she simpleminded? "With some thought."

Susanna flashed a smile as she approached the counter. The clerk behind the register was already writing up the paperwork. "I did think."

The woman was impossible. "I mean, more than half a minute." The clerk gave Flynn a curious look, but he ignored it.

Susanna didn't understand why he was getting so worked up. This was natural to her. "It doesn't take me very long to make up my mind, Flynn. Something is either right, or it's not." *And when will you get that through your thick head?*

It just didn't compute. You didn't make decisions that were binding on a whim. This was a pet they were talking about, not a stuffed animal. "What kind of an actuary are you?" Actuaries were supposed to be a logical, pragmatic breed, not whimsical.

She watched as the attendant brought the dog out. Billie and Michael fell upon it, one boy on either side, both trying to get their arms around the dalmatian. She turned to look at Flynn. "A very happy one."

With dog food, a squeaky toy and various other doggie paraphernalia, they left the pet shop with the newest member of Susanna's family in tow. Getting into the car was a feat, but they managed.

The matter of a name was a little trickier. Billie wanted to name the dalmatian Manfred and Michael thought that Marmaduke would be a good name.

Susanna twisted around in her seat and cocked her head, studying the dog. "George," she pronounced, as if divinely inspired. "We'll call him George."

"George?" Both boys groaned at once.

Susanna nodded. "George. I like it."

"George," they chorused in a surrendering sigh.

Flynn was surprised at how quickly they retreated. But then, children had a remarkably keen sense of survival, he thought. They knew when the odds were against them. Sometimes adults lost the ability to see that when they grew older.

No sooner had they arrived at Susanna's house than the boys begged to show off their new acquisition to Aunt Jane. Flynn noticed that Michael referred to her as Aunt Jane, as well. The boy was doing his damnedest to fit in, Flynn thought. But they weren't meant to, not into this family.

Damn, she was making it hard to keep that in mind, he thought, watching Susanna putter around the kitchen.

Jane was in the house within moments. The dog bounded behind her, joyously laying claim to the entire house, leading the boys on a merry chase.

"Hi, handsome, nice to see you again," Jane tossed off to Flynn as she entered. "Susanna in the kitchen?" He nodded and she walked past him. Jane looked at her niece, shaking her head, hands on her hips. "I don't suppose you know what you're in for."

Flynn leaned against the doorjamb, his arms folded across his chest. "I tried to warn her."

Jane nodded. "Like talking to a wall, though. She has a mind of her own. Don't know where she gets it from," she told him with another shake of her head. The puppy rose up on his hind legs, his paws on Jane's legs. She petted him absently, looking at Susanna. "Lucky for you I know how to train dogs." She glanced at Flynn and saw his surprise. "Kyle trained animals for the movies."

"Kyle?" Flynn looked at Susanna for an explanation.

"Her first husband," Susanna said, getting the coffee cups from the cabinet.

Flynn shook his head, amused. First a baseball player, now an animal trainer. "You have a husband for all occasions?"

If she saw his amusement, Jane didn't show it. "Pretty nearly." Jane took a firm hold of the dog's leash and kept him from bounding off again. "Actually, I came over to borrow your boys."

"Borrow?" Susanna repeated.

"Overnight." Jane smiled at the boys who looked at her eagerly. Their expressions seemed to say that this was turning out to be a super day. "I've been waiting for you to get back. I just rented two great horror videos, but I'm too afraid to watch them on my own."

Flynn could have sworn a sly, satisfied look slid over the older woman's face, then disappeared.

Jane looked down at the small faces. "I'm going to need two brave men, one to hold each hand. What do you say, are you up to it, men? There's all the popcorn and ice cream you can eat in it for you if you agree."

As if they needed a bribe. "Aunt Jane..." Susanna said warningly.

"You can have some, too, if you want," the woman offered innocently.

Billie looked at George, who was trying to chew his leash. "Can George come, too?"

Jane nodded solemnly. "I'm counting on it." She looked over the boys' heads at Susanna. "Is it all right?"

"It is with me." Susanna glanced to her left. "Flynn?"

He had already vetoed buying a dog, he wasn't about to play the heavy twice in one day. "Sure, why not?"

They were gone before he finished the sentence.

Chapter Fifteen

Flynn watched the door close behind the boys. He shook his head, turning to look at Susanna. She had already retreated into herself and started taking out an assortment of different herbal teas. Undoubtedly for her "pleasure," he thought with a smile, remembering the way she had phrased it before.

Susanna felt him staring at her and looked up. Flynn nodded toward the front door. "Subtlety doesn't run in your family, does it?"

She plopped a packet of spiced cider into the midst of the teas. "No, but honesty does." She placed the assortment on the table before him.

"You want me to be honest?"

His voice was low. Anticipation crackled in the air. Susanna knew she was asking, almost demanding this confrontation, yet she was afraid of the results. She took a breath and held it. "Yes."

"Brutally honest?"

She flipped the kettle on and then turned. There was nothing else for her to do, no more busy-work to fidget with. "You're not the type to tiptoe around things."

No, he never had been. "You're driving me crazy."

She relaxed a little. "You've already told me that before." She shrugged and was surprised when he took hold of her shoulders. Tilting her head back, she saw that his eyes had grown dark.

"No, really crazy." He felt the slight tremor that pulsated through her body. God, he wanted her. It wasn't fair to himself, to her to let this happen. And yet, he couldn't stop it. "I can't get you out of my mind, out of my blood. I close my eyes and I see you."

"Sounds like a man who's haunted." But she was smiling when she said it. She couldn't help it. It felt wonderful to know that she wasn't alone in this, that his emotions were as churned up as hers.

"Haunted?" he repeated, rolling the word over in his mind. Yes, that was the best way to describe it. He was haunted and she was the haunter. "Yes, I'm haunted. Haunted by the way you felt against me. Haunted by that damn perfume you wore." He sniffed. She was wearing it now. "What is it?"

Susanna grinned. She didn't wear perfume. There was an assortment of bottles on her bureau, but they were almost all full. She could never remember to put any on in the morning. "Soap."

Flynn raised a lock of her hair. It was in his way. He pressed his lips to her throat and felt her quiver. Felt himself quiver.

"Soap and you. A heady combination." He trailed his lips along the side of her neck, touching just the tip of her ear. She gripped his forearms. His own knees felt weak.

"This was all I could think about since Saturday. Having you like this."

Susanna fought her way to the surface. He was making her mind drift, fantasizing. "You could have fooled me."

"I doubt it." He took a step back before he couldn't. "The only one I was trying to fool was myself."

"And did you?" She searched his face for the answer.

"I'm here, aren't I?"

Not enough. It wasn't enough. She needed to have him say something more, to verbalize his feelings, his commitment. "Yes. So is the dog."

He pulled her toward him. The hell with safe. His arms didn't feel complete without her in them. "No one put a collar around my neck and dragged me." She had to know how much he wanted her, he thought.

"No," she agreed slowly, watching his eyes. Why was he torturing himself this way? Why couldn't he just accept things and take it one step at a time? No one was rushing him. "No one did."

Maybe she needed a declaration, but he couldn't give her one. It wouldn't come. He was afraid to let it come. "Susanna, if I make love to you—with you," he stumbled over the phraseology and she found it endearing, "what does that make us?"

She touched his cheek. "Happy."

He pressed her cool fingers to his face, then kissed them one by one. "But later—"

She covered his lips with her fingers, stopping him before he could say something to spoil the moment. "Later will work itself out later," she promised. Then, because she thought he wanted to hear it, she lied. "No twenty-year plans, Flynn. Just here and now. You and me."

He glanced toward the front door. If he didn't miss his guess, Jane wouldn't let the boys come back for anything. "Has anyone nominated your Aunt Jane for sainthood?"

"I'm thinking about it." The kettle went off, whistling insistently. Susanna reached behind her to shut off the burner. Flynn kept her within the circle of his arms. Susanna leaned back slightly, amused. "Can I get you anything?" She nodded at the tea packets on the table.

No thoughts, he promised himself. No consequences. Just here and now, as Susanna had said. "Yes."

"What?"

He brushed his hand along the outline of her T-shirt, his fingers just touching her breast. "Guess."

The laugh caught in her throat. "I need a hint. I'm kind of slow."

He pressed another soft, lingering kiss on her throat, losing himself in the feel, the taste of her skin. He skimmed his fingers along her spine and felt her arch against him. "Hardly."

The passion sizzled instantly, demanding tribute, leaving him in awe. Leaving him breathless. Flynn had sought an explanation for the last time. It had been over a year since he had made love to a woman, perhaps he had just been carried away physically, made more of it in his mind than it was. It was possible, he had argued. He was here to prove his theory. Dispelling the myth, he would get himself back under control.

This time, he assured himself, he was prepared for her. Prepared for what was about to happen between them.

There was no way to be prepared for plunging out of an airplane without a parachute.

She had missed him. Lord, she had missed him. Knowing he was only a few miles away had made it even worse. A few miles away and not here. Not with her. Of his own volition. She hadn't been ready for the kind of pain that had generated.

She shivered as he impatiently drew her clothes from her, first the T-shirt, then the jeans. He was trying not to tear them off. His fingers got tangled in the straps of her teddy. With a soft laugh, she moved his hand away and slid the straps from her shoulders, watching him watch her. Hot sensations poured through her, like lava spilling from a volcano. There was nothing but pure desire in his eyes.

When the delicate white lace had slipped to the swell of her hips Flynn stopped her. "I think I can take it from here." His voice was thick from wanting her.

She said nothing as she took his hands and placed them on her hips. Watching only her eyes, Flynn pulled away the teddy. He let out a small sound of appreciation as the material slipped off and he looked at her, his eyes touching her everywhere. She felt the touch as surely as if his hands had been there, instead.

"My turn," she murmured thickly, pushing his shirt from his shoulders, tossing it to the floor.

When he felt her long, tapering fingers slide against his hips, urging both his jeans and briefs down at the same time, he could feel his blood surge through him, pounding in his loins. He pulled himself free of the confining clothes, anxious to feel her against his naked body, to have her flesh warm his.

"My room still free?"

"No one's checked in yet." As an afterthought, she grabbed the clothing, taking it with her just in case the boys had to come back for something. But if she knew Jane, they wouldn't be back before morning.

"Keep it that way." He swooped her up in his arms. "I'm making a permanent reservation."

She thought of his operation. He shouldn't be carrying her like this. "Flynn, be careful."

"Too late for that."

And it was. Too late for caution, for thought. Too late for anything but getting lost in the taste, the feel, the lure of her.

Gently, he laid her down on the bed, then drew close to the haven that only she could create for him. The covers became tangled around their bodies as they sought the pleasure they knew was waiting, the pleasure each could give to the other.

She had lied, Susanna thought as she felt his moist, open-mouth kisses outlining the hollow of her abdomen, making it quiver. She had lied when she'd told him that tomorrow would take care of itself. She wanted him today, tomorrow, forever. And it grieved her that he didn't need her the way she did him, in every part of her life.

Coherent thoughts vanished, evaporated by the heat created by his lovemaking.

Flynn couldn't believe it. It was even more overwhelming than before. More satisfying even as it continued to be arousing. He plunged himself into her after holding back longer than he thought humanly possible. A half-dozen times she had almost pushed him over the ragged edge, but he had restrained, held back. Now, he couldn't. He had to have her, had to take her. There was no more time. He drove himself up to the pinnacle, taking her with him. She cried out his name as her nails dug into his shoulders. They both tumbled from the cliff together.

Exhausted, Flynn tried to keep from crushing Susanna by balancing himself on his elbows. She shifted beneath him and he wanted her. Again. Though he had no strength with which to take her, he wanted her.

He'd never have enough of her.

Dependence. He was growing dependent again in a way he never had before. Addicted to the way she made him feel: happy, whole, eternally young. He was afraid. Hell, he was scared out of his mind. How had it happened, when he swore it wouldn't? When he was so sure that it wouldn't?

She saw the look, the doubt, enter into his eyes. *Too soon,* she thought. *Too soon. Be mine for a little while longer.*

"What's the matter?" she asked.

He couldn't tell her, not now. He smiled, framing her face in his hands as he drew himself up. "Were you ever a gymnast?"

It wasn't what she had expected to hear. She laughed with relief. "No, why?"

He indulged himself and nipped at her lower lip, sucking slightly. He felt her shift beneath him, his arousal growing. Maybe he wasn't as exhausted as he thought. "I never knew anyone who could bend that way."

It was on the tip of her tongue to say that love could make her do incredible things, but she knew he wasn't ready to hear the word, even though she ached to say it. Now that she knew, she wanted to tell him. Instead, she shrugged. "I'm double-jointed."

He shifted slightly so that their bodies remained touching, but his weight was on the bed. His hand rested possessively on her thigh. "Anything else I should know about you?"

"I have all my own teeth, I love children and sometimes, I tend to take charge." She slanted him a look beneath hooded lashes.

"Sometimes?" he echoed with a laugh. She was a soft general.

All right, maybe all the time, she thought. "Sometimes, I sleep."

He laughed. She was extraordinary. "Tell me, why aren't you married yet?"

Why? So I wouldn't pose a threat to you?

She wouldn't let him see how much his question bothered her. "You sound like Aunt Jane." Susanna turned her head away from him, hoping she wouldn't cry.

She was evading him. He wondered why. What had kept someone like her, someone with such optimism for life from marrying? He cupped her chin and made her look at him. "Seriously," he pressed.

"Seriously?" *All right,* she thought. *You asked for this.* "Because I never met anyone who made bells ring since Brett." She raised her eyes. "Until now."

Before he could shut it away, he felt a tenderness sprout within him in response to her words. Flynn sat up. This had to stop before she was hurt. Before they both were. "Susanna, I'm not going to get married again. I'm not going to have another relationship."

Susanna scrambled out of bed and grabbed the closest article of clothing. With a muffled oath, she struggled into the teddy. The man was impossible. "In case it escaped you, there's more happening here than washing socks."

"This isn't a relationship," he said quietly, damning himself for being so weak. For needing her.

T-shirt in her hands, she swung around to look at him. "It's not? Then what is it?" she demanded. If she cried now, she'd never forgive herself. Or him.

"An anomaly." He pulled on his jeans, then tried to take her by the shoulders. She hit his hands aside. "Susanna, it can't be a relationship."

She raised her chin pugnaciously. If she took a swipe at him, she knew it wouldn't hurt, not anywhere close to the way his words had hurt her. But still she wanted to. "Why?"

He wished she could understand, wished he wasn't the cause of the hurt in her eyes. He had never wanted to hurt her, just to save himself. "Because in a relationship, my guard will slip and I can't have that." He yanked on his shirt, then dragged a hand through his hair. "I can't be dependent on someone else for my happiness. Not again."

She stood before him in a T-shirt hanging down to her thighs, her eyes blazing. A delicate Fury.

How dare he run from this? How dare he push everything into her hand? "I think you have something twisted here. We don't depend on others for our happiness. Happiness comes from inside." She poked at his chest. "From you. Not me."

She lowered her voice, struggling to get her emotions under control. "I'd like to think I add to it, but I'm not the source. That's inside of you. I can't change you. I can't make you into something you're not." She wouldn't have wanted to try. What she was trying to do was reach the person she thought was buried inside. The person who made love with her and needed love in kind. "If I can't do that, how can I possibly make you dependent?"

It was so simple. Didn't she see? "Because a day without you is empty. Because I want to see you, hear you, touch you. If that's not dependency, I don't know what is."

Her anger melted. The look in his eyes had made it burn away. "So you're swearing off me?"

Her hair was still tousled from the wild, breathtaking ride they had been on. Her lips were slightly bruised from the imprint of his. He had her scent along his body. And she had his on hers. How was he supposed to resist that? How was he supposed to resist her? With a halfhearted effort, he tried.

He wasn't surprised when he lost.

Muttering an oath, Flynn pulled her to him roughly, a groan on his lips. "No, just swearing at you." He buried his face in her hair. Soft, silky. Tangling his common sense into knots. "Do you have to look so damn desirable all the time?"

She grinned. He had the oddest way of giving her a compliment. "No, I don't have to. But right now it helps."

"Only one of us, Susanna. Only one of us." He pulled off her T-shirt again, knowing he was plunging over the falls once more. Knowing, too, that sometime soon, the barrel was going to smash against the rocks.

* * *

He was going to handle it. There were no two ways about it. Flynn had made up his mind to handle it and he would. As long as he kept that in mind, kept a tight rein on his feelings and allowed himself only so much slack, everything would be all right. He could see her. Even make love with her and not get himself hopelessly lost. The trick was to do it in small doses.

The trick was remembering his plan.

It seemed that everything conspired against him. Stephanie and Julia surprised him the following Saturday, arriving before noon and announcing that they were taking Michael and Billie to Disneyland.

"I'm not included?" Flynn asked, amused. He watched Michael help Julia gather the necessary "supplies" that would make an outing to the Magic Kingdom complete. Michael had stopped eyeing him warily, as if Flynn were going to evaporate the next moment. He was no longer worried about Michael. The boy was going to be just fine.

"No, you're going to be busy," Julia told him, depositing several cans of soda into the backpack.

"Doing what?" Flynn asked suspiciously. "Your car acting up again?"

"The car's fine." Stephanie threw a light jacket for Michael to Julia. She looked at her father. "You're going to be busy taking Susanna out for a proper dinner." She shook her head.

Flynn followed Stephanie as she walked into the bathroom, where she rummaged through the medicine cabinet until she found a bottle of sunscreen. It amused Flynn that Stephanie managed to be so thorough while giving off this careless image. "Proper? What is that supposed to mean?"

Stephanie cocked her head, her dark hair spilling over her shoulder. "She's always cooked for you, the least you could do is pay for a meal." Finding everything she wanted, Stephanie crossed back to the family room.

Did this bossy streak come naturally to all women? he wondered. He was beginning to think so. "For your information, I already have."

"Terrific." Julia's eyes brightened as she accepted the half-empty bottle of sunscreen and tucked it into one of the myriad zippered compartments on the blue-and-red backpack. "Where?"

"Hamburger Heaven," Michael put in, coming to Flynn's defense. The smirk on Stephanie's face had him mystified. How had he struck out?

"Indigestion in record time," Stephanie proclaimed. She placed her hands on her father's arms, giving him a patient look. "I think Susanna would like to go somewhere where the meals don't come in individual containers on plastic trays, Pop."

He could spend the afternoon arguing with them, but that would keep them from the amusement park and he didn't want to disappoint the two boys. Besides, he supposed that his daughters did have a point. Susanna had technically saved his life. He owed her a night out.

Moreover, if they were in a restaurant, he couldn't very well give in to temptation. "All right." He started to go call Susanna when he caught the girls giving each other a high five. Michael leaped up to add his small hand to the celebration.

Time to nip this in the bud. "Look, everyone, this is just dinner."

Stephanie crossed to him, an affectionate smile on her lips. She straightened his collar. "There's another *D* word that's applicable here." He raised an eyebrow quizzically. "Date, Pop. Date."

He removed her hands from his collar and held them firmly. His expression was very serious. "I don't date,

Stephanie." Lord, he didn't even know how anymore. Up to now, there had been no need.

"Then you should, and it should be with Susanna."

She sounded so positive about it, the way only the very young could. It amused him despite himself. "Have the church picked out?"

"No," she said cheerfully. "That we'll leave up to you."

They were going to leave other matters up to him, too, he thought. This was his life, not theirs, to work out. "Come here." He moved farther out of the room. The subject was too serious to discuss in front of Michael. "I'm not about to get married again."

"Not with this attitude."

"Not with any attitude." He looked into her eyes and saw some of himself, saw the optimism that had once resided in his soul. Before he had learned. "Stephanie, I'm forty-five years old."

"You're the youngest forty-five I've ever known." To emphasize her point, she tapped his biceps. "If you weren't my father, I'd give Susanna a run for her money."

He was going to make her understand if it *did* take all afternoon. "Be that as it may, think logically for a minute. I'm ten years older than Susanna. If I did marry her now, in fifteen years, I'll be sixty."

Stephanie looked at him, her expression growing somber. "And how old will you be in fifteen years if you don't marry Susanna?"

The simplicity of her question confounded him. He had no answer for her. "Anyone ever tell you that you have a smart mouth?" he asked affectionately.

"I come by it naturally." Impishly, she patted his face. "I have a smart pop. Until now." She swung around. "Ready?" she called to Julia and Michael.

"No," Flynn murmured to himself. "But that doesn't seem to matter to anyone."

He didn't seem to have a say in any of this, Flynn thought as he drove to Susanna's house later that evening. Everyone was trying to take it out of his hands. Everyone was eager to propel his life down the track. Stephanie, Julia, Michael, Susanna's aunt, they were all behind him, pushing. But only he would come to the station at the end of the line. Only he would face the loneliness after all was said and done, the way he had once before. He had no desire to reach that destination again.

Flynn parked the convertible at the curb next to her mailbox and got out. He didn't care how beautiful Susanna was, how desirable she was and how much everyone else liked her. He simply wasn't going to be railroaded into doing anything he didn't want to do. And that was that.

The trouble, he thought when she opened the door, the porch light bathing her in an ethereal glow, was that he did want to. Desperately.

Damn, even he was fighting against himself.

Of course, it was hard not to want her when she was wearing minimal clothing disguised as an evening dress. Her shoulders were bare and tempting. Her hot-pink halter dress was completely backless with a straight skirt that emphasized every curve he had already memorized with his fingertips.

"What's this all about?" Susanna pulled the door closed behind her and went down the walk. When he had called earlier, asking her out in that noncommittal way of his, she had been pleased, but completely surprised. Seeing him in a suit and tie was even more surprising. He looked stunning.

Flynn opened the car door for her and waited until she got in. "It's about conspiring daughters and grandsons and aunts.'' He shut the door, then came around the hood to his own side.

She didn't understand. "Is this some kind of classified information you're giving me in code?"

He wove his way to the main drag in Bedford. The familiar path toward the mall seemed different in the dark. He had done it five days a week for eight years, half-asleep. Traveling down this road with Susanna, dusk painting the sky shades of muted pink and purple, made it seem unusual. Romantic.

He was going to have to steer clear of that kind of thinking if he was going to survive. "Everyone thinks we're good together."

He made it sound like a life sentence. "It doesn't matter what everyone else things. It matters what you think."

If he could blame his being here on someone else, it wouldn't be as difficult for him to accept. Knowing he was acquiescing of his own free will put another light on the matter. And she knew it, too, he thought, glancing at her. "You fight dirty, you know that?"

"I fight to win." She settled back. "So, where are we going?"

"That restaurant I keep talking about but never seem to take you to. Robert Burns."

"The one at the mall?" He nodded. She had the impression that this wasn't his idea. It wasn't any good unless he wanted to do it. "Sounds wonderful, but you don't have to."

There she went again. "I wish you'd stop telling me what I can or can't do."

Susanna could hear the shift in his tone. She was tired of always worrying if she was saying the right thing and second-guessing his reaction. She wasn't trying to lead his life for him; she was just making a suggestion.

"Sorry," she said tightly. "I thought this was a dialogue. I keep forgetting you want to be autonomous." She felt her temper flaring. Dammit, she wasn't throwing a lasso over him. She thought he *wanted* to be with her. "You know, for a fee, I read somewhere that you can declare yourself your own country and be as damn independent as you want." With a huff, she crossed her arms before her and stared out the window.

If he lived to be a thousand, he'd never understand the opposite sex. "What set you off?"

If he wanted to fight, he was going to get one. "You. The damn wall you keep rebuilding every time I find a chink to crawl through." She drew herself up as he slowed down at the light. "You know, you might call what you want independence, but I call it being lonely." Incensed, Susanna suddenly got out of the car and slammed the door behind her, making it vibrate. As Flynn stared, stunned, she started to walk away.

"Get back into the car," he ordered. Crazy. The woman was positively crazy.

Susanna just kept walking. It was probably two miles to her house and she was in three-inch heels, but she didn't care. Anything was preferable to being in the car with that heartless brute, even if he was the best-looking thing she had ever seen in a suit.

Flynn did a U-turn in the middle of the road, grateful that there were no cars behind him. When he called to her again, she just raised her chin higher. Her pace never slowed.

She wished she had taken a shawl with her. The wind was beginning to pick up. "I don't have to listen to you."

Any second now, a policeman was going to pop out of nowhere and give him a ticket. Is that what she wanted? "Susanna, I'm driving on the wrong side of the road."

She didn't even spare him a glance. "Shouldn't bother you. You're just showing off your independent streak."

Letting go of a string of choice words, Flynn jumped out of his car, abandoning it. Susanna began to walk faster, but he quickly caught up to her. Grabbing her arm, he jerked her around. "What is it you want?"

How could he ask her that? Shutting her out at every turn, how could he ask that? "To get in, Flynn."

He looked back at his car. He hadn't thrown her out. What was she talking about? "What?"

She didn't want to have to spell it out. "I don't want to be your mother, I don't want to baby you, I want to be there for you. There's a difference. It involves trust and caring and, oh yes, the *L* word." Her lips twisted in a mirthless smile. How could he be like this after they had made love? "The one that'll make you choke if you say it."

What he wanted to choke was her, but he kept his temper bridled. "What are you talking about?"

She shook her head, her eyes shining with tears. "You haven't a clue, do you, Flynn?" Pulling away, she began to walk again. "Tell your daughters and everyone else involved that I had a very—enlightening time."

Incredulously, he fell into step. "You're going home?"

"Watch me."

"It's two miles. In the dark." And she was hardly dressed for a stroll. That dress would stir the imagination of anyone with any kind of libido.

Susanna swallowed past the lump in her throat. "We independent people are very resilient. You ought to know that."

His patience at an end, he pointed behind him. "Get in the car." To his astonishment, she just kept walking. "I said, get in the car."

"Make me."

He wasn't about to let something happen to her because she was so damn pig-headed. For tonight, she was his responsibility. "Okay."

The next thing she knew, she was being lifted in the air and then slung over his shoulder. "What the hell do you think you're doing?"

Carrying her fireman style, he began to walk back to the car. "Taking you out to dinner."

"You idiot, you'll break your stitches. Put me down!" She tried to wiggle off, but he had a firm grip on her.

"They're my stitches to break."

Unceremoniously, he deposited her into the car. Coming around to his side, he got in and turned on the ignition. With effort, he let out a breath, trying to calm down. He'd never acted that rashly before and it left him as stunned as it probably did her. He glanced toward Susanna. "Still hungry?"

That he cared enough to *make* her come made her smile. Perhaps there was hope for him yet. "Why not? Playing cavewoman always makes me hungry."

He supposed he should apologize. He hadn't a clue what had come over him. "I didn't mean to do that."

She grinned. "Too bad. It was the most spontaneous thing you've done so far, other than have your appendicitis attack."

No, he wasn't going to understand women, Flynn decided. Not if he lived forever.

Chapter Sixteen

He had no idea that the restaurant had dancing on the weekend. The announcement was posted outside the building, which had been designed to resemble an old Scottish castle. Leaning his hand against the cool, smooth, gray stones, Flynn read the notice and was tempted to alter his plans. But the look on Susanna's face made the decision for him. They went in.

Flynn held up two fingers in answer to the maître d's unspoken question. The genial-looking man in the red-and-green plaid kilt turned wordlessly and led them to a table just off the dance floor.

"Will this do, ma'am?" A soft Scottish burr enveloped every syllable.

"It's lovely," Susanna answered as the man helped her with her chair.

Flynn saw the appreciative expression on the maître d's face as he took a long lingering survey of Susanna's bare back. The man looked up at Flynn and there was a congratulatory note in his eyes as he waved him to his seat.

Flynn scanned the wine list. "I suppose you want to dance." He hadn't danced in years. Probably no longer knew how, he thought.

Resting her chin on her raised, linked fingers, Susanna looked at the dance floor. A lovely ballad echoed softly through the restaurant as a lone couple took advantage of the romantic atmosphere. They looked very much in love, she thought wistfully. "You're getting good at reading my mind."

"No, not really." Flynn selected a wine and indicated his choice to the young, slight waiter who had appeared at their table to take their order. Like the maître d', the waiter wore a kilt. "I don't think I have a clue about what goes on out there."

He made it sound like no-man's-land. "Nothing that complex," Susanna assured him. "It's all very simple, really."

Flynn uttered a short laugh. She clearly underestimated herself. "Any woman who can juggle as many things, as many roles as you do, can never lay claim to the word simple."

Susanna smiled at the waiter as he returned to serve her first, then pour a glass for Flynn. He left the bottle on the table. She waited until they were alone again. "That's your problem, you make things far too complicated. Like the dog."

He took a sip and let the light wine curl through his system. It hadn't anywhere near the kick that she had. But then, she was far more potent. He looked at Susanna over the rim of the glass.

"The dog," he echoed, not having the slightest idea what she was driving at.

"George." Absently, she sipped her wine, then smiled. "It's a simple matter, Flynn. Boy, dog. Dog, boy." She indicated each coupling with a wave of her hand. "They belong together."

He failed to see the simplicity she obviously thought was so evident. To him the purchase of the animal had a great many complications attached to it. He tossed one at her. "How about the vet bills?"

She shrugged. He watched the candlelight play along the slope of her shoulders. He remembered the way her skin felt there, delicate and silky. "Those will belong to me. It's a small price to pay for happiness."

"Whose?" Was she talking about herself now, or her son? Or both?

"Billie's. George's." She thought of the look on his grandson's face when the puppy licked him. "Michael's." All of which made her own heart glad. "Mine."

All this because of one dog. Only she could pull that off. And she had even included the dog in this group. "That about covers the whole bunch, doesn't it?"

She looked at him pointedly. "Almost."

There was some hidden message here that he didn't quite fathom. And he didn't want her to spell it out for him, either. "It would take more than just a dog to make me happy, Susanna."

"Tell me about it. Maybe we can come up with something." What was it? she wondered. What would bring the lights back into his eyes on a permanent basis?

She was digging and he didn't want her to. He didn't want to talk about the past, or the problem that gnawed away at him. The fear. He didn't want to burden her with it. "No."

He was closing the doors again. One step forward, two steps back. Susanna sighed, looking down into her wineglass. The crystal shimmered and sparkled, but gave off no warmth. An illusion. Was that what they had between them? Only an illusion? "Looks like the big guy pitched another shutout."

Now she was talking to wineglasses. Maybe he had jarred something loose before, carrying her over his shoulder the way he had. "What are you talking about?"

"Never mind." Her smile was tight, to keep herself from unraveling. "I don't think someone as complex as you would understand."

There was only one way out of this. He rose. "Care to dance?"

She took the hand he offered. "I'd love to." She smiled at him, striving to maintain her sense of humor. It was the only weapon she had. "This way we're both satisfied. You get to move and I get to stay with you."

He led her to the dance floor and took her in his arms. "Love Is A Many-Splendored Thing" was being played by the three-piece band. He pressed her closer to him and felt her sigh vibrate against his chest. Her bare skin made his fantasies take flight despite his resolutions to the contrary. Every minute with her was a struggle of some sort, he thought.

"Susanna, someday you're going to have to print a code book so the rest of us can understand what you're talking about."

"The one who really counts will understand. He won't need a code book."

Then it probably wouldn't be me, Flynn thought. And that was just as well. For both of them.

It was all right, Flynn assured himself. There was just a week left before the end of his leave of absence. It was all right to indulge a little, all right to let his guard slip. Once he was back at work, things would get back to normal. For now, he'd let them drift.

He thought he was safe.

For the next week, Flynn saw life, his and Michael's, fall into a pattern. Though Mrs. Duffy had turned out to be every bit as resourceful, every bit as competent as Mrs. Henderson had been before her, Flynn found himself eating dinner at Susanna's house. The fault was Michael's.

Susanna still came by each morning to pick him up for school. She insisted on it really, saying his house was on her way to the school. Since going with them made Michael happy, Flynn agreed.

Because George was there, Michael begged to be allowed to go over to Billie's house every day after school. Jane was more than willing to bring Michael along when she picked Billie up from school in the afternoon. Since the arrangement was only temporary until he went back to work, Flynn saw no reason to deny Michael this small pleasure, either.

Around five o'clock, Flynn would drive the short distance to Susanna's house to pick the boy up. Once there, Flynn found himself being subtly persuaded to stay for a while. He never refused.

George, Flynn noted, was coming along by leaps and bounds. The leaps were mostly aimed at Flynn. Though he didn't want to, Flynn found himself growing fond of the gregarious dalmatian. He became involved with Jane's short training sessions, acting as her less-than-willing assistant. Since his protests fell on deaf ears, he complied. Besides, watching the dog's progress was rewarding. The rest of the time, he spent coaching Billie on his batting technique. He found that to be rewarding, too.

On Saturday and Sunday, it seemed as if they spent the entire time with Susanna, Billie and Jane. And Jane was more than willing to take the boys and the dog off their hands for long stretches of the afternoon. Because he had the shelter of knowing it would all change soon, Flynn allowed himself to relax and enjoy Susanna.

He wasn't growing dependent on this feeling of contentment, he argued silently. It was just a vacation of the spirit, nothing more.

They sat on the sofa, watching *Wuthering Heights*. Susanna astonished Flynn by reciting whole blocks of dialogue along with the main characters. Watching old movies was one of her hobbies. He had no idea when she found the time.

Susanna nestled in the comfortable crook of his arm, her feet curled up under her. "Billie's really coming along with his hitting."

Flynn couldn't resist playing with a lock of her hair, winding the silken threads around his finger. "He has a lot of natural ability going for him. He was just a little afraid, I think."

There was a lot of that going around, Susanna thought. She turned so that her mouth was just below his. "Still, thank you for taking the time to help."

He didn't want her making too big a deal of it. Gratitude was something that still made him feel uncomfortable. "I had nothing else to do."

She tugged on his shirt until their eyes met. Hers were impatient. "Can't you just say yes, I did a good deed and I'm proud of it?"

"Okay, yes, I did a good deed and I'm proud of it." He slid his tongue lightly over her lips and felt the shiver that had come so familiar so quickly. "Satisfied?"

Curling her fingers farther into his shirt, she kissed him with breathless feeling. "It's a start."

It was an end.

As he drove away from Susanna's house that Sunday, he told himself that he had to make a break here and now. Tomorrow he would be returning to work. Perforce he would have to return to his old routine. The routine didn't include Susanna.

He'd have an excuse to stay away from her. There was no doubt in his mind that while he had been out, six weeks of work had piled up on his desk, waiting for him to plow through it. Mrs. Duffy could drop Michael off at his games and pick him up. There would be no opportunity for Flynn to do it himself. He'd see to that. He needed time away from Susanna to regain his senses, his bearing. He was getting to look forward to seeing her too much.

Getting?

All right, he thought, pressing the button for the automatic garage-door opener. It yawned open in front of him. He had *gotten* used to seeing her every day. And that was very, very dangerous to his survival. He had to draw the line here, before it was too late.

Before he was completely lost, completely emotionally dependent on her.

If he wasn't already.

"We're home, champ," he said, nudging the sleeping boy next to him. But if they were home, he thought, why didn't it feel that way?

Just further evidence, he assured himself as he took Michael by the hand and guided the sleepy boy inside, that he needed this break.

Flynn stared at the neatly printed letter in his hands. Linen. Top-grade linen, he mused. Nothing but the best for the corporation's vice-president. The letterhead proclaimed Worth Aerospace's logo. Neatly embossed beneath was the vice-president's name.

Flynn sighed, fingering the letter. His transfer was approved. The position he had asked for a hundred years ago, before his life had been upheaved, was his. The relocation expenses involved in moving to San Francisco were all going to be paid for by the company. The new position entailed a promotion and more money.

Added to that, he'd be near Michael's old neighborhood.

And away from Susanna and the chaos she represented. On that single sheet of paper was everything he wanted. Everything he *thought* he wanted.

So where was the relief? Where was the satisfaction?

Flynn stared out the window, one of the few on his side of the building. It had been a coup, getting this spot. So was getting this transfer.

Why didn't he want it?

He knew the answer to that.

Oh God, woman, what have you done to me?

When she saw him approaching the field at the end of the game, Susanna felt her heart begin to beat double time. There was a fleeting burst of joy before she recovered and took herself to task for it.

She was an idiot, she thought angrily, turning to take down the banner. A hopeless, romantic idiot. The man obviously could do very well without seeing her. He hadn't been around for over a week, hadn't called, hadn't attended either of the games. And he hadn't been to this one.

What he had been, she thought with the sting of angry hurt tormenting her, was avoiding her like the plague. She shouldn't be wasting her time on a man like that. And certainly not her heart.

So why was she doing it?

Easy. Stupidity, pure and simple.

To her far left, Billie and Michael were helping to hand out the after-game treats and all the little boys were forming a ring of outstretched hands around them. Normally, Susanna would hurry to try to get them into order. But she wasn't up to it right now.

The boys were resourceful, she thought. They could handle it. It would prepare them for later hurdles they would have to take. The kind presented by hard-hearted, hardheaded jerks.

The banner was giving her trouble. Billie had asked to help her put it up. Somehow, he had bent one of the stakes so that it now refused to budge out of the ground. She wiggled the slim iron rod to no avail.

She could feel him behind her, but didn't turn around. "Need help?" Flynn asked.

Susanna set her jaw rigidly. "No. I can handle it myself."

He was tired of her Tarzan approach. "Move aside, woman, and let someone help you for a change." Her head jerked up and he saw that her eyes were blazing.

"You could do with a dose of your own advice."

He began to answer her, then stopped. Holding on to the stake, he yanked hard, bringing it up and a plug of dirt, as well. He handed the iron rod to her. She looked as if she could spit nails, he thought.

"Could I come over?" he asked as she threw the stake on top of the other one and then rolled up the banner. He jumped aside as she accidentally dropped the hammer near his foot. A sting like an asp, he thought. He'd have to keep that in mind. "I'd like to talk to you."

He was being formal. This wasn't good. For the first time, Susanna felt a clutch of panic, then forced it away. She had promised herself never to panic. Never. He was probably going to tell her: Thanks for the six weeks, but now I have to go back to my life as a design engineer, or something of that ilk. Well, if that was the way he wanted to play it, then fine. Who needed him? Who the hell needed him?

She did, that's who.

"Sure," she said tonelessly. "Door's always open."

She worked at fixing a smile on her face. Under no circumstances was she about to let him see how this was hurting her. She didn't want his pity, just his love. She waved to Billie and Michael, who had finished handing out treats and were eating themselves. They scrambled over, raising dust as they came.

"Why don't you two ride with me?" she suggested. "I could use the company."

Michael looked to Flynn for permission. "Okay with you, Pop?"

"I'll follow in my car," Flynn told him. He glanced at Susanna. Why was she insisting on taking the boys with her? And why was she acting as if he were an investigating IRS agent?

She arrived at her house first, but Flynn's car was only half a beat behind. Susanna had a sense of doom as she got out of the car. Flynn was already beckoning the boys over. He pointed across the street, to Jane's well-lit front porch.

"Why don't you ask Aunt Jane to take you two out for a nice ice-cream cone?" he suggested to Billie, handing him a ten dollar bill.

Billie's eyes grew large and he turned the bill around and around in his hands. "This is going to buy some big cone," he cried.

Flynn patted the boy's shoulder. "I know you guys are up to it. Tell her to take her time." The two were off and running, debating their first choices of flavors.

Susanna squared her shoulders as she opened the front door. The silence hung like a heavy curtain between them as they walked in. She heard him shut the door behind him. Busy, she needed to be busy. Susanna made for the kitchen. If her hands were busy, she couldn't beat on that hard head of his.

"So, what would you like to talk about?" Her voice sounded so stilted and she hated herself for not having better control. She should have waited until he started. Let him feel the pressure.

Upbraiding herself silently, she yanked out the box of herbal teas and slammed it on the table.

He saw the tension in her shoulders. Maybe she was afraid of what he was going to tell her. Maybe he shouldn't tell her yet. No, he'd come too far, thought about it too much. "My transfer came through."

She was right. Twelve points for the lady with the broken heart. She refused to turn around as she put the kettle on the burner. "To San Francisco, wasn't it?" She wasn't going to break down if it killed her.

"Yes."

She pressed her lips together. *You don't care, remember,* she ordered herself. "Well—" she turned around to face him, smile in place "—it's what you wanted. I'm very happy for you."

It wasn't what he expected. Her words felt like a slap in the face. "Really?"

Maybe he had been wrong about her feelings, after all. Maybe he had been wrong about everything. He could stand, he now knew, her independence, possibly even the fact that she didn't need him for anything. He had already resigned himself to the knowledge that he was as emotionally dependent, as tangled up inside as any man could ever get. He could handle all that.

But not the fact that she didn't care. Had he driven her away? he asked himself.

"Really." She put on the water. Susanna took a deep breath, trying to find the strength to go on with this charade. It didn't come.

She whirled on him, fire in her eyes. "No, dammit, not 'really.' I'm not happy for you. And I'm not happy for me, either."

Hope began to rear its head. "Why? You don't need me."

She felt the tears coming and damned herself for it. "A hell of a lot you know."

His eyes narrowed as he studied her. It was time to iron out the double-edged problems between them. "I've never met a woman who was so self-sufficient, so on top of everything. Every time I turned around, you were competently handling everything. Taking over."

Annoyed that her emotions showed, she angrily brushed a tear from her cheek with the back of her hand. "It seemed to me you had enough to handle without having a clinging vine on your hands."

She was crying, he realized. Crying. Over him? It didn't seem possible. Tenderness flooded over him. "Not a clinging vine," he said softly. "Just someone who needed me."

The big jerk! Didn't he understand what the word *need* meant?

"I *do* need you, you idiot. Not to pull up stakes for me or to help load the dishwasher. That's fine and dandy, but I don't *need* it. I just need you to be there for me, to let me lean a little if I want to. Because I do need to lean once in a while." She placed her hands on his chest, pressing her words in. "I need you to trust me with what's in your heart. And I need you to need me. You want to toss around the word *self-sufficient*? Mister, in the dictionary, the word has a picture of you."

A mental image of that flashed through his mind and he almost laughed. Maybe he had come on a little strong on that subject. Maybe they both had. "I just didn't want to grow dependent again, the way I had the last time."

"We all need each other sometimes, Flynn, that's what it's all about. Risks and needs. And loving." She sighed, her hands dropping to her sides. She was getting herself worked up and he was trying to say goodbye. "But you wouldn't know about that."

"Oh yes, I would." He pulled her to him. She wanted to resist, but couldn't. This could be the last time and pride had no place here. "Ever since I met you, I've done nothing but need you, no matter how hard I tried not to. I needed to see you, hear you, touch you. I still do. I need you inside of each day, or else it's empty. It scares the hell out of me, Susanna," he admitted. "Needing you."

"It shouldn't. I'm not going anywhere." She'd be here if he needed her. Always. "You are."

He shook his head. "No, I'm not."

He wasn't making any sense. "The transfer—"

Flynn began to think of undressing her slowly, inch by inch. Of making her skin heat, her body arch against his. Nothing else mattered. "I turned it down."

"You turned it down?" She laced her arms around his neck, hope flashing high. "Why?"

"I thought that four hundred miles would be a hell of a nightly commute."

Maybe her brain was getting foggy. "I don't follow you."

"That would be a first for you. You always seemed to know more about me than I did." His hands fitted about her hips easily. As if they had always meant to be there. "I discovered that I like this fathering business. So, while I'm at it, I might as well do it for two. Billie," he added when her eyes grew large with confusion. "I'm asking you to marry me."

"Marry—?" Her voice vanished in shock. "I don't understand."

It hadn't really come home to him until this afternoon, when he held the transfer in his hand. "When the transfer finally came through, when I realized that it meant not seeing you, *really* seeing you, I had to turn it down. I knew what this short separation had done to me. It didn't get you out of my system. The separation totally backfired. It just made me want you more."

The tea kettle whistled, reminding Susanna of the herbal teas she had set out. She had banged it down so hard, the various packets had flown out of the box. She looked at them now. "What's your pleasure?"

He finally had the right answer, he thought. He had had it all along, he just hadn't known it. "You, Susanna. It's always been you since the first day I saw you. I love you, for now and for always."

Susanna grinned. "Bingo."

He pulled her closer. "I haven't held you in over a week."

"One week, two days, four hours and ten minutes, but who's counting?"

"I am." He lowered his head. "And the countdown starts now."

She stood on her toes, her lips brushing his teasingly. "Ready to blast off when you are, Flynn."

* * * * *

Silhouette

SPECIAL EDITION

THE DONOVAN LEGACY
from Nora Roberts

Meet the Donovans—Morgana, Sebastian and Anastasia.
They're an unusual threesome. Triple your fun with double
cousins, the only children of triplet sisters and triplet brothers.
Each one is unique. Each one is . . . special.

In September you will be *Captivated* by Morgana Donovan. In
Special Edition #768, horror-film writer Nash Kirkland doesn't
know what to do when he meets an actual witch!

Be *Entranced* in October by Sebastian Donovan in Special
Edition #774. Private investigator Mary Ellen Sutherland
doesn't believe in psychic phenomena. But she discovers
Sebastian has strange powers . . . over her.

In November's Special Edition #780, you'll be *Charmed* by
Anastasia Donovan, along with Boone Sawyer and his little
girl. Anastasia was a healer, but for her it was Boone's touch
that cast a spell.

Enjoy the magic of Nora Roberts. Don't miss *Captivated,
Entranced* or *Charmed.* Only from
Silhouette Special Edition. . . .

SENR-1

Silhouette
SPECIAL EDITION™

VOWS
A series celebrating marriage
by Sherryl Woods

To Love, Honor and Cherish—these were the words that three generations of Halloran men promised their women they'd live by. But these vows made in love are each challenged by the tests of time....

In October—Jason Halloran meets his match in *Love* #769;

In November—Kevin Halloran rediscovers love—with his wife—in *Honor* #775;

In December—Brandon Halloran rekindles an old flame in *Cherish* #781.

These three stirring tales are coming down the aisle toward you—only from Silhouette Special Edition!

TAKE A WALK ON THE DARK SIDE OF LOVE

October is the shivery season, when chill winds blow and shadows walk the night. Come along with us into a haunting world where love and danger go hand in hand, where passions will thrill you and dangers will chill you. Come with us to

In this newest short story collection from Silhouette Books, three of your favorite authors tell tales just perfect for a spooky autumn night. Let Anne Stuart introduce you to "The Monster in the Closet," Helen R. Myers bewitch you with "Seawitch," and Heather Graham Pozzessere entice you with "Wilde Imaginings."

Silhouette Shadows™
Haunting a store near you this October.

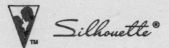